Praise for *Black Powder, White Smoke*

"Absorbing . . . Estleman combines action, suspense, and a twist of humor in this satisfying drama full of Western lore."
—*Publishers Weekly*

"Estleman writes about master craftsmen, whatever his theme, and then shapes sentences like prose poems to the craft at hand, his details sharp as metal shavings, in a voice all his own."
—*Kirkus Reviews*

Praise for *The Master Executioner*

"The tale of a master executioner written by a master story-teller: What more could you ask for?"
—*Elmore Leonard*

"Estleman's prose snaps like fresh linen Treasury bills, using a Cold-Eye-of-God style for a type of fiction-truer-than-fact stretching back to Defoe's true-fact novel, *Journal of the Plague Year*."
—*Kirkus Reviews* (starred review)

"Hauntingly poignant despite its reserved protagonist and morbid subject matter . . . Mr. Estleman has done impeccable homework on the finer points of what Stone would regard as a lost art. . . . Mr. Estleman movingly conveys the brutalizing effects of killing for the law, even when you are terribly good at it."
—*The Economist*

"One feels and smells the gallows and hears the snap of the second cervical vertebrae. It is a remarkable book and one I would urge you to read."
—*The Amarillo News & Globe-Times*

Books by Loren D. Estleman

*A Forge Book

PORT
HAZARD

A Page Murdock Novel

———————————

Loren D. Estleman

A TOM DOHERTY ASSOCIATES BOOK

NEW YORK

PORT HAZARD: A PAGE MURDOCK NOVEL

Copyright © 2004 by Loren D. Estleman

A Forge Book
Published by Tom Doherty Associates, LLC
175 Fifth Avenue
New York, NY 10010

www.tor-forge.com

Forge® is a registered trademark of Tom Doherty Associates, LLC.

ISBN-13: 978-0-7653-4111-2
ISBN-10: 0-7653-4111-5

First Edition: January 2004
First Mass Market Edition: February 2008

Printed in the United States of America

0 9 8 7 6 5 4 3 2 1

For Louise A. Estleman:
September 13, 1918 – June 30, 2002.
A swell prim, and now with God.

PART ONE

The Double Eagle

1

I was killing a conductor on the Northern Pacific between
Butte and Garrison when my orders changed.

He wasn't a real conductor. They all have bad feet, to
begin with, and the three-inch Texas heels poking out of his
serge cuffs caught my eye just before he tried to punch my
ticket with an Arkansas toothpick the size of a sickle. I was half
out of my seat and used the momentum to grasp his wrist,
deflect the blade, and butt him under the chin, crushing the
crown of a good pinch hat and making him bite through his
tongue. He bled out both corners of his mouth. I drew my
Deane-Adams awkwardly with my left hand, jammed it into his
crotch, and fired.

He fell on top of me, there not being any other place to fall
in a sleeping compartment. I had several pounds on him and
I'm not a big man, but deadweight is deadweight. I was still
climbing out from under when someone knocked at the door.

In the throbbing echo of the .45's report, he might have been tapping on a door at the other end of the train.

I was plastered with blood from collar to knees when I opened the door. The Negro porter paled beneath his deep brown pigment at the sight of the blood and the revolver in my hand, but he had an old scar on his cheek that looked combat-related, a saber cut, and in any case, they're trained by Pullman not to panic easily. He held out a Western Union envelope.

"Wireless for Deputy Murdock," he said.

I holstered the Deane-Adams, tore open the flap, and read while he took in the heap on the floor:

RETURN TO HELENA AT ONCE STOP YOUR LIFE
IS IN DANGER

                              BLACKTHORNE

"That man ain't a conductor on this train," said the porter.

"I guessed that when he tried to hack me open. Is there a detective aboard?"

"No, sir. We ain't been robbed on this run all year."

"When do we get to Garrison?"

He had a little trouble thumbing open the lid on his turnip watch. "Eighteen minutes."

"The town marshal's name is Krueger. He knows me. Send someone to tell him I'll need help with this extra baggage."

"I needs to tell the conductor."

"If that's his uniform, you might have trouble getting an answer."

He dipped a knee and turned the dead man half over on his side. Then he stood.

"Yes, sir. Mr. Fenady was missing that there third button this morning. You reckon this fellow kilt him?"

"He didn't strike me as the bargaining kind. What's that?" I pointed to something on the floor that glinted.

He bent and picked it up. "It must of dropped out of his pocket when I turned him over." He handed it to me.

It was a double eagle, solid gold, the size of a cartwheel dollar. It threw back light in insolent sheets, and the edges of the eagle's wings were sharp enough to cut a finger. "See if there are any more."

If I expected the porter to balk at the prospect of rifling a dead man's pockets, I was disappointed. He knelt again, and in less than a minute he rose, shaking his head. He was used to searching drunken passengers for their tickets to find out where they belonged.

I felt the coin, reading SAN FRANCISCO, CALIFORNIA, with the ball of my thumb. "Is your Mr. Fenady the kind to carry around uncirculated double eagles?"

"No, sir, he sure ain't. That, or he lied about not having the cash to replace that lost button."

I pocketed the coin. He watched without expression. I said, "You want a receipt?"

"No, sir." He turned to go.

I put a hand on his arm, stopping him. It was hard under the uniform sleeve, roped with muscle from carrying trunks and hoisting fat women aboard parlor cars.

"Thirty-sixth Infantry?" I asked.

"No, sir. Tenth Cavalry. Buffalo soldiers. I was too young to serve in the War of Emancipation."

"That doesn't look like a tomahawk scar."

He grinned joylessly. "Wasn't always the red man we was fighting, sir."

"What's your name?"

"Edward Anderson Beecher."

"Did you ever consider serving the law, Beecher?"

"What's the pension?"

"No pension. Congress covers the cost of your burial."

"Thank you, sir. I reckon I'll go on taking my chances with Mr. J. J. Hill."

"That's the problem. The good ones are too smart to serve for the money."

He said nothing, saying plenty.

"Don't forget to tell Marshal Krueger about the double eagle," I said.

That took a moment to filter through. This time when he grinned, the sun came out. "Yes, sir."

"Did you think I intended to keep it a secret?"

"It ain't my place to think, sir."

"I'm a killer, not a thief."

"Yes, sir."

"Stop calling me sir. I quit the army in sixty-five."

"Yes, boss."

After he left, I took the coin back out and weighed it on my palm. Its face value was twenty dollars. That bothered me more than the attack. I'd thought my life was worth a little more.

2

They found the conductor, Tim Fenady, a twenty-year man with a wife and four minor children, in the baggage car wearing only his long-handles and lace-ups, with a single stab wound between his shoulder blades that matched a rip in the uniform the man I killed was wearing. They couldn't tell me the hired killer's name in Garrison. When his own clothes were found, the pockets were empty, which meant that either he was a professional or there had been one more crook aboard the train. By the time they dumped him into a hole in potter's field—burial cost two dollars out of my pocket, a policy of the U.S. District Court, Territory of Montana—I was riding an express back to Helena, sitting up in a chair car. Apparently I'd lost my compartment privileges by not dying.

That season, Judge Harlan A. Blackthorne was smoking his cigars and studying his cases in a room at the Merchants Hotel, his chambers at the courthouse having been gutted by one of

Helena's frequent fires. His desk had been rescued, albeit charred on one corner, and the room's bed had been removed to make room for it. When I reported there directly from the station, the clerk in the lobby told me the judge was in court, but that Marshal Spilsbury was expecting me.

Spilsbury was a Montana native, the son of a Scots farmer, and a decent man who had no liking for me. This wasn't entirely his fault. At the time of his appointment, he'd vowed to rid the federal service of killers, and placed me third on the list for termination. He'd found out quickly that Blackthorne didn't share his views. A bit less quickly— letters of complaint to the White House in 1883 carried an average turnaround time of three weeks—he'd learned that a United States marshal's position in that territory was redundant as long as Blackthorne ran the court. To Spilsbury's credit, he made no more attempts to circumvent recognized authority, and in fact listened attentively when the judge, with uncharacteristic patience, pointed out to him that if all the killers in the district court system were let go, the deputies who remained would be of insufficient number to deal with the throngs of homicidal parties who would suddenly have returned to the civilian population.

"Your Honor, these are jackals we're discussing," he'd argued.

"Very true," Blackthorne had said. "However, they are *our* jackals."

I found the marshal studying his pocket Bible in a straight-back chair, the only place to sit in the room apart from the great overstuffed horsehair that stood behind the desk, another aromatic survivor of the courthouse fire. There was no indication that he'd even entertained the notion of changing seats in the judge's absence. He was a lay reader with the Presbyterian church, and although he could quote the gospel chapter and verse, he never did. His restraint carried the respect of the most blasphemous among the deputy marshals, who theorized that he was settling the account for the sins of some father on some haunted moor three generations back.

He raised his long narrow face from Revelations to greet me. He wore all black from neck to heels except for his white collar and the plain six-pointed star pinned to his broadcloth vest. He'd been in mourning three years for a wife dead of diphtheria in populous St. Louis, which may have explained his decision to decamp to a region less settled, and there was about him a quality of gentle brooding that caused men several years his senior, me included, to address him as an elder.

"I hope your journey back was more pleasant than the one out," he said.

"The one out wasn't so bad, if you don't count the stretch between Butte and Garrison." I didn't shake his hand. He didn't offer it. He wasn't being rude, just unhypocritical. You couldn't hate him for that.

"I suppose you had no other choice but to kill the man."

"I might have. I wasn't thinking about choices at the time."

He glanced down, saw nothing on that page to comfort him, and closed the Bible. He poked it into his watch pocket. Then he drew a fold of stiff paper from inside his coat and held it out. "Is this the fellow who assaulted you?"

I took the paper and unfolded it. It was a wanted reader issued by the Department of Justice in Washington, D.C. I read the description and handed it back.

"Tobias Mimms," I said. "It could have been. When you're on the scout, you're sure to lose a little weight. 'Wanted in Missouri.' Who isn't? He's too young to be a former guerrilla, but back there they serve that up with the beans and fatback. Murder, conspiracy to commit murder, and aggravated assault, which would have been a murder interrupted. Paid killer?"

"It doesn't say. But then there is no specific charge for that." He put away the reader. "I understand you found a gold piece on his person?"

I fished out the double eagle and put it in his hand. He studied both sides as carefully as he read Scripture. "This was minted very recently. Gold stamping needn't pass through many hands before it begins to lose definition. Have you ever been to San Francisco?"

"No, sir."

He looked at me for any sign of irony in the address. "Mimms has. He was seen there last month. Agents from the Pinkerton office there obtained a federal warrant and mounted a raid on the disorderly house where he was staying, but he'd disappeared. Ten days ago he resurfaced in Montana." He returned his attention to the coin. "You were on your way to Bannack to identify a prisoner. Is there anyone who can perform that duty in your place?"

"Treadway was the deputy he made the break from, but he's on furlough. His wife is expecting."

"Yes. Well, unless she's expecting something other than a child, I am of the opinion she can spare him. Nothing in his history says he trained as a midwife."

I nodded. That made one more reason for Treadway not to buy me a whiskey on my birthday.

"There are other ways for a coin to make its way here from California," I said. "It didn't have to be in Mimms's pocket. We don't know for sure it was Mimms on the train."

"The day you left for Bannack, I received a wire from Sheriff Matthias in Granite County. Do you know him?"

"Only by reputation. He has a peg leg and his own private army of deputies to do his footwork."

"Evidently an efficient system. One of them overheard a drunken conversation in a saloon in Phillipsburg, something about a number of law dogs fit for muzzling. Your name came up."

"My guess is it comes up often in that kind of conversation."

"The sheriff thought this one worthy of repeating. The fellow doing the talking is a notorious Copperhead. He was sentenced to hang for treason in seventy-two, but was pardoned by President Grant. He announced his retirement shortly afterward, but Matthias holds the opinion a case could be made for another trial based on his activities since."

"There are plenty of people who won't let go of the war. They're about as much of a threat as these blowhards who still say the earth's flat."

"It's a comforting analogy, but specious. Have you ever heard of the Sons of the Confederacy?"

I shook my head.

"They're a loosely knit organization, founded in Richmond in 'sixty-six, on the first anniversary of the surrender at Appomattox. The charter members were Confederate veterans, dedicated to electing Southern sympathizers to high office and effecting by peaceful means what four years of bloodshed could not—namely, the secession of states and territories whose leaders share their vision."

"It seems to me the same thing was tried in sixty-one."

"Hear me out. Today the group contains a significant number of noncombatants, many of whom were too young to serve; some, in fact, who were not born when the war ended. These youngsters are easily influenced, with emotions untempered in the crucible of cruel experience. Former spies like this fellow in Phillipsburg talk a good fight and fill their heads with poison. They could or would not take up arms, and so are content with persuading others to take them up in their stead. They have created a rift in the ranks between those who counsel lawful action and those who would spill blood yet again. In the last three years, the Sons of the Confederacy have accounted for twenty-seven murders, including the assassination of a Massachusetts senator and the ambush slayings of three peace officers attempting to arrest members upon various charges. Their aim is to spread panic and distrust in the Union and set the stage for a second war on behalf of states' rights."

"I don't know what it has to do with Mimms and me. I don't make it a practice to arrest rebels. Not for being rebels."

"That would be a salient point, if Tobias Mimms were not the fellow the Copperhead told to muzzle you."

I found a growth of whiskers my razor had missed and scratched it. I can't get a decent shave aboard a moving train. "If they're that dangerous, why hasn't Chet Arthur sent troops into Richmond?"

"Virginia represents the peaceful element. The firebrands have taken up residence on the Barbary Coast."

The smoke began to clear.

"You're proposing sending me to San Francisco to weed out the bad apples?"

"You're mixing metaphors, Deputy, in addition to being a damn fool. I'm sending you there to widen the rift."

This was a new voice, or rather a new one in that conversation; harsher and more sardonic. Judge Blackthorne had entered, and now he took his place behind the desk with an air as if he were calling the court to order.

3

Small men often have a way of filling a room, mainly out of spite. Harlan Blackthorne obliterated rooms; not by compensation or by denying his lack of stature, but by sheer force of the conviction that most of the men he met were unnecessarily large. Those of normal height felt unwieldy in his orbit, while tall men were made to consider themselves freaks. He was a dandy who had his suits cut too youthfully for him, and there was a lot of speculation among the deputy marshals, with considerable money to back it up, that he dyed his glossy sable hair and beard. Strangers who didn't know who he was smiled behind their hands when he strutted into a room. Two minutes into conversation with him, the smiles withered and blew away. He had more enemies in Washington than Jefferson Davis and held absolute authority over a region as large as Middle Europe.

An empty glass and a pitcher of water awaited him on the

desk. Without ceremony, he filled the glass from the pitcher, removed his false teeth, and submerged them in the glass, where they grinned at Spilsbury and me throughout the interview. He only wore them behind the bench, not that either his speech or his dignity suffered in their absence. If anything, without them his rare smile gave him the tight-lipped, diabolic look of a Satanic Mona Lisa.

"The schism that exists between the law-abiding new Confederates and their violent brethren is their problem, not ours," he continued, not bothering to greet either of us. "In fact, it offers the rest of us our first opportunity to destroy the organization, or at the very least, render it superfluous. In five years it will pose no more threat to these United States than the Knights of Columbus."

Whenever the judge made reference to "these United States," it sounded as if he had them right there in his watch pocket. He'd fought for them in Mexico, served their military as an advisor during the Civil War, losing his teeth in battle and his digestion in politics, and seemed to consider these sacrifices some kind of down payment on proprietorship. He had opposed Southern Reconstruction in favor of punishment, and behaved in general toward the eleven former seceding states as if they'd deserted him personally. Alarmed, the moderates in his party had conspired to arrange his appointment to a territorial post as far from Capitol Hill as was available. There he continued to make his opinions known by sentencing former rebels who were convicted in his court far more severely than those who had never declared war upon the Union. Of those who appealed, only two got as far as the Supreme Court, which had reversed one sentence and upheld the other by a narrow margin. The common belief in Montana, that there was no appeal between Blackthorne and Jehovah, remained unshaken.

"What makes me the one to insert the wedge?" I asked. "I'm just a target, and a cheap one at that. Twenty dollars and train fare."

Blackthorne snapped his fingers at Spilsbury, who leaned forward and passed the double eagle across the desk. The Judge glanced at it and smacked it down on his blotter as if he'd flipped it. "This is a symbol, not remuneration. It pleases them to commission murder for the Confederacy with the token of a Yankee goldpiece. Mimms offered his services gratis."

Now I was being discounted. The longer I stayed in that room, the less my life was worth. "How did I come to be on their list to begin with? It's been almost twenty years since I took my licks for the Union."

Spilsbury spoke for the first time since Blackthorne had entered.

"You're rather a notorious character. Evidently there are scores of schoolboys who ought to be reading Matthew Arnold who are instead persuaded by the example of a number of ten-cent shockers that you roped and skinned the elephant. That's a tempting mark for a cause looking for space in the public columns."

"I didn't write the dime novels. I barely met the man who writes them before I ran him out of Helena. There isn't a word of truth in any of them."

"Whoever said 'a lie cannot live' never saw one dressed in

yellow pasteboard with a lurid title," the marshal said. "These fellows are not known for their discernment."

"Gentlemen, you're both wrong, as well as in contempt for speaking out of turn. The court is in recess, not adjournment. It goes where I go." Having swung this gavel, the judge favored me with his Luciferian smirk. "You are exalted, Deputy. Marshal Spilsbury doesn't feel called upon often to pay you a compliment. However, he overestimates your importance. These are not unruly schoolchildren, hungering for adult attention. They never strike without reason.

"It's true you're the most infamous officer of this court," he said. "However, it's my court, and your extermination was intended as a message for me. My opinions of this treasonous trash are widely known. If they can kill my most ferocious dog, the reasoning follows that they can kill me. It's first-form Machiavelli at best, but rather impressive for a band of inbred plug-chewers and pickle-stickers."

I found this intelligence more of an irritation than a testimonial. In one choice phrase I'd gone from dime-novel hero to slaughterhouse mutt. What made it more irritating still was the conviction that he was probably right. For all their prominence in the telegraph columns and bookstalls, gun men were pawns, shuttled about by judges, senators, and owners of railroads. Those were the only three groups whose members were difficult to replace.

I said, "How am I supposed to pull off this parting of the Red Sea? I'm not even first form."

"That's a point in your favor. Disregarding Emancipation,

the principal result of four years of war was to scatter spies across the continent. Southern sympathizers are no longer to be found solely in the South. You'll find them piloting a ferry in Kansas City, bookkeeping in Philadelphia, pumping a black-smith's forge in Texas. They're in Congress and medicine and law enforcement. An army dispatched to destroy the Sons of the Confederacy would be observed and reported upon throughout its march. By the time it reached the enemy stronghold, the enemy would have vanished, slithered down its network of holes, to reassemble elsewhere later and force us to commence gathering intelligence all over again. One man, or a small group, might slip past these Copperheads unnoticed, or if noticed, might be dismissed as no threat. How you manage the parting itself is your affair. Your experience in sowing discord in this court may show you the way."

"Where do I start? San Francisco's a big place."

Blackthorne directed his gaze to the marshal, who pro-duced a memorandum book from the same pocket that con-tained the wanted circular on Tobias Mimms. He forked a pair of spectacles with egg-shaped lenses onto the thick bridge of his nose. He hadn't needed glasses to read his Bible, but then he knew most of its passages by heart.

" 'Daniel Webster Wheelock,' " he read. "Have you ever heard this name?"

"Two thirds of it," I said.

"It seems his parents had lofty hopes for him in the profes-sion of law. If so, their disappointment was abysmal. Half of every penny that vanishes into the bagnios and deadfalls on the San Francisco waterfront finds its home in Wheelock's purse. In return, he keeps the peace, such as it is. Those who breach it either pass from sight or end up snagging some fisherman's net in the harbor. There is a name for such fellows."

"Back East, they're called captains of industry."

He went on reading as if I hadn't spoken. "He's sixty, a club-foot, with a classical education obtained at Harvard University; a Boston native with an ancestral connection to the first pilgrims. Rather a curious background for a Tammany hack. However, he's the man to see if you want to do any sort of business in Barbary, legitimate or otherwise."

"Am I to call him out or shoot him from ambush?"

"Neither, if you can avoid it," put in Blackthorne. "Killing Wheelock would only stir up the hive and scatter its contents further. In any case, there's no evidence he's connected with the Copperheads. They're under his protection, along with every other active citizen out there, lest the top blow off and Washington declare martial law to contain the damage. Wheelock has the most to lose in that situation. As a peacemaker, he's more conscientious than the army and the Church of Rome. You need to befriend him if you're to find out who's behind the Sons."

"How I do that is my affair, too, I suppose."

"The marshal's notebook will provide pointers. He's made rather a study of The Honorable D. W. Wheelock."

" 'Honorable'?"

"He's a city alderman, as well as a captain in the fire brigade," Spilsbury said, thumbing through his pages. "He also holds—"

The Judge's teeth bumped against the side of the water glass, cutting him off. Blackthorne was fishing them out. "I've heard all this before. At present, I have a murderer to try. The marshal can give you everything you need." He worried the teeth into place and stood. "Don't forget, Murdock, you're still a target. Take along a deputy to stand at your back."

"I'll take Staderman."

"Staderman's laid up with a broken pelvis. That big roan of his put its foot wrong last week and rolled over on him. He should have shot the clumsy beast years ago. He has a soft spot where horses are concerned."

"His only fault."

"I thought you hated each other."

"I didn't choose him for company. What about Partridge?"

"He's testifying next week. Kearney's available."

"Kearney can't hit Montana with a shotgun."

"That's the lot, Deputy. Thirty-six men, one hundred forty-six thousand square miles. If you know a civilian you can trust, whom you can persuade to risk his life for posse pay, have at it."

"I can think of one," I said. "One I think I can trust. The rest of it may take some work."

4

The difficult part about tracing Edward Anderson Beecher was he worked for the railroad. The easy part was he worked for the railroad.

A fellow who earns his living carrying luggage, making up berths, and delivering messages to passengers aboard the Northern Pacific could make his home in Portland or St. Paul, Boise or Salt Lake City. All I had was a name and description, and an area of search as big as the Indian Ocean. All I needed was the name.

Chicago knew where every piece of rolling stock was sided and where every employee was keeping himself. When I told Judge Blackthorne who I wanted to stand behind me on the trip to San Francisco, he wired the name and a one-sentence request East and got a reply within six hours. The porter with the friendly saber scar was working a ceremonial excursion organized to commemorate the completion of the rairoad line and was expected in Gold Creek Saturday, along with a herd of generals, bankers, congressmen, newspaper reporters, and Ulysses S. Grant, former president of the United States.

There were four trains in the excursion, pausing at every whistle-stop for speeches, libations, and gifts of wildflowers tied with ribbon and delivered by pretty little girls in white dresses to dyspeptic old goats in stiff collars. Three had already passed through Helena. I was told I'd missed several displays of fine elocution and the spectacle of a senator's fat secretary being hauled aboard a rolling caboose by his britches after he slept through the departing whistle with one of the young creatures at Chicago Joe's. Beecher, according to the wire, had boarded the first train west of town. He must have turned back from Garrison just ahead of me to accept the assignment. The fourth and last train was due in one hour and I was expected to be on it.

I got to the station with my valise just as the locomotive shrieked to a leaky stop, hung all over with flags and garlands and gents in beetle hats leaning out the windows, firing pistols at the clouds and waving at the throngs and the firehouse band, for whom the enchantment of "O, Susanna" sounded as if it had begun to wear thin. The first team, including Grant and the railroad brass and Washington's best speechmakers, had been aboard the first train, and by the time it came to stock this one, all that was left were the wardheelers and second cousins; people not considered important enough to ride up front but too dangerous to leave behind. I swung aboard a day coach against the stream of alighting passengers, found a seat near the back, and let down the window to thin out the atmosphere of twice-smoked cigars and Old Gideon.

In due course, the electioneering blathered to a finish, reinforcements were brought aboard in the form of crates of champagne and the odd giggling girl in bright satin. The train lurched ahead, pulling away from the tinny strains of "Garryowen," and buried the end of Custer's dirge under the razz of its whistle. An old campaigner in a sour-smelling suit with tobacco juice in his beard went to sleep with his head on my shoulder. I wasn't sure whether he was too important to shoot, and by the time we rolled into Butte, my left arm was numb. We overnighted there, for no good reason except to let the excursionists nurse their headaches and to sample some more of the local fauna. All the hotel rooms were taken, so I got back on board and gave a porter a dollar to make up a berth and wake me an hour before the train was scheduled to embark. He did that, and for another dollar brought me biscuits and gravy from the Silver Bow Club, leaving the tray outside the water closet as I was shaving. I asked him if he knew Beecher and where I might find him in Gold Creek.

He frowned. He was a handsome lad of eighteen or so, with aristocratic features and skin as black as a stove. "I can't say as I've heard the name, sir, but a lot of the coloreds keep theirselves at Danny Moon's Emporium on the Benetsee."

"Do they serve white men?"

"I wouldn't know, sir. I keep temperance myself."

"How long before the yahoos start boarding?"

He looked at his watch. The entire transcontinental system would fly to pieces without its pocket winders. "Fifteen minutes, if we're leaving on time. We're sure to hear from Mr. Hill if we don't."

I gave him another dollar. "Would an abstemious gentleman such as yourself object to learning whether there's a quart of good whiskey left in town and bringing it to me?"

He took off his cap, poked the coin under the sweatband next to the others, and put the cap back on. "Mr. Drummond at the Silver Bow Club keeps some Hermitage in stock for patrons of good character."

I sighed and wiped off the last of the shaving soap. "What do you charge for a reference?"

The porter stiffened. The cap came off and he fished the silver dollars out of the band and held them out. "I ain't a grafter. You'll find plenty of them in town."

"Sorry, friend. Most people I meet, when they find out I work for Washington, start thinking they can get a little of their own back. It destroys your faith in good fellowship. I'll get the bottle myself."

After a moment he returned the coins to his cap and his cap to his head. "I'll get it, sir. These bankers and politicians will try your patience. One of them slapped me when I wouldn't fetch him a woman."

"Did you slap him back?"

"Mr. Hill wouldn't approve of that. The gentleman wouldn't approve of what he ate for supper that night, either." He touched his cap and went off on his quest.

Gold Creek was in a fever. It had never lived up to its name, the nuggets coughed up by Benetsee Creek never having compared to the strikes in Bannack, Alder Gulch, and Last Chance, and for twenty years had stood only on the loose foundation of the hopes of those residents who had gambled everything on their claims and had nowhere else to go and nothing to get them there if they had. The coming of the Northern Pacific had rekindled some of that early optimism. Fresh clapboard, glistening with new paint, had been nailed up over the log walls of the assayer's office and the general merchandise, and the horse apples swept out of sight for the first time in a decade. The street, in fact, was faintly greenish, paved as it was with the uncollected droppings of a generation. The population was five hundred, but only if you counted the flies.

Today the transient numbers were considerably higher. People had come from all around to get drunk and slap the back of the victor of Appomattox, to round up votes, fleece the sheep at the gaming tables, and lift the occasional poke in the press of flesh. There wasn't a room to be had in any of the hotels, as I found out when I went looking for a roof. Most of the private homes had temporary boarders, and tents had sprung up like mushrooms all over the foothills. The whole place looked like the night before Gettysburg.

Stepping down from the train I squeezed past a gang of Eastern Republicans handing out leaflets opposing protective tariffs and shoved aside a rodent in a striped jersey who tried to wrestle my valise out of my hand. This put me off balance, and I jostled a portly, gray-bearded gent in a suit that smelled of mothballs. I put out a hand to steady us both and muttered an apology. Someone barked at me and I turned my head that way just in time to be blinded when a heap of magnesium powder went up in a white flame. I had my Deane-Adams in my hand before I realized my photograph had been taken. Years later an acquaintance asked me how I'd come to know General Grant, and when I said we never met, he told me he'd seen a picture of me in a book with my hand on the shoulder of the eighteenth president of the United States. That made me feel bad, because if I'd known I was that close I'd have told him it was my privilege to have fought with Rosecrans at Murfreesboro. I never got another chance. Grant died two years later, penniless, a victim of his business associations.

The third hotel I tried was full up like the others, but the clerk agreed to let me leave my valise there for a consideration. My expense book threatened to create a shortage of dollar coins in Denver. I asked where I might find Danny Moon's Emporium. The clerk, a horse-faced Scandinavian, too young for his drinker's rosy nose, looked me up and down from hat to heels, then mumbled something about following the creek south until it got dark. It wasn't noon yet, but I took his meaning.

It was built of logs without benefit of clapboard, with a long front porch supported on more logs, like a raft. Boards suspended from the roof with letters burned into them advertised whiskey, lunch, and cold beer. I stopped to let a bull-necked, bald-headed Negro in dungarees and a wool flannel shirt soaked through with sweat carry a streaming bucket of beer bottles up the front steps from the creek, then followed him inside, moving aside an oilcloth flap that covered the doorway. That old familiar mulch of tobacco, burned and chewed, sour mash, stale beer, and staler bodies greeted me in the darkened interior. I let my eyes adjust to the pewtery light struggling in through panes thick with grime, then made my way to the bar, towing a path of silence through the whirr of conversation. Mine was the only white face in the establishment, and I had on the only white shirt. My entrance had interrupted a game of dominoes atop a table made from a packing crate and an argument at the bar, which was made from a door laid across a pair of whiskey barrels.

The bartender turned out to be the man I'd seen carrying in beer from the creek. He paused in the midst of unstopping one of the bottles to look at me from under a brow like a rock outcrop. I groped a nickel out of my pocket and laid it on a door panel. "I'll have one of those beers, if they're not all spoken for."

A gray tongue like a toadbelly came out and slid the length of the bartender's lower lip. "You lost, mister. You gots to follow the creek north till it gets light."

That seemed to be the joke of the town. I said, "It's a long dry walk."

The customer to my right reached over and pinched the sleeve of my travel coat between thumb and forefinger. He had on overalls with a big safety pin keeping one strap in place over a pair of red flannels gone mostly gray. "That silk?" he asked.

"Not for thirty a month and four cents a mile. What about that beer?" I was still looking at the bartender.

His eyes moved from side to side, couldn't find a quorum. He slammed a thick glass onto the bar and filled it from the bottle, not bothering to tilt the glass to cut the clouds. I thanked him and took a drink. It was homemade stuff, bitter, with hops floating in it, but I felt the cold of it drying the sweat on the back of my neck. I asked the bartender how he kept people from stealing the bottles out of the creek.

"Water moccasins."

"I didn't think we had water moccasins in Montana."

"Benetsee's got everything in it. Except gold." He opened a mouth with no teeth in it and let out air in a death rattle of a laugh.

"Maybe you just spread the story around to protect your beer."

The mouth clapped shut, then opened a quarter-inch. "Maybe I is a liar in your eyes."

"No, sir. Just a good businessman."

A full little silence followed, like a fire gulping air. A drop of sweat wandered down my spine, stinging like molten lead. I had five cartridges in my revolver and thirty-two pairs of eyes on me, if the dusty mirror strung from a nail behind the bar wasn't missing anyone in the shadows. Then someone laughed, a shrill, bubbling cackle, with no irony in it. A hand smacked the bar, hard enough to create a tidal wave in my glass.

"He's snared you, Danny." This was a voice I recognized. "I'm so scared of snakes in general I never once thought you was bluffing about them water moccasins. What you need now's a wolf trap. Man's got to be thirstier'n Christ on the cross to trade his fingers for a sip of that piss you stir up in back."

Another silence, shorter than the first. Then someone else laughed. That started a rockslide. The room shook with guffaws. I extracted a fistful of coins from my pocket and laid them on the bar in a heap.

"Pour each of these fellows a beer," I said. "If there's anything left, you can put it toward that wolf trap."

Danny joined the others this time, showing his pink gums.

"I'm thinking bear. You don't know these boys when they's parched." He scooped the coins into a box with Pallas Athena on the lid and started pouring.

I picked up my glass and moved to the end of the bar, where a gap had opened in the rush to take advantage of my generosity. Edward Anderson Beecher leaned there on his forearms with one hand wrapped around his glass, a cigarette building a long ash between the first two fingers. He had on his porter's outfit, the cap tilted forward and touching the bridge of his nose—a violation of the Northern Pacific uniform code. The scar on his cheek looked like a curl of packing cord caught in fresh tar. He was smiling into his beer, his lips pressed tight.

I said, "Prefer to buy your own?"

"Don't take it as an insult. Two beers and I'm a bad risk. If it gets back to Mr. J. J. Hill I even showed up in a place like this in my working clothes, I'll be back shoveling horseshit."

"You railroad men all talk about Hill like you've met face to face."

"Could have. One white man in a beard looks pretty much like all the rest."

I drank, spat out a hop. I hoped it was a hop. "Thanks for the shove. That could have gone another way."

"I come here to drink, not see my friends kilt. I seen how handy you are with that iron."

"You make friends quick. Or is Gold Creek home?"

He dragged in smoke, the ash quivering but not falling, blew twin gray streams out his nostrils. Shook his head. "I know all the places at all the stops, is all. Spokane's home. I ain't been lately. Last time I was I had a wife."

There was nothing there for me. At forty-two, I was one of the oldest deputies in Blackthorne's string, but the younger ones had given up trying to tell me about their dogs and women. Sooner or later, all confidences were regretted; resentment set in, and always when you needed the disgruntled party to deal you out of a bad hand.

Then there was the chance of getting to like one of them. Given my choice, I'd bury a stranger.

"How was the ride out?" I said.

"Better than some. That General Grant sure can put away the rye."

"Lincoln asked him what brand he drank so he could send a case to all his generals."

"I heard that. You reckon it's true?"

"Likely not. I understand Honest Abe wasn't born in a log cabin, either."

"I was born between cotton rows myself. Maybe I ought to throw my hat in the ring."

"I'd set my sights lower to start."

"I started out a slave. What's lower than that?"

I wasn't going to get a better invitation. I fished the deputy's star out of my shirt pocket and laid it on the bar between us.

5

He shifted his tight-lipped smile from his glass to the star, then put two fingers on it and slid it back toward me, as if he were anteing up.

"We had this conversation before," he said. "I'm a porter, not a deputy."

"I'm not offering that. I don't have the authority to deputize anyone. That was just for show." I returned the star to my shirt pocket. "It's posse work; fifty cents a day and four cents a mile."

"Last time you said I got free burial."

"You still do. Of course, if you kill anyone, his burial comes out of your pay."

"That's backwards. Cheaper to get kilt than stay alive."

"Isn't it always?"

He parted with his cigarette ash finally, in a peach tin set on the bar for that purpose. He took one last pull and tipped the stub in after it. "Who you hunting?"

"It's not a who. It's a what." I turned my back on the man to my left, tall and thin with an Adam's apple that measured his swallows of beer like the stroke of a steam piston. He was eavesdropping without making any effort to hide it. "Is there a quiet place to drink? I've got a bottle of Hermitage in my valise at the hotel."

"You found a room?"

"Just for the valise. Looks like I'm sleeping at the train station tonight."

"You want to use the floor. It's softer than them benches." He emptied his glass and pushed away from the bar. He didn't invite me, but I followed him out.

When I turned in to the hotel for the whiskey, he told me to get my valise. I came out carrying it and accompanied him to the station, but we didn't go into the building. I followed him to a siding, where he gripped the rail on the back of a caboose and swung himself onto the platform without using the steps. I used them. Inside was a potbelly stove with a cold coffeepot on top, a pair of cots made up neatly, military fashion, three folding chairs, a water crock with dipper, a table holding up a checkerboard, and a brass cuspidor the size of an umbrella stand with N.P.R.R. embossed around the rim. The car smelled of hickory and tobacco juice and cigars and felt like the parlor of a private club. Which it was: the most exclusive in the egalitarian United States, open only to members of the railroad fraternity. Here the conductors retired to put up their sore feet, and the porters and brakemen gathered to play cards and checkers and read newspapers and complain about unreasonable passengers.

There was a checker game in progress on the table, although the players were absent. To avoid disturbing the pieces, Beecher removed a pair of tin cups from a built-in cupboard and set them on the stove to fill from the bottle I took out of my valise.

"What's Mr. Hill say about drinking on railroad property?" I asked.

"What you expect. I'm supposed to have a room, but Chicago kind of forgets how to count where the colored employees are concerned."

"You sleep here?"

"Just till one of them checker players shows up and boots me out. But I figure they got better games to play in town. You can take the other cot. If anybody asks we'll tell 'em you're on railroad business." He picked up one of the cups and sat down on a chair.

I got mine and took another chair. "I thought you were a bad risk after two beers."

"That's why I stopped at one. This stuff drinks like milk." He poured down half his cup in one draught. "This *what* you're after, that ain't a who; it got anything to do with that fellow you kilt?"

I nodded, and told him about the Sons of the Confederacy.

"I never made it to Frisco," he said. "I know some who did. They say Dan Wheelock's the man to see there if you got a misery. I can't feature doing that. I likes to keep my miseries close to home. I'm not good as a spy. Can't even bluff at poker."

"I'll do the spying. I just need somebody to stand behind me on the trip out."

"I ain't your man. I don't even own a pistol."

"Got anything against them?"

"Only that they don't hit what I aims at. I ain't so bad with a rifle, but it's been years."

"Any shooting you're likely to do will be at close range. I know some pistols where marksmanship doesn't count so much." I took my first sip, a dainty one. Good liquor affected me quicker than the watered-down slop you found in most saloons.

"Why pick me? Ain't you got no friends?"

"A friend can be as bad as an enemy when it comes to staying alive. I liked the way you carried yourself on the train. Also it occurred to me you wouldn't approve of the Sons of the Confederacy any more than the man I work for does."

He shook his head and drank. "I don't fight old wars. Anyway, I got a job. It pays a pension and I can't remember the last time anybody got kilt doing it."

"I can't match that."

"All right, then." He got up, topped off his cup, and plunked himself back down. "You like your job?"

"Some parts. Getting killed isn't one. How about you?"

"It's as high as I can go, mister. I disremember your name."

"Page Murdock."

"Scotchman?"

"My father was. He came here when there wasn't anything between Canada and Denver but a lot of Blackfeet and Snake. I was raised by him and a quarter-breed Snake who may or may not have been the bastard granddaughter of Merriwether Lewis, who may or may not have been my mother. Now you know more about me than I do about you."

"I doubt it. That I does. I don't know who my grandfather

was. When I was little, I liked to think he was a chief in Africa. He was likely a slave like all the rest."

"You're a little more than that. The Tenth Cavalry didn't step off the boardwalk for anyone."

"I stepped off plenty since." This time he drained the cup in one gulp.

"Ever miss it?"

"Some parts."

I drank a little more. The stuff was already softening the sharp edges. I choked back a yawn. I didn't sleep well on trains. They were always taking on and dropping off cars, and making all the noise of Shiloh as they went about it. I might have dozed off. I stirred when he stood to refill his cup, and again when he lit the wick on a lantern hanging from a hook on the wall. The ends of the caboose were dark.

". . . scalped a man once," I heard him saying at one lucid point. "A boy, really. Shames me now to think on it. He was a Cheyenne brave, maybe fourteen, scrawny but a scrapper. Raped his share of white women, I expect. Still."

"Not one of the parts you miss."

"I was young and full of piss and corn liquor. Custer weren't cold yet, so I considered it personal. It weren't as if that long-haired hard-ass wouldn't of had me flayed if I kicked one of his damn greyhounds for stealing my rations."

"That happen?"

"Not to me. You hear stories when you're on sentry duty. It could of, though, if I ever got closer to him than three hundred miles of prairie. I don't like dogs or officers. Straw bosses in brass buttons."

"What parts did you like?"

He tapped his fingers on the side of his cup. It was a rolling rattle, like a military tattoo. "Parade."

"Parade?"

"Yeah. Most times you're bored, or your feet hurt, or some white officer's giving you misery on account of your galluses is showing. Everybody's bellyaching about something. On parade you ain't got time to think about all that. You're too busy keeping your chin up and your back straight and your horse from shying, and so's the man next you and the man next him, all the way from the head of the column to the rear. All that counts is keeping the line straight. So long's you do that your color don't matter."

"Parade's one of the things I left the army to get away from."

"*Your* color don't matter whatever you do. I'm talking about being part of something bigger than you."

"If you miss it so much, why'd you quit?"

"Last fight I was in, we raided a Arapaho village. It was on Buffalo Creek, down in Wyoming Territory. Don't bother looking it up, it weren't the Rosebud. When the main column took out after them that got away, I was left behind with some others to burn the lodges and shoot the ponies. Them ponies never done nothing to me. When my enlistment run out I run out with it."

"You like horses?"

He shook his head. "Sons of bitches bite. I reckon I would, too, somebody tried to throw a saddle over me. I wouldn't shoot one because of it."

"You might have to, if you're outnumbered and you need something to hide behind."

"I done that, only not at Buffalo Creek. We was the ones doing the outnumbering."

I remembered my whiskey and drank. It had grown warm from the heat of my hand gripping the cup; I hadn't been so insensible I'd dropped it. "Well, I can't offer anything like parade. I don't care if your chin's in your lap, so long as you keep me alive."

"I'm thinking that's a twenty-four-hour hitch."

"And no time off on Sunday. The Barbary Coast isn't the First Baptist Church."

"Even Mr. Hill knows a man's got to sleep."

"Your job will be waiting when you get back. The man I work for will write him a letter."

"If he ain't J. P. Morgan I don't know how it'd help. Mr. Hill wouldn't change the way he runs his road for anybody less."

"You've never read one of Judge Blackthorne's letters."

He smiled, again without showing his teeth. I was beginning to realize it wasn't connected with anything like amusement on his part. "You ride for Hangin' Harlan?"

"He prefers 'Your Honor.' "

The floor shifted slightly. Someone had mounted the platform outside the door. Beecher said, "Somebody's done come back to finish out that game of checkers. I reckon I can't offer you that other cot after all."

The caboose shifted again, this time closer to the opposite end.

"Douse the light," I said.

He got up without hesitating, raised the chimney on the lantern, and blew out the flame. In the sudden black I stood and drew the Deane-Adams.

The door at the rear swung open and banged against the wall. I fired at the silhouette I saw in the gray rectangle of doorway and swung the other direction, far too slowly, because that door had opened just behind the first, and just as violently. The man on that end fired. My shot was a split second slower, but his missed because Beecher had swept the chair he'd been sitting in off the floor and hurled it the length of the car, striking the second man and throwing off his aim. My bullet snatched him out of the doorway. I pivoted again, but that one was empty also, except for a heap on the platform. The inside of the car stank of brimstone. It had lost its club atmosphere all at once.

Beecher relit the lantern and strode over to cover the second entrance, armed only with the light, which he held out from his body. I kept the revolver in my hand and went the other way.

"This one's still breathing," Beecher called out.

"Get his gun."

The man on the rear platform sat with his back against the railing and one leg pinned under him. He had on a canvas coat, too heavy for the mild early-autumn night, but long enough to cover a firearm, which came away from his hand with no effort when I bent to take it. There was no need to feel for a pulse. In the light from the station, there was a glistening cavern where his left eye belonged. I'd still been coming up from the chair when the door flew open, and had fired high. I couldn't tell if he was young or old. A face in that condition doesn't offer much to go by.

I knelt in front of him and went through his clothes. I felt something and pulled it out.

Beecher called out again. "Three chances what I found in this one's pocket."

"One's all I need." I was looking at the gold coin glinting on my palm.

6

The man I'd killed at the back of the caboose was named Charles Worth, if the letter in his pocket signed, "Your loving sister, Wilhelmina," didn't belong to someone else. I'd never heard of him or his sister. The letter was mostly about the fine weather in Baltimore, but it told me more about him than I found out about his partner, whose punctured lung filled with blood and drowned him before the doctor could get inside. He looked to be in his early thirties and had nothing on his person to identify him; even the labels in his ready-made clothes had been ripped out.

The doctor, a young man himself but with the broken look of a professional who had come west hoping to make his fortune off the anemic wives of wealthy miners only to find himself pulling bullets out of prospectors shot in drunken duels, came out of his examining room wiping his hands with a towel. He scowled at the faces pressed against the windows of his office—bearded and clean-shaven, scrubbed and filthy, locals and visitors—and drew down the shades. The core group had followed us there from the train station. The rest had been growing up around it for twenty minutes.

"He didn't say anything," the doctor said. "You don't when your throat's full of blood and mucus. My work would be a great deal less messy if you fellows would aim for the heart."

I said, "Mine would be, too, if they'd give me time. Did you know the man?"

"I never saw him before, and I know all the residents here at least by sight. He probably drifted in with this new mob. This is my fourth shooting in two days."

"It's them politicians." Beecher was studying a diagram of the human circulatory system on a chart tacked to the wall.

The doctor noticed. "You can take that with you, if you like. It's one of God's miracles. Maybe next time you'll think twice before you blow a hole through it."

"Talk to Mr. Murdock. I ain't shot nobody since the army."

"I was thinking about my own circulatory system when I shot him," I said. "What about the other one?" I gave the doctor the letter I'd found folded in Worth's shirt pocket. A little blood had trickled onto it from the hole in his head, mixing with the yellow-brown ink.

He glanced at it, handed it back. "I knew Charlie. I never worked on him, but he kept me busy, wiring shattered jaws and patching up holes. He liked to pick fights with Yankees. You'd think he served with Robert E. Lee himself, except he was only twelve years old when the war ended."

"Local recruit." I put away the letter. "His friend didn't lose any time looking him up. He must have come in on the same train as me, maybe all the way from Helena."

"If I were you, I'd take the next train out. You, too," he told Beecher. "Charlie had friends."

"Yankee baiters, too?" I asked.

"I doubt they had a creed. In every place, there's an element that falls in behind the man with the loudest manners. They run with the pack because no one else will have them."

"Being part of something that's bigger than themselves?" I was looking at Beecher.

"Ain't the same thing." He'd turned away from the chart.

The doctor rubbed his bloodshot eyes. "I agree with your man. Any group they join is as small as its least-significant member. That's what makes them dangerous."

Beecher said, "I ain't his man."

We went from there to the city marshal's office, which was laid out more like a parlor in a private home than a place of business. A fussy rug lay on the half-sawn logs of the floor, tables covered with lacy shawls held up bulbous lamps with fringes on the shades, homely samplers and pictures from Greek myth hung in gilt-encrusted frames on the walls, which had been slathered with plaster and papered to disguise the logs beneath. The marshal, a basset-faced forty with an advancing forehead and Louis-Napoleon whiskers lacquered into lethal points, sat behind a table with curved legs he used for a desk, examining my deputy's badge for flaws and tugging an enormous watch out of the pocket of his floral vest every few minutes to track the progress of the hands across its face.

"There'll be an inquest," he said. "You'll both have to give evidence."

I said, "We can give you statements right now. I need to be on my way to San Francisco tomorrow."

"No good. You can't ask questions of a written statement in open court."

"Wire Judge Blackthorne. An attack on a deputy U.S. marshal is federal business. It's only your jurisdiction if you want to oppose him."

"I don't expect to go to hell for it. He isn't God."

"Put that in your wire. He might even pay you a personal visit."

"What about the colored man? He federal business?"

Beecher was seated in an upholstered rocker next to an open window, through which the noise of crickets sounded like thousands of violins having their strings plucked. I guessed he'd chosen the spot for the fresh air. The smell of fust in the room was strong enough to stand a shoe up in. "I is with the Northern Pacific, boss. I belongs to the right-of-way."

"Beecher's a civilian employed by Blackthorne's court," I said. "He's U.S. property same as me."

"Gold Creek isn't Tombstone or Deadwood. We're an incorporated city, with a charter and two churches. The local chapter of the Grand Army of the Republic meets in the basement of the Unitarian. When two men are killed, the incident is investigated and adjudicated. This is a civilized community."

I said, "According to the doctor, killing is daily business. Do you seriously intend to claim two more when Helena is offering to take them off your hands?"

"My appointment's up for review at the end of this year. I don't want to be accused of stuffing something behind the stove." He didn't appear to be listening to himself. Washing his hands of the thing appealed to him, but there was a gilt-edged Bible in plain sight on his desk. No Christian wants to be compared with Pilate.

"Blame it on de gub'ment, boss," Beecher said. "Everybody else does."

The marshal pulled on his whiskers. His neck creased like a concertina. "I don't recall asking you for counsel, boy. I can't see any time I would."

Beecher shrugged and inhaled air from outside.

However, the argument was through, and it was his suggestion that finished it. The marshal wasn't going to let things look that way, so I changed the subject, to give him time to form the conclusion independently.

"Did you get to meet General Grant?"

The creases disappeared. He held up a set of red and swollen knuckles. "Right here's the hand that shook the hand. When I told him I served with the quartermaster corps, he thanked me for the boots that took him all the way from Fort Henry to Appomattox."

"He could probably use a new pair. I hear the business world hasn't been kind to him."

"Me neither, comes to that. I ran a mercantile in Albany, best in town. I closed it up and came out here to sell picks and shovels, and I sold plenty, all on credit. I figure to be a rich man just as soon as all those markers come in. Meanwhile, I break up fights and shoot rats and stray dogs to put meat on my table."

"What's a rat taste like?" Beecher asked.

I bulled ahead before the marshal could pull his chin back in. "Everyone I talk to came out here to make money off miners. Didn't anyone come for the gold?"

"They're still out digging."

The weapons we'd taken off the men at the caboose lay on the marshal's blotter. Worth's was a short-barreled Colt. The stranger had fired a wicked-looking revolver at me, equipped with a second barrel whose bore was larger than the one on top. I pointed at it.

"I'll be taking the Le Mat with me," I said.

"That's evidence."

"Blackthorne would just send someone to collect it. I'll save him the trouble."

"What about the Colt?"

"I don't need the Colt."

"What do you want with a Confederate piece?"

"They didn't lose the war because their weapons weren't good. They just didn't have enough men to carry them. I'll give you a receipt."

He shoved it across the table at me. "Anything else I can do for you, seeing as how all's I got pressing on my time is a town full of drunken Easterners?"

I checked the load. There were four live .42 cartridges in the cylinder, someone having taken the trouble to convert it from cap-and-ball, and a 20-gauge shell in the shotgun tube. He'd fired one cartridge and kept an empty chamber under the hammer. I was grateful he'd chosen not to use the buckshot on me. "You can direct me to a gunsmith's."

"How many weapons does a man need?"

"No more than he has hands, but guns aren't much use without ammunition."

"You want Joe Hankerd at the Rocky Mountain General Merchandise, only he's closed now. I don't know if he carries anything for a rebel gun."

"Both sides used the same calibers."

We got directions. It took five minutes of door-kicking to bring down a red-faced runt in handlebars and a nightshirt, and two more to get him to lower his sawed-off double-barrels and let us in. He charged me twice the going rate for two boxes of shells, one for each of the Le Mat's firing features, and locked up loudly behind us.

"Frontier's famous for its hospitality," Beecher said.

"That's just from sunup to sundown."

We were still towing a percentage of the local population, but they thinned out as we left the saloons behind and continued walking toward the mountains. The only light ahead of us belonged to the lanterns and campfires of the mine sites in the distance. Our breath frosted a little in the crisp air of coming autumn. Beecher asked where we were headed.

"Away from the crowd."

We lost the last straggler to a hotel whose latecomers were camped out on the floor of the lobby. Shielding the movement with my body, I handed Beecher the Le Mat and the two boxes of ammunition. "Keep them out of sight. A Negro with a gun can draw a lot of hell most places."

"I told you I'm no good with a pistol." He held the items in both hands like a balance scale.

I took back the revolver, adjusted the nose on the hammer, and returned it. "That fires the shotgun round. Scatterguns were designed with you in mind."

"I ain't said I'm throwing in with you."

"You threw in when you threw that chair. By this time tomorrow, every depot lizard from here to the Pacific will know about the colored porter who helped kill two men in Gold Creek. You're branded either way."

He touched the scar on his cheek with the Le Mat's muzzle. "I reckon I am."

"I didn't mean that."

"I know. But a nigger with a scar has a hard time blending in with the black crowd."

"Getting out of that uniform will help. Got any civilian clothes?"

"In my duffel. In the caboose."

"We'll collect it in the morning. It'll just be another caboose by then. A couple of killings won't draw attention long with Grant in town."

"*That's* what's been stinging me. I couldn't think. If these new Johnny Rebs want to make a stir, why choose you? Grant's the bigger target."

"That's the reason. Too many people around him. These boys aren't interested in making themselves martyrs for the cause. Getting away's as important to them as hitting what they aim at."

His teeth caught the light from a window. It was the first time he'd shown them. "If that's the case, they didn't think it through where you're concerned."

I didn't smile back. "My odds just got a little shorter. Meanwhile, we've got eight hundred miles to cover before San Francisco."

"You ain't asked me why I threw that chair."

"I didn't figure you gave it any thought. That cavalry training dies hard."

"I ain't no trick dog."

I blew air. "Are we going to have this conversation all the way to California? Because if we are, I'd just as soon we rode in separate cars."

"We probably will anyway."

"That's between you and Mr. Hill. Do we leave this conversation here or not?"

"I reckon," he said after a moment. "I don't see any sport in it."

"I didn't get around to thanking you for throwing that chair."

"No need. I didn't give it any thought." He stuck the revolver under his belt and the boxes in his pockets. "Where we sleeping tonight?"

"Take your pick." I swept a hand along the weak lights wavering in the foothills.

"Them miners'll likely shoot us as claim-jumpers."

"They might, if their claims were worth the filing fees. That's the thing about frontier hospitality. The poorer a man is, the more he's got of it."

I started off in the direction of the fires. Beecher caught up, his pockets rattling like a peddler's wagon. We weren't sneaking up on any prospectors that night.

7

The first train had pulled out with General Grant aboard by the time we got to the station the next morning. There were no seats on the second, so I bought a ticket on the third—Beecher showed his employee's pass—and we ate breakfast at a place called the Miner's Rest while waiting for departure. The proprietor sent us around to the kitchen, whether because of Beecher's color or the clothes I'd slept in up in the hills, I didn't know. In his corduroy coat, cotton twill shirt and trousers, flat-heeled boots, and slouch hat, my companion looked the more respectable member of our party.

The conductor, a stranger to Beecher, directed us to separate coaches, assigning the Negro to a twenty-year-old chair car well back of the Pullmans containing the dignitaries, most of whom required a porter's assistance to climb the steps from the station platform through a haze of whiskey and stale perfume. I recognized some of them from the train I'd come in on; promoted from fourth to third to fill vacancies left by those who'd taken the express back East.

I started to say I'd take the chair car, too, but in response to an infinitesimal shake of Beecher's head I asked for a pencil and paper, and when they were brought by a porter I scribbled a message and gave him a dollar to send a wire. Beecher and I separated. I lowered a window against the stink of cigars and digested barley, swung down the footrest, and got to work catching up on the sleep I'd lost lying on the iron earth under a borrowed blanket in the hills. Ten years more and I'd need a featherbed. Just plain surviving is fatal in the end.

Shortly after the train started moving, a fat fellow with a bad sunburn plunked himself down next to me, introduced himself as a reporter with a New York newspaper, and asked if I'd heard anything about a double shooting in Gold Creek. I said I hadn't.

"Someone said there was a renegade nigger involved," he said.

"I wouldn't know."

"Late night last night. I slept right through it, didn't catch wind of it till the train was pulling out. Any Indian trouble along the line?" He sounded eager.

"Not anymore. They're all on reservations."

"What about train robbers? I understand they're thick as fleas in Montana."

I said I didn't think the fleas in Montana were thicker than anywhere else, but he didn't take the hint. When he started in on grizzlies I changed seats.

In Deer Lodge, the porter I'd asked to send my wire shook me awake and handed me a Western Union envelope. I read the telegram and made my way back through the snoring payload to the ancient chair car, where I found Beecher jammed in between a mulatto in a valet's livery and a Chinese with a wooden cage on his lap containing a sitting hen. The car was so hot the flies were asleep in midair. I told Beecher to join me up front. He started to shake his head again, then thought better of it, got up, took down his duffel from the tarnished brass carrier, and followed me.

Five minutes after we sat down in the Pullman, the conductor appeared. He had a drinker's face, shot through with broken capillaries, and cardamom on his breath. Why anyone west of Chicago was in any business other than drumming whiskey was a puzzle.

"I'm sorry, sir," he said. "I guess I didn't make myself clear in Gold Creek. The other, er, gentleman—"

I stuck the telegram under his nose. It read:

DEPUTY MURDOCK
BE ADVISED EDWARD ANDERSON BEECHER
NEGRO OFFICIALLY ASSIGNED DUTIES DEPUTY
U S MARSHAL EFFECTIVE THIS DATE STOP
ENTITLED SAME CONSIDERATION AUTHORITY
ALL OTHER DEPUTIES
                 CHESTER A ARTHUR
                 PRESIDENT
                 UNITED STATES OF AMERICA

He sawed the flimsy back and forth, caught the focus, and paled a little behind the magenta.

"How do I know this is real?" Pricklets of sweat stood out like boiler rivets on his upper lip. He fanned himself with the paper, without any visible effect. "Anyone can send a wire and call himself the King of Prussia."

I showed him my deputy's star. "Wire him back. He ought to be sitting down to dinner with General Sherman about now."

For all I knew he was having his toenails painted by a harlot sent by the New York Port Authority, but the conductor knew even less than I did. He handed back the telegram and left the car, wobbling on his sore feet.

Beecher asked to see the telegram. I gave it to him. He read it and looked up. "Arthur really send this?"

"It's doubtful, but you can ask Judge Blackthorne next time you get to Helena. If he's in a generous mood he might even give you a straight answer."

"What did you tell him?"

"You're the only thing keeping me alive."

"He set this much store by all the help?"

"A good carpenter takes care of his tools."

He read the flimsy again. Then he returned it. "My luck, it'll be this same train I work when I get back. I'll be emptying spittoons come the new century."

"I wouldn't brood on it. If we make San Francisco, chances are we'll both end up on the bottom of the bay."

"That being the situation, I believe I'll ask one of these here colored boys to bring me a cigar."

"Open a window if you do. I'd as soon sit next to a chicken." I put the telegram in a safe pocket. I had an idea I'd be drawing it as often as the Deane-Adams.

PART TWO

The Hoodlums

8

Three days and as many train changes later, we rolled into San Francisco aboard the Southern Pacific through a swirling mulch as brown as brandy and nearly as thick, a combination of fog from the harbor and coal smoke from a thousand chimneys. The globes of the fabled gas lamps, their posts obscured, lay like fishermen's floats on its surface, glowing dirty orange. On the depot platform the porters wheeled trunks and portmanteaux with lanterns balanced atop the stacks toward waiting hotel carriages; the lanterns illuminated little but themselves, but they gave passengers something to follow and avoid stepping off the edge and breaking a limb. Telegraph Hill was an island in a dun sea, pierced here and there by the odd church spire and the tall masts in the harbor.

Beecher and I were looking for a porter to direct us to a hotel that didn't care which colors it mixed under its roof when a dandy materialized out of the mist in front of us. He was thirty or younger, with longish flaxen hair curling out from under a Mexican sombrero, wearing an olive-colored frock coat over an embroidered vest that looked as if it had been cut out of the carpet in the lobby of an opera house. His trousers were fawn-colored and stuffed into knee-high boots and he was carrying a walking stick too short to lean on, made for swinging when he walked. It was all good material but needed cleaning; and had for some time, from the smell of him. The stick, however, had been polished recently, gleaming in what light there was like the tongue of an exotic reptile.

"Carry your bags, cap'n?" He pointed at my valise with his stick. He was holding it by the handle, a heavy-looking blob of silver shaped into the head of some animal.

"I've just got the one," I said.

"Half a hog for my trouble? I'm past two days without gruel."

"What's half a hog?"

"A nickel, cap'n. First time in Frisco?" He showed me a gold tooth, which would have made a better impression if the one next to it weren't black.

"Is there a tax on that?"

He giggled, and twisted the handle off the stick.

He did it one-handed, with a neat, practiced flick of his wrist, but he'd have done better to use both hands, because it called attention to itself. The rest of the stick fell away from eighteen inches of bright metal narrowing to a point. I got my valise in front of it just as he underhanded it at the center of my rib cage. It sheared through the leather like a lance through a blister. Before he could pull it back out and try again, I gave the valise a twist, snapping the shaft clean in two.

He had good reflexes. Six inches of jagged metal still stuck out of the handle, and without hesitating, he drew back to jab it at my face. I swung up the valise, but the contents shifted, throwing off the angle, and in that instant I saw myself walking through the rest of my life sideways with my empty eye socket turned to the shadow. Then something cracked, a sharp, shocking explosion like a chunk of hickory splitting in a stove. The dandy's sombrero fell off and he followed it down to the platform. In his place stood a sad-faced stranger with black bartender's handlebars under a leather helmet. He had a blue uniform buttoned to his chin and an oak stick in one hand, attached to his wrist by a leather thong. His expression as he examined the results of his action looked as if he'd bashed in the head of a kitten.

However, young skulls are hard to break. The dandy pushed himself into a sitting position and blinked up through the blood in his eyes. "You can't pinch me! I'm a Hoodlum!"

The man in uniform appeared to consider this. Then he leaned down and tapped the young man behind the right ear. The arm the dandy was supporting himself on went out flat and he fell onto his back. His eyes rolled over white and a thread of drool slid out of one corner of his mouth. Apart from that, nothing moved.

I remembered Beecher then and looked his way just as he pulled out his shirttail and dropped it over the butt of the Le Mat stuck under his belt. A bit more practice and he'd have it in his hand the next time a foot and a half of sword let out my intestines. He was more reliable with a chair.

"This one ain't much older than my sister's boy," the policeman muttered. His Irish was as thick as stout. "They're getting too small to keep. Ah, me." He stuck his stick under one arm, produced a pair of manacles from a loop on his belt, and bent to work.

"I'm obliged, Officer," I said when he straightened.

He had a bulge in one cheek, which he emptied into a brown mess on the platform near where the dandy lay on his stomach now, with his hands linked behind his back. "You gents need to check those weapons first stop you make. You have run out of wilderness when you're in San Francisco."

Our pistols were out of sight, but there is no overestimating a policeman's eye. I told him my name, which meant nothing to him, and showed him my star, which meant very little more.

"What about your man?"

Beecher said, "I ain't—"

I snapped open the telegram with Arthur's signature for the policeman to read. He grunted, shifted his plug from one cheek to the other, pursed his lips to spit, thought better of it, and mopped his mouth with the back of a broken-knuckled hand. "I voted for Hancock. Come to clean up Barbary?"

"You seem to be doing a fair job of that all by yourself." I put away the flimsy.

"This?" He toed the inert man in the ribs. "This pup wandered out of his yard. Past Pacific Street I'd of wanted the militia. Just because these Hoodlums own the waterfront don't mean they hold title to the rest."

Beecher asked what a Hoodlum was. The policeman appraised him, worked up a fresh head of juice, and defiled the crown of the young man's sombrero lying on the platform.

"Dips and thieves what like to dress up like toffs," he said.

"That poetist fellow Oscar Wilde hared through here last year, piping up beauty for its own sake and decked out in purple velvet, which is milk and sugar to these lads. Come sunup next day, you couldn't find a bolt of brocade that wasn't spoke for, nor an unslashed pocket to pay for it. It's how they know each other. Going in after 'em's the same as putting your fist through a paper nest of hornets. This far inland all you got to do is step on 'em."

"Are you sure he's a Hoodlum?" I asked.

"He ain't Wilde. I know, because the wife dragged me down to Platt's Hall to see him. I never wasted fifty cents worse in all my born days."

"Would you mind checking his pockets?"

"What for, iron knuckles? He didn't need 'em as long as he had that trick stick."

"I'm looking for a double eagle."

He barked a short laugh. "Twenty crackers in his pocket, and he tries to nick you for a five-cent piece?"

"It could have been an excuse to get close."

The policeman spat, sighed, knelt, and performed the chore. The young man moaned when he was jostled, but didn't wake up. He might have had a fractured skull. The policeman rose with his bounty displayed on his palm. "Two coppers and a busted watch. Fellow he nipped it from probably fell on it. If he ever had a double Ned, it's spent. Not on soap." He pocketed the items and mopped his palm on his trousers.

"These coins aren't for spending. He's just a thief, like you said."

"Wheelock's Wards, we call 'em here."

I perked up at that. "Daniel Webster Wheelock?"

"If there's more than one, it's a bigger country than they told me when I shipped over. These lads are Cap'n Dan's eyes and ears outside the Bella Union. Employing unfortunates, he calls it. I wouldn't know. The only unfortunate thing I see about these lads is they're as many as ants. I wouldn't drop my drawers in a Donegan on Kearney without a squad to stand behind me."

I remembered Wheelock was a fire captain as well as a city alderman. I only half understood the rest. I thanked him again for stepping in and hoisted my valise. The broken sword-end came loose of the rent in the leather and clattered to the platform.

"Thank Mr. Callahan," he said, slapping his palm with his stick. "It's the only English these lads savvy. Where you gents billeted? Magistrate might need you to swear out a complaint, on account of the fog."

"The fog?"

"If he's a Wheelock man, he might say I couldn't see what I saw. That's what makes these boyos so chesty when Callahan comes to call."

"No billet yet," I said. "All suggestions are welcome."

He thought for a moment. "The Slop Chest on Davis is the crib for you. It ain't so bad as it sounds; Nan Feeny inherited it from her husband, the Commodore, who was soft on sailors and named it after a captain's tackle. Twelve cents the day, eighty the week if you pony up front. Either of you gents smoke tobacco?"

Beecher said he did.

"You'll want to run the tip down the mattress seams. Discourages the active citizens."

" 'Active citizens'?" we said together.

The policeman spat and shook his head. "That's any with at least four legs more than you. Come morning, you'll think you was cut up by the tongs. You frontier folk might know your Injun palaver, but if you don't learn the local office, you'll finish up feeding fish in the bay."

The Hoodlum was coming around, moaning something about taking the jolly off, or something equally enlightening. The policeman reached down and hauled him to his feet by his shackles. This brought a howl that made me feel as if my own arms were being torn from their sockets, which the policeman silenced by punching the young man in the ribs with his stick. As he was being pulled toward the end of the platform, the Hoodlum said, "My roofer," which was the first thing he'd said that I could translate without help. The policeman bent, scooped up the tobacco-stained sombrero by its crown, and jammed it down over the prisoner's ears. Then he led him off into the fog.

Beecher said, "I didn't follow but one word that man said in ten."

"Maybe Nan Feeny has a dictionary." I tucked in the torn flap of my valise and started off in the path of the policeman and his captive.

The first cabman I told to take us to the Slop Chest ordered us out of his carriage. Since he was holding his whip we didn't argue. I told the next one in line before we got in, and we didn't get in. The third driver, who was the most polite, pretended he was too busy getting his cigar burning to hear me. When I spoke to the next one down I held up the late Charlie Worth's double eagle, turning it until it caught the light from the corner gas lamp. It brought no smile.

"That's too much." He was a lean fifty in an old-fashioned stovepipe hat and neckstock, with the sandy complexion of someone who spent most of his time sitting out in the elements.

I said, "I thought if I showed it, you wouldn't think I was luring you out there to nip you."

I must have got the vernacular wrong, or maybe amused contempt was the only other expression he had. He pointed his chin at Beecher. "He with you?"

I said he was. I'd already dismissed this driver and was thinking ahead toward the last carriage in the line. I wondered how long the walk was to Davis and what kind of hell the fog contained on the way.

"Twenty-five cents. I don't split fares."

We got in.

Either the haze was lifting or my eyes were becoming accustomed to the stingy light that managed to penetrate it. We watched ornate gingerbread buildings sliding past, a stout, homely little brick box whose sign identified it as the United States Mint, which belatedly I realized was where the coin in my pocket had come from, and to where it had returned by way of circumstances unsuspected by the men who operated the stampers. Shortly after that, the gimcrackery faded out and even brick became scarce, replaced by buildings made of clapboard and scrapwood bearing unmistakable stains from exposure to the sea; ships that had sailed their last missions, broken up for what profit could be obtained from their corpses. A dozen or so blocks of that, and then the carriage came to a stop.

"Slop Chest," the driver said.

"Holy Jesus," Beecher said.

"Home," I said; and loosened the Deane-Adams in its holster before getting out.

9

—

The Slop Chest—this on the basis of the driver's declaration, since there was no sign to identify it—looked at first as if it had floated in on a devastating flood, and settled on its present foundation when the waters receded. It was built to resemble an oversize flatboat, with a cabin on the deck and part of the railing removed for visitors to enter by way of three warped steps and a door that might have been cut out of the side with a bucksaw for all the attention that had been paid to plumbs and levels, and hung with leather hinges. What appeared at first to have been a hit-or-miss whitewashing of the boards turned out on examination to be a couple of decades' worth of sea salt, washed up on deck during storms and allowed to dry into a crust as hard as limestone; seasons of rain had washed some of it onto the strip of bare earth that separated the structure from the boardwalk, forever preventing the growth of so much as a single blade of grass. A dilapidated rocking chair and glider occupied the deck—I suppose it could be called a front porch—and these, together with nearly every square inch of the floor, were covered with bodies flung about in loose-rag positions that suggested either a massacre or a bacchanal of ancient Greek proportions. These men were clad in peacoats, striped jerseys, and baggy canvas trousers, sailors' garb. Their snores were loud enough to rock the old boat on its moorings.

"Looks like the Little Big Horn," said Beecher.

"Or Hampton Roads," I said. "Who's minding the ships in the harbor?"

"Twenty-five cents," said the driver.

I paid him. He stuck the coin between his teeth and gave the reins a flip. I stepped back just in time to save my toes.

Beecher slung his duffel over his left shoulder, unbuttoned his shirt to clear the path to the Le Mat under his belt, and we climbed the steps.

The interior was a saloon, better appointed than the outside would indicate. There were a couple of gaming tables covered in green baize, an iron chandelier suspended from the ceiling, beneath which a mound of pale wax from the dripping candles had begun to grow into a stalagmite on the floor, and a carved mahogany bar with a pink marble top. Behind it, above the bottles aligned on a back bar nearly as ornate, hung a canvas in a gilt frame as wide as a fainting-couch, upon which sprawled at full length a hideously fat woman amateurishly executed in thick paint. It was the lewdest thing I'd seen outside of the upstairs room of a brothel, and wouldn't have existed half an hour in any public establishment on the frontier before the decency squads poured in with their axes and wooden truncheons.

Beecher stared at the painting. "Man must of used up every drop of pink in town."

The room wasn't as crowded as I'd expected on the evidence of the front porch. A blue-chinned tinhorn in a frayed cutaway and dirty top hat was dealing himself a hand of Patience at one of the tables and three men, two of them dressed as sailors, the third in a faded wool shirt and filthy overalls worn nearly through at the knees—a miner's kit—leaned on the bar, nursing glasses of beer and conversing not at all. The hour was too early for celebration and too close to midday for the gainfully employed. It was a depressing time to drink. Gloom hung overhead like the chandelier, dripping dejection into a sullen mound.

There was no sunshine to be had from the bartender, an old salt who at one time might have been cheerfully fat, but whom life had rendered down until the gray skin hung in sheets from his cheekbones and bare forearms, blue as old china with aging tattoos of indeterminate character. His bald head was as white as polished bone above the line where a hat protected it from the sun when he went outside; the first indication I'd seen that the city was not perpetually wrapped in smutty fog. I bought two beers, which he poured from a tap covered with green mold, and asked if Nan Feeny was on the premises.

"Who for, you or your man? She don't favor pumpernickel."

Beecher clapped the Le Mat on the bartop, which at close range was far from pristine. The marble was mottled all about with odd saucer-shaped depressions with cracks radiating out from the centers. I couldn't decide what could have caused them. "Next one calls me his man won't be one much longer," he told the bartender.

The old sailor looked at the pistol as if it were a fresh spill. "Hodge."

He barely raised his voice. I was still puzzling out where this latest new word belonged in the regional lexicon when a section of the back bar swung away from the wall and a dwarf entered the room through the opening.

He impressed me as a dwarf. From his beltline to his bowler-topped head he was normal size, built thick as a prizefighter through the chest and shoulders, his biceps straining the sleeves of his yellow-and-black-striped sailor's jersey. From the waist down, he was no larger than a six-year-old boy, and one stricken with rickets into the bargain. He paused this side of the opening, then came forward, swaying from side to side on shriveled bowlegs draped in black broadcloth. His feet kept going when he reached the bar, pumping him up until he was facing Beecher at eye-level. I went up on the balls of my feet and spotted the three-foot ladder nailed inside the bar. His face was unlined, late twenties at the oldest, with a closely trimmed black beard covering the lower half, grown probably to prevent strangers from mistaking him for a child.

An explosion shook the bar, slopping beer over the rims of the glasses perched on it and draining a trickle of plaster from the ceiling. Beecher and I jumped; the other patrons at the bar didn't stir, except to lean on one elbow to watch a show they'd seen before. I looked down and saw a fresh depression in the marble. It was occupied by a black-enameled iron sphere half again the size of a billiard ball, attached by six inches of chain to a ring poking out of the little man's right sleeve. There was no hand there. With a practiced gesture he'd swung the ball in a short arc ending in a loud bang when it struck the bar, just short of crushing Beecher's hand where it rested next to the Le Mat.

"No firearms in the Slop Chest, mate." He had a broad cockney accent, but his voice was low and silken, unlike the bray of a small man with something to prove. He didn't need it as long as he had that ball and chain. "Either check 'em here or leave 'em home."

The bartender scowled at the new dent. "Damn it, Hodge, I told you before I'm responsible for this bar. Nan said she'd dock me next time."

"I'll stake the whole bloody whack. A bar oughtn't be marble to start. It stains like cotton drawers. What's it to be, mate?" He kept his eyes on Beecher. "Lay up the snapper or take one in the brain-box?" He twirled his wrist. The ball made a shallow orbit and landed where it had started. Slivers of marble jumped up and skittered across the bar.

"Jesus, Hodge!" the bartender complained.

Very slowly, Beecher slid his hand forward and nudged the revolver's handle inside the little man's reach. Hodge scooped it up with his good right hand and thrust it toward the bartender, who took it and placed it on a high back shelf lined with backstraps of every make and model. There were more confiscated weapons there than patrons in the saloon; evidence that the place indeed took on boarders. Hodge's gaze slid my way. "What's your story, mate? Try me on?"

Using two fingers I drew the star from my shirt pocket and laid it on the bar. He barely glanced at it.

"Tin's cheap," he said. "What else you got?"

I took out the telegram and spread it on the bar. The edges were tattering. I was considering having it framed and hanging it around my neck. Beecher probably wouldn't volunteer for that.

"What's it say, Billy?"

The bartender read aloud, stumbling over "officially" and "consideration." It might have been signed by the man who emptied the spitoons for all the impression Arthur's name seemed to make on either of them.

"Paper's cheaper." Hodge looked patient.

I slid the Deane-Adams out of its holster and held it toward him butt-first.

"On the bar. I heard about the border roll in Brisbane."

I laid it down, retrieved the star and the telegram, and pocketed them. He picked up the revolver, thumbed aside the loading gate, and rotated the cylinder to inspect the chambers, all one-handed. "English piece. Limeys transported me old man's old man for picking an earl's pocket, but I ain't one to stroke a grudge. What's a Yank want with a barking-iron made in Blighty?"

"I don't care for Colts. The five-shot's lighter and packs the same fire power."

"What happens when you face six men?"

"I run."

He grinned in his beard. His teeth looked too white and even to have grown inside his mouth. I asked him if he lost his hand in Australia.

"Coming over. Worked my way across. Mainsail bust loose while I was striking it and took me rammer with it. Had me a regular hook till I rolled over on it in me doss and near crushed the old cobblers. Got a smithy on Battle Row to run me up this rig. I count me rise in the world from that day. You don't need to be as tall as Jack's hat when you got four pounds of Michigan iron slang off your fam."

"How do you sleep?" Beecher asked.

"Like a rum angel, cock's-crow to day's arse."

I said, "Sorry we got you out of bed. We need a couple of rooms. A policeman at the train station told us to ask for Nan Feeny."

His porcelains gleamed. "Best be mum about that with Nan. She wouldn't appreciate a fly-cop giving her the oak."

"Does anyone in this town speak American?" I asked.

"Nan's your mollisher. She was a governess in Boston till they caught her up to her petticoats in the master of the house. He's still rhino fat up there on Beacon Hill, but the booly-dogs stunned her right out of her regulars and she took it on the rods. She's fly to the patter when it suits."

Now he was just showing off. "You're the bouncer here?"

"Keeper of the keys, and Nan Feeny's knees. Axel Hodge is the chant, and Black-Spy take the cove says it ain't. You're this bloke Murdock?"

"Page Murdock."

"Horseshit," said Billy the bartender. He was the most articulate man in the place.

Hodge's face was an opaque sheet. "Well, you may be flush gage out in country, but here you're just herring. Frisco's a bufe what eats anything."

I'd had my colorful fill of Axel Hodge. I nudged Beecher's

foot with my boot, alerting him, then took hold of the iron ball where it rested on the bar and jerked it across and over the lip of the marble on my side. Hodge's arm came with it. His chin hit the bar with a snap that was going to send him back to his dentist for adjustments. Billy reacted, reaching under his side of the bar for whatever weapon waited there, but before he could straighten up, Beecher wrenched the Deane-Adams out of Hodge's startled grip, rolled back the hammer with a gesture that told me he'd been practicing with the Le Mat while I wasn't looking, and took aim at the spot where the old sailor's eyebrows met above the bridge of his nose.

The other patrons took their elbows off the bar and slid out of ricochet range, but not so far away they wouldn't be able to witness what happened next. This was something new at the Slop Chest, worth repeating when they were back at sea and the tall tales had spun themselves out.

Hodge tried to pull away, but I leaned my hip against the iron ball, pinning it against the mahogany on my side. He couldn't get leverage with his short legs.

"I was told folks are friendly in California," I said. "If this is how you treat all your customers, I'm not surprised they'd rather draw flies on the front porch than come in and wet their whiskers."

The air stirred. Weatherbeaten boards moaned and shifted, leather scraped wood, a dozen voices howled in protest. In a small advertising mirror tilted on one of the shelves behind the bar, I saw sunburned, unshaven faces plastered against the windows and jammed together between the doorjambs leading to the front porch. I thought at first the sleeping sailors had been roused at last by the commotion inside. Then the bodies in the doorway separated as if someone had pried them apart with a pinch-bar and ten yards of taffeta and silk petticoat rustled in through the space, wrapped around six feet of female.

Movement rippled through the crowd, and caps and hats came off heads that had been breeding lice in darkness for weeks. That was impressive.

"What's the row, Hodge?" the woman said. "I could hear you punching holes in my bar all the way from Pacific."

"Cly your daddles, Nan. It's all plummy." With his chin nailed to the bartop, the rest of Hodge's hard-hatted head had to move up and down to get the words out.

Nan Feeny—what I could see of her while dividing my concentration among Hodge, Billy, and the woman's reflection in the mirror—had a handsome head on a long neck with a choker, topped by an elaborate pile of hair—startlingly white, against a face that was still too young to need as much paint as had been applied to it.

"Plummy as a bag of nails," she observed, and unslung a pepperbox pistol from the reticule she carried.

"Red lady," muttered the tinhorn seated at the table, laying the queen of diamonds on the king of clubs.

10

Just the one, and you're lucky to have it. Them pegos wasn't sleeping on the deck for the fresh air. Twenty-five cents a day." Nan Feeny opened the door and stepped aside.

"We were told twelve." I waited for my eyes to adjust. The room, one of several opening off a short hall behind the barroom, was a windowless den no larger than a ship's berth, with two narrow bunks built one atop the other into the wall, which I thought was carrying the nautical theme too far.

"Twelve apiece, and a penny tax."

"Who collects the tax?" Beecher took his turn looking at the accommodations. There wasn't room for two men to stand inside.

"Little squint-eyed ponce stinks of lilacs, and you don't want to turn him away without his copper. I was burned out once. That's the price of pride in Barbary."

We'd settled our differences in the saloon. Beecher had

checked his revolver and I'd given Hodge back his arm, and when she'd put up the pepperbox we'd straightened out the reason for our visit. Face to face, or almost—the proprietress had two inches on me in my high-heeled boots—she had bad skin, hence the paint, and strong bones that wouldn't give up her age short of another decade. However, she was still two young for her white hair, which didn't look like a wig. She wore it in a chignon that added several unnecessary inches to her height.

I asked her how much for a week, which surprised her. Her natural eyebrows went up almost as high as the ones she'd brushed on.

"Cartwheel dollar. I don't take paper. There's more queer cole hereabouts than treasury. If it's coniakers you're after, I'd best quote you the rate for a year." She had a granite brogue with no green pastures in it.

I'd shown her the star and the telegram. "We're not interested in counterfeiters, if that's what you're asking. Tell me if this means anything." I handed her the double eagle.

She studied the coin on both sides. I thought for a moment she was going to bite it, but teeth were scarcer than gold in that neighborhood. She gave it back, and it was my turn to be surprised. I thought I'd have to wrestle her for it. "I ain't even seen one of them in lead. If you take Nan's advice you'll keep it in your kick. There's tobbies'd settle you for spud and lurch your pork in the brine."

Any way I worked that out didn't sound attractive.

Beecher said, "This one was stamped right here in San Francisco."

Nan studied him before answering. I couldn't tell where she stood on the subject of conversing with Negroes.

"Strictly speaking you left Frisco behind when you crossed Pacific Street. There's some as would say you passed right on through America and out the other side."

I said, "You're telling us you'd know if someone was walking around with one of these in his pocket."

"There's nary a thing Nan don't know what goes on between here and blue water."

"What about the Sons of the Confederacy?"

She twisted a lip. "I'd swap a week's peck to see one of them Nob Hill noddles try on Barbary. There'd be rebel red from Murder Point to North Beach."

"I was told they're thick here."

"I ain't saying you can't spot 'em, all got up in lace goods and lifting their roofers to the mollies as like to give their active citizens some sun. Past dark they don't show their nebs outside the Bella Union. Sons of the Confederacy, my aunt's smicket. They couldn't make war on Queen Dick."

"They've done a fair job of making war on peace officers," I said. "Is that the same Bella Union where Daniel Webster Wheelock hangs his hat?"

"There ain't but one." She took my measure from under her eyelids, one of which drooped a little like a broken windowshade. The powder she used by the pot hadn't quite eradicated an old scar that ran diagonally across its top. "What's your business with Cap'n Dan?"

"I heard he's the man to see in Barbary."

"That's no packet, though you'll not see him without he

gives it his benison. He posted the cole to the Commodore to start the Slop Chest. He's also the cove what sent the squint-eyed ponce and the slubber de gullions what set fire to the place."

The stubborn fog had found its way into the hallway through the gaps between the boards. I held up the double eagle. "I like to listen to your Irish. Where can we go to hear more out of the draft?"

Her private quarters was three times the size of the room where Beecher and I had left our bags, which didn't make it spacious. There was a barrel stove for heating and cooking, a pair of mis-matched chairs, one with a broken-cane seat, a cornshuck mat-tress on an iron frame, and a portrait of Nan's late husband, the Commodore, who had been twice her present age when it was painted and looked like just the kind of old walrus who would undertake to support a woman not yet born when he sprouted his first gray hair. The cut of the men's clothes in the doorless wardrobe—a number of sailors' jerseys and a full-dress suit—bore out Axel Hodge's boast that he was the keeper of Nan Feeny's knees. A seam in one wall showed where the back bar opened into the saloon. The room might have belonged to the master of the ship, if the Slop Chest had been a ship instead of a facsimile thrown together from the corpses of genuine vessels. The carpenter in charge was incapable of building anything that would float in a gentle pond.

Sitting up on the bed with her high-laced ankles crossed and peach brandy in a cordial glass in her hand—Beecher and I

declined an invitation to join her in the sticky-sweet beverage—
our hostess lowered her guard sufficiently to modify her language and, more revealingly, offer her colored guest a cigar from
the Commodore's private stock, which she kept fresh by storing
the boxes in a cupboard with fresh bread. He accepted it and
made himself as comfortable as possible on the chair with the
broken seat, puffing up gray clouds that found their way out
through the spaces in the siding. Because the place was as private
as a cornrick, we kept our voices low and Nan got up frequently
to rewind the crank on a phonograph with a morning-glory
horn the size of Joaquin's head. "Beautiful Dreamer" drifted out
of the opening, interpreted by a tenor with bad sinuses.

Nan, for all her stature and presumed experience with
strong drink, became candid under the influence of the peach
brandy. We learned that the Commodore, whose given name
was Cornelius, had not spent a day at sea, but had profited in
Chinatown through the opium smuggled in by way of the pockets of common seamen so far as to have developed an affection
for the briny breed. The policeman who had recommended the
place had been mistaken about how it got its name. The Sailor's
Rest, as the combination saloon and rooming house had origi-
nally been christened, had been rebaptized shortly before the
Commodore's death, and without his consent, when the leader
of a press gang who was variously known as Shanghai Mike,
Mike the Crimp, and St. Michael the Persuader (after the effective methods by which he recruited reluctant hands for sea
duty) smashed a bottle of green rum over the skull of an opponent in a game of *Rouge et Noir* and proclaimed that he had
thus "launched" a new vessel he called the *Slop Chest*. No one

dared oppose his fancy until his corpse was found in a China-town alley with its face caved in, ostensibly by a tong hatchet-man, but by then a couple of generations of patrons had come to know the establishment by no other name. It stuck, although in respect to her deceased husband Nan had stubbornly refused to take down the much-defaced sign the Commodore had commissioned. After the first structure was burned to the ground for nonpayment of the penny tax and replaced by the current building, there was no need to hang any sign at all, since the patrons themselves had contributed most of the construction work in return for free grog.

I noticed she still referred to the place as The Rest, and never without lifting her glass to the Commodore's bilious like-ness. He had taken her off the line at a place called the House of Blazes to make her his wife, and whatever the old man may have wanted in the way of romantic attraction, he had made a lady of her ("swell mollisher" was the phrase she used), and she observed the ceremony of buying a round for the house every year on the anniversary of his birth. The fact that he'd been a solemn teetotaler all his life failed to strike her as ironic. Nan was a woman of contrasts, as well as handy with the portable Gatling she carried in her reticule. She got up once and turned back a corner of the threadbare Oriental rug to show the stain where she'd shot an old acquaintance who'd failed to grasp the significance of her retirement from the horizontal trade.

"Kill him?" I asked.

"He took his own sweet time, but infection done for him in the end."

"Where was Hodge?"

"Tobing lushies in Brisbane would be my guess. Axel wandered in here a year ago Independence Day, dragging that slag and thimble off his flapper, cute as cows and kisses. You wanted to palm him like a pennyweight. The Commodore was gone to Grim ten years and then some, rest him. Axel ain't a patch on his articles, but an old ewe like me can't be too particular. Any old dwarf in a storm, I say.

"That scrub I put to bed with a shovel was a square citizen," she went on, refilling her dainty glass from the decanter. Some of the contents slopped over, seasoning further the blot on the floorboards at her feet. "I'd of scragged for it sure as blunt if Cap'n Dan himself didn't stand in with me at the inquest. That hedged the sink he played me on the other, where I'm concerned."

I actually understood most of that. It was like border Spanish; it made sense if you didn't think too hard or try to speak it yourself. I couldn't tell where Beecher stood. He was enjoying his cigar.

"Why do you think Wheelock spoke up for you?" I asked.

"Who knows what goes through a nob's knolly? I put on this neckweed every day so as not to disremember how near I come to mounting the ladder." She touched the ribbon at her throat. "I don't mind saying it takes the sting out when the ponce comes for his copper."

"Does he ever come around?"

"The ponce? First and fifteenth, regular as a yack."

"Wheelock."

"What for? The knock-me-down at the Bella Union don't burn holes in the glass and he don't have to break Tommy with sea-crabs. Which don't make him no jack cove in my thinking.

God rest him, I never seen what the Commodore did in them fish." She toasted the portrait and drank.

"Do your customers know what you think of them?"

"I ain't said pharse in here what I'd say out front. They think it's top-ropes after eight months on pannam and bad swig. Ask the first duffer you see if Nan don't amuse."

I followed only part of that. I wondered if she made it up as she went along.

"Most politicians make it a point to get out and shake hands with the hoi polloi," I said. "What makes Wheelock so shy?"

"Most politicians ain't blessed with Hoodlums. Come ballot day they'll mark your X for you. You don't even need to ask." She gave the phonograph a thoughtful crank. "If guessing was my game, I'd say it's on account of his bully crab, what the squares call a club foot. He don't flash it about."

I asked if an appointment could be arranged.

She laughed. She was back in bed with her brandy. Two-score years later and I can't hear "Beautiful Dreamer" without picturing every grubby detail of that room.

"Stifle a Hoodlum," she said. "They've a place in his panter, and he might be peery enough to want to cut his eyes on you before he sends his tobbies to ease you over."

Beecher looked at me through the smoke of his cigar. "I forgot what's stifle."

"Put him to bed with a shovel," I said.

Nan laughed again. "You're a fly one, that you are. I'll wear weeds when you take scold's-cure. See if I don't."

11

For the next three days I did what Judge Blackthorne would consider nothing, or as close to it as one could come in a lively place like the Barbary Coast.

Both our berths were as uncomfortable as they appeared; after our first night, Beecher and I traded places just to make sure. The ticks were as bad as advertised, although after our inaugural experience with them my companion burned two packs of ready-made cigarettes exterminating the ones he could find hiding in the seams by daylight. Smacking the survivors and scratching their bites gave us the benefit of taking our minds off the slats gouging holes in our hides. It all gave me a more friendly opinion of Shanghai Mike and his decision to rechristen the place: This was no Sailor's Rest.

The morning after that first night, while Beecher was using the community washbasin behind the building, I found a place down the street that served biscuits and gravy that would have passed muster anywhere I'd been, a pleasant surprise, and a cup of coffee that was not. I paid too much for the meal and went back to the saloon, where I sat down to a fast, losing game of blackjack with the resident gambler. When he excused himself to use the outhouse, Beecher sat down in his chair.

He was irritable, and with good reason. In his world, Pullman porter was as high as a man could climb, and the Slop Chest could only remind him how short the fall was to stony bottom. Then again he might have been just tired and hungry. I told him about the place where I'd eaten breakfast, but he appeared to be just waiting for me to stop talking so he could start.

"What we doing today?" he asked.

"We're doing it."

"What about tomorrow?"

"Same thing."

He scratched at a bite on his wrist. He looked as haggard as I felt. "Ask you something?"

"Why stop now?"

"How long you been on this job?"

"About eight years."

He examined the bite, a tiny, white-rimmed volcano erupting from dark skin. "Ask you something else?"

"I'm still here."

"How you know when it's done?"

I didn't answer. He didn't have to know what I was waiting for until it was here. His cavalry experience would not have prepared him for it or its necessity. I trusted him with my life, but not the truth; not yet.

The fog, at least, was less persistent than the vermin. It was always there in the morning, although not as thick and choking as it had been on the afternoon of our arrival, but it burned off by midday. However, the presence of the sun did little to brighten Davis Street and its tributaries. The ramshackle saloons, bagnios, and rooming houses didn't cast shadows so much as drain the sunlight of its energy, and the streets were puddled with slops tossed out through their open doors and upstairs windows the night before. The flies that overhung them in dense clouds barely stirred to make room for the hooves and wheels that churned through the offal, buzzing impatiently until they passed.

Deprived of forgiving gaslight, the harlots who prowled the boardwalks—where there were boardwalks—demonstrated only too clearly that they found it convenient to paint one face on top of another without removing the previous application, often to a depth of as much as a quarter-inch. The pimps, gamblers, and cutpurses were hardly an improvement. Smallpox, knives, and coshes had left their marks on man and woman alike. On my first stroll around the block, I passed a half-dozen pedestrians, all of whom didn't total a complete specimen of human being among them. A good man with modeling wax, glass eyes, and timber legs could have made his retirement in six months in that neighborhood, if someone didn't bash him over the head and turn out his pockets at the end of the first day.

The maze of sagging, paint-peeling buildings created an impression of incredible age, yet the oldest of them was barely thirty, and most were much newer, their predecessors having burned to the ground in the five great fires that had shorn through the city in the space of eighteen months. Carelessness and arson had failed to eradicate the kind of physical and spiritual corruption that in most cases was centuries in the making. The boomtown years had encouraged construction to the point where two vehicles could not pass in some blocks without risking locked hubs and the inevitable altercation that ensued. The tight quarters bred confrontation and vice, which in turn bred more confrontation, and there seemed not a square yard of earth that hadn't been baptized in the blood of generations of innocents; which in the local dog-Latin was defined as corpses, mortals removed to a plane beyond guilt. Years later, visiting the East End of London, I was struck by that same perception of ancient evil, but there the process had been going on for four hundred years. By the late summer of 1883, I'd spent a year of wary days in cowtowns, miners' camps, and end-of-track helldorados, nearly lost my brains to a stray bullet while taking an honest bath on the other side of a wall belonging to an assayer's office when a client caught him with his thumb on the scale, but had never seen a place to compare with shanty San Francisco for unvarnished wickedry. The place wallowed in it.

I was encouraged by the law of percentages to believe there were decent people living within hailing distance of the Slop Chest: locksmiths and laundresses, bookkeepers and barbers, wet nurses and wheelwrights, glaziers and governesses; the usual mix of honest laborers struggling to pay the greengrocer from week to week. The difference here was they kept their trades behind closed doors like embezzlers, locked themselves in with their families at night, and scurried by first light and last dusk between hearth and forge, slinging frightened glances over their shoulders as if they were transporting stolen goods.

Day was night in Barbary. Killers and pickpockets ran free while the law-abiding paced their cells.

Different day, same conversation:

"What we doing today?"

"We're doing it."

"What about tomorrow?"

"Same thing."

Inside Nan Feeny's place of business, the faces of the clientele kept changing. One set of sailors stopped in for a beer or twelve, gambled, fought, were thrown out by Axel Hodge or staggered off to their rooms, shipped out on the morning tide, and were replaced by another set. Mates, boatswains, swabs, cookies, ships' carpenters, and the odd captain—the aristocrat of that society, distinguished from the others by his tobacco pipe of unblemished clay and no missing buttons—tramped in and out. By the third morning, Beecher and I were the senior residents. The only constants were Nan, Billy the bartender, Hodge, the proliferating damage to the bar's marble top, and the tinhorn in the soiled topper and shabby cutaway, who slept under some other roof after he'd skinned his last sea-crab of the evening.

He called himself Pinholster. I didn't ask, and he didn't volunteer, whether he was born with the name or if any other went with it. Frontier etiquette had taught me better than to pursue the point. When he got tired of fleecing me, he confided that he'd served aboard the U.S.S. *Minnesota* during the late unpleasantness, which was the reason he gave for keeping his game at the Slop Chest when he could have tripled his fortunes at any of the better places on Pacific Street or Kearney. He said he had an affection for sailors—"a place in his panter," as Nan would have put it—and in any case an old widower such as he didn't need much to keep himself, just a dram and a plate of hot food and a soft place to stretch out while his nervous stomach processed it.

I figured he wasn't quite forty, but there were streaks of gray in his chestnut beard and his face had the tobacco-cured look of a lifetime spent shut up in saloons and fandango parlors. The beard needed trimming, his hat a good brushing, and there was no way left to turn his collar or cuffs that hadn't been tried, but as to the things that applied directly to his vocation—his hands— they were smooth and white and the nails pared and buffed. He could cut a deck one-handed without showing off, and so far as I could tell he dealt from the top and never palmed a pasteboard. However, he might just have been minding his manners when playing with me. Rumors infested Nan Feeny's little enterprise like ticks and I wouldn't have bet a dollar to a dead dog there was a beggar or a spiv between there and the harbor who didn't know two deputy U.S. marshals were in residence.

"Here's a show," Pinholster said without looking up from the deck he was shuffling.

I thought he was getting ready to demonstrate a card trick, but just then a hand touched my shoulder. I reached for a revolver that wasn't on my hip. I hadn't heard so much as a footfall.

"Chinee papah, mistuh man?"

A young Chinese stood next to the table. In his pillbox hat, black smock, and shapeless trousers he was scarcely larger than Hodge, but his limbs were all in proportion and the square lines of his jaw said he was no boy. He wore the queue of his class and held out a folded newspaper covered with Chinese characters. I was about to tell him I didn't read the language when a loud report and a rattle of shattered marble told me the bar had lost a little more of its value.

"'Ey!" Hodge's accent was up on its haunches. "Wun Long Dong! Speel to your crib, chop-chop!"

"Stubble your red rag, Jack Sprat!" snarled the Chinese.

Hodge hopped down from his ladder and came around the end of the bar, twirling the iron ball over his head on the end of its chain. The intruder padded out.

"Two, three times a month that same celestial comes in here peddling his papers," Pinholster said. "Sometimes he makes a sale or two before Billy or Hodge hares him out."

"I didn't know Nan served Chinese customers."

"She doesn't. The Hoodlums wouldn't stand for it. You may not think there are rules of behavior in Barbary, but you're mistaken. Chinatown for Chinamen, the waterfront for the Sydney Ducks, and so forth. Just because you can't see the lines doesn't mean you won't bleed if you cross one."

"If that's true, who buys his papers?"

"It isn't the papers. It's what's inside." He cut out the ace of spades and held it up. "Black dreams."

"Opium? The Commodore built this place selling dope to the Chinese."

He flicked a crumb off his moustache that had been there all morning.

"You might have noticed Nan's her own creature. In any event, that was all before Captain Dan. He settled the last tong war by negotiating a licensing agreement between Chinatown and the Hoodlums. The jack dandies don't peddle dope and the celestials stow their wids outside Chinatown. That means—"

"Don't raise hell."

"You learn fast," he said. "You ought to apply that brain-box to cards. Part of not raising hell is keeping their hop inside their own jurisdiction. This fellow that Hodge just prodded out's a spunk looking for black powder, and he'll find it if the tongs catch wind. Wheelock doesn't maintain the peace because the sneak-thieves and swablers are afraid of him or his Hoodlums. They're afraid of each other, and they all turn to him because he's one of them."

"One of who?"

"Whoever he's with at the time."

I said, "No wonder the police can't enforce order. They aren't politicians."

"He's got the gabs, all right, but they're no good without teeth. If he thinks Nan's violating the agreement, she'll think that fire she had was love's own sweet song."

"The Hoodlums."

"They're what answers for a police force in Barbary." He dealt himself a hand of poker: four bullets and the king of clubs.

"Where does Wheelock stand with the Sons of the Confederacy?"

He lifted his brows. That was one piece of intelligence that hadn't filtered through the walls of Nan Feeny's room.

"About where he stands with the Benevolent and Protective Order of Elks, which is not at all. The baby rebels aren't a force here. If they're what brought you all this way you wasted the price of a train ticket."

"That's what Nan said. My information is this is their head-quarters."

"Not knowing who gave it to you, I wouldn't call him a liar. The Salvation Army's on every street corner, but I've been here a spell and I've yet to see a soul saved. If numbers counted, we'd have a Chinaman for mayor."

I asked to see the deck. He made a face of mild disappointment and said it wasn't marked, but he slid it my way across the baize. I picked it up, shuffled, and dealt a heart flush.

Pinholster smiled for the first time. "You didn't learn that chasing mail robbers in the territories."

"I owned a faro concession and part of a saloon in New Mexico for a little while. You can get good at anything if you do it often enough. Quicker still if you don't like starving."

"You've been losing for a reason," he said. "I think I can guess what it is."

I scooped up the cards, cut the deck one-handed, and slid it back toward him. "It won't take long. You've already told me everything I needed to know except one thing."

I was drinking a beer at the bar when Beecher came in from the street and checked his revolver with Billy; in the Slop Chest, the municipal ban on firearms only went as far as the door. Beecher was unsteady on his feet and his eyes were hot. He'd found another place that served beer to Negroes.

"What we doing today?" he said.

I waited until Billy moved down the bar to fill a sailor's glass.

"What's the date?"

That gave Beecher pause. "Fourteenth."

"Fifteenth. We got here on the twelfth and we've been here three days."

"What's the difference?"

"The difference is today's the day Wheelock's tax collector comes to call."

" 'Squint-eyed ponce what smells of lilacs.' " His impression of Nan's brogue was faulty.

"I got a more complete description from the tinhorn. Also a time and place. That corner table's as good as a window on Barbary."

"What'd it cost?"

"Only my reputation as a cardplayer."

He steadied himself on the bar. He was on the verge of asking a question he didn't want to know the answer to. Then he changed directions. "Just what *is* a ponce?"

"We'll ask him when we see him."

12

We smelled the Hoodlum before we saw him.

This was no small miracle, given the variety of stenches that had laid claim to the venue. The alley between the Slop Chest and the warehouse next door—home to an illegal and unadvertised game of Chuck-a-Luck that Pinholster swore had been going on without interruption, through fire and famine and fanatic reform, since 1851—was so narrow a man could put out his hands and touch both opposing walls at the same time. Beecher and I resisted the temptation. Mold and green slime coated the warehouse brick and a wriggling heap of rats covered whatever had been flung out the side door of Nan Feeny's establishment.

Somewhere in the direction of the respectable part of the city a tower clock gonged out the hour of eleven. The last chime reverberated on the damp air like a coin wobbling to rest on a plank bar. The spill from a corner gas lamp illuminated the far end of the alley, but fell short of the bricked-in doorway where we waited, a rectangular recess six inches deep in the warehouse wall. The shadows were as thick as poured tar and a light ground fog—light for San Francisco—tickled our ankles. We took turns breathing in the close atmosphere of that medieval corridor.

The lilac smell when it came was unexpected, and oddly more repugnant than the stink of slops and garbage; it didn't belong, and like a drop of honey on the tongue when lemon was expected, it struck me as unpleasant, nauseating. It was followed by a low, inaccurate whistling, some tinpenny tune that had swept across the frontier faster than the transcontinental, and had already been forgotten in Montana, and then an amphora-shaped shadow, slung across the Slop Chest wall by the distant gas lamp. The shadow grew smaller and more distinct as its owner came around the corner of the warehouse. Something kicked a loose stone rattling across the hardpack and a wrenlike figure followed it into the alley.

There the foul odors met him and he paused to draw something from his right sleeve and press it to the lower part of his face. A fresh puff of lilacs reached us. Beecher stirred, blew air out his nose. I touched his arm and he grew silent. We watched the newcomer return his scented handkerchief to his sleeve and continue walking. He wasn't whistling now. We could hear him breathing through his mouth.

He was my height, but lighter by at least forty pounds, buttoned snugly into a black frock coat with the kind of peaked sleeves that thrust up above the shoulders where they're stitched to the yoke and make the wearer appear as if he's hunching himself against a stiff wind. The lower three buttons were unfastened to expose a velvet vest that looked ruby red even by outdoor gaslight, and he wore calfskin boots to the knees of his pale trousers and a narrow-brimmed black hat with a low flat crown. The clothes differed in some details from those worn by the Hoodlum who'd accosted us on the train platform, but the effect was identical. They were the regimentals of a strict society. I knew then that the whispers about Wheelock were true; only a man of singular influence and determination could compel a ragtag gang of hugger-muggers and slash-throats to leave their roomy pickpockets' overcoats and anonymous black watchcaps at home and parade the streets in uniform. It went against centuries of conditioning, of lying low and playing things close to the vest. "You can't arrest/revile/annoy me," the clothes said. "I'm a Hoodlum!"

He stopped before the side door of the Slop Chest and rapped out a jaunty knock; part of the tune he'd been whistling. The door sprang inward and Nan Feeny's white head showed against the light from inside. She wore voluminous skirts, and a white shirtwaist buttoned to her throat, surmounted by the vigilant ribbon.

"'allo, Nan," said the Hoodlum. "Where's that skycer what shares your crib? Go to blow his conk and bash in his neb?"

His cockney was even broader than Hodge's. It had come straight from London and lost nothing during the voyage.

"He's tending bar tonight. Billy's got Venus' Curse." She thrust out a sack. Coins shifted inside.

The Hoodlum didn't take it. "Don't lope just yet. Let's inside and break a leg." He laid a hand on her hip.

Nan raised the pepperbox pistol from her pocket.

He withdrew his hand. "I ain't so spooney as you think. You wasn't always no iron doublet."

"Who says I am? You're Molly's goods. Take your pony and scour back to Queen Street."

He snatched the sack from her, hefted it. "The game's flush this trip. You ain't been flying hop, by any chance? Cap'n Dan wouldn't like that by half."

"I don't even let celestials in the place. It's been a rum week, is all. I've got aces over sevens."

"Full house is the word. You got tappers in your crib. Two U.S. coves. Been squeaking?"

"Go hoist a huff, you kept jack." She stepped back and banged the door shut.

"Old cow." The Hoodlum bounced the sack of coins a couple of times on his palm, then slipped it into a side pocket and turned away, whistling.

Beecher's clothing rustled. I touched his arm again, settling him. When the Hoodlum was halfway up the alley, I drew the Deane-Adams and stepped out of the doorway. Beecher slid the Le Mat out from under his shirt and joined me.

We were within ten feet of the Hoodlum when he stopped and reached across his body. We thumbed back our hammers. The crisp double-click racketed off the walls.

The Hoodlum turned, holding his scented handkerchief. When he saw us, he dropped it and reached for a pocket. I fired a round over his head. Both hands shot upward, palms empty.

There was an awkward pause. I'd never robbed anyone before; I wasn't sure about the order of events. During this space, no windows or doors opened, no one came running to investigate the report. A night in Barbary without at least one unexplained gunshot would have been worth half a column in the *San Francisco Call.*

The Hoodlum's face was narrow and pinched, old pox scars visible in the gaslight reflected off the Slop Chest's salt-stained wall. Small clumps of stubble sprouted like Indian paintbrush between the craters. He blinked incessantly—not, I was sure, from fear. Nan had called him squint-eyed.

"You blokes can't stick me up," he said. "I'm—"

I said, "I know what you are. Molly's goods."

His face went dead. It was a young face. A woman with narrow options might have considered it handsome, despite the scars and his predisposition against razors. I was pretty sure I knew what a ponce was now. Someone had bought him his red vest and it wasn't Daniel Webster Wheelock.

"Throw the sack at my feet," I said.

He blinked more rapidly. "Cap'n Dan—"

I snapped a slug into the dirt between his feet. He jumped straight up and down like a startled rabbit. Looked down at his boots to count his toes.

"The sack."

He lowered his hands. One went into his pocket. I made a motion with the five-shot.

"If anything comes out of there besides a sack of coins, you can ask Axel Hodge who fitted him with his ball and chain."

He drew the sack out slowly and gave it an underhand flip. It clanked when it hit the earth.

"Empty all your pockets."

Again he hesitated.

"Pepper his legs with buckshot."

Beecher lowered his aim a notch.

"No!" The Hoodlum turned out all his pockets and threw the contents after the sack: a squat-barreled pistol, brass knuckles, a weighted sock, three clasp knives in assorted sizes.

I asked him if he was expecting trouble.

"Just looking after me regulars. Times are dusty."

"Stay away from the waterfront," I said. "If you fall in they'll need a crane to pull you back out. What's your chant?"

"My what?"

"Your name. Your monoger. What do people call you when they're not mad at you?"

"Tom Tulip."

I took aim at his red vest.

"It's me name!"

"Well, Tom, tell your friends there's a new tax in Barbary. Penny a head for every Hoodlum who shows his face outside the Bella Union."

"You ain't the tickrum to collect it! When Cap'n Dan gets drift of this, you'll be whiffling out the hole in the back of your nob!"

"He'll want names. Mine's Murdock. This is Beecher."

"And who in Black Spy's skipper is Murdock and Beecher, if you please?"

I slipped the deputy's star out of my pocket and flung it at him. He caught it against his chest in both hands, turned it toward the light.

"Tell Wheelock to take good care of it," I said. "I'm responsible for it."

"U.S. coves." He leaned forward and spat on the ground.

"Bang on, Tom. Tell him to send the swag to the Slop Chest. We're cribbed up there this week."

"He'll send the whole bleeding Bella Union! The frogs'll fish your black ointment out of the briny."

"Put out this spunk," I told Beecher.

He tilted the Le Mat a few degrees and emptied the shotgun barrel over Tom Tulip's head. In those tight quarters it sounded like a powder keg blowing its top. The Hoodlum spun on his heel and took flight, coattails fluttering. We heard his pounding feet long after the echo of the blast faded.

Beecher changed hands to blow on his fingers. He was chuckling. "I believe I missed my right calling. How much you calculate we got?"

I stepped forward, picked up the sack, and gave it a couple of shakes. "Dollar and a half and change. If we're going to make a living at this, we'd better hold off till Tom finishes his rounds."

"Drop the swag."

This was a new voice. I looked up to see Nan Feeny standing in front of the open side door with her pepperbox trained on my chest. I dropped the sack.

"I offered to topper 'em both in their dosses the first night," Hodge said.

"Shut your mummer and let me think."

The little man stood swinging his iron ball rhythmically back and forth and watching Nan pace the floor of her room. His eyes beneath the brim of his bowler were as expressionless as a shark's.

Beecher and I were the only ones sitting. Tom Tulip's pocket arsenal occupied the bed, along with my Deane-Adams, Beecher's Le Mat, and the sack of pennies, which had surely established a record for depth of feeling for so small a sum. Hodge had done the disarming and carrying. We had our legs crossed.

"The swag and Tom's trinkets blow back to Cap'n Dan, that's settled," she said. "If they don't he'll hush us all and burn the place for spite. *How's* the thing what's got me smoky. If we come a-crawling with the skep in hand, he'll hoist the tariff, and who's to stubble him? We're scraping close to shinerags as things stand."

Hodge said, "Send it to him in an eternity-box with these two inside. That ought to show him we're plumb."

"I ain't turned up the toes of so much as a slingtail hen in forty years of grief, and I ain't about to set precedent. What was that game about? You both gone cranky?" She'd stopped pacing to stand in front of us.

I said, "I got the idea from no one but you, right here in this room. 'Stifle a Hoodlum,' you said; but I'm not that blood-thirsty."

"I was just pecking words. I never thought you'd try it on, I'll smack the bishop's calfskin I didn't. Anywise, you'd of done better to twist his nub and give him an earth-bath than buzz him and leave him leg to peach to Cap'n Dan. We'll be up to our arses in Hoodlums come morning."

"Take the air, Nan," Hodge said. "Sluice your gob down at Haggerty's. When you come back, it'll all be rub." He smacked his widow-maker against his open palm.

She said nothing. Her face was impossible to read. I wondered if I could get to the weapons on the bed before Hodge caught up to me and swung his ball, and if Beecher had the reflexes to slow him down. Then there was Nan and the eight loaded chambers in her pocket. I was thinking about all this when someone knocked. The sound came from the direction of the side door to the alley.

Nan looked at Hodge.

"Could be a fish looking to flop," he said.

She shook her head. "Tide's out."

The knocking came again, louder. Someone was kicking the door.

Nan picked up Tom Tulip's bulldog pistol and gave it to Hodge. "If it's more than one, empty it. Then leg it for the front door. I'll be scarce by then."

"What about these two?"

She took out the pepperbox. He nodded and withdrew.

Beecher started to say something. Nan eared back the hammer. He fell silent.

The knocking ceased. A powder-charged silence followed. Voices rumbled. Another silence, longer than the first. None of us was breathing.

A floorboard yelped outside the room. Nan swung her pistol that way. Hodge came in. He had the bulldog stuck under his belt and an envelope in his hand.

"Just a cove with a stiff."

Nan took the pistol off cock and put it in her pocket. She snatched the envelope. The address side was blank. She frowned at the signet on the crimson seal, cracked the wax, and fumbled with the flap. She frowned again and tipped something out onto her palm. It was a deputy's star.

Hodge snorted. "Crikey! The old town's full to the facer with tin. Who's minding the store?"

I said the star was mine. He told me to shut my mummer.

Nan unfolded a square of paper, read what was written on it, and held it out toward me. I got up from my chair and took it.

The letter was written in neat copperplate on heavy linen bond with gold edges.

P. Murdock, Deputy United States Marshal
The Sailor's Rest

Dear Deputy Murdock:

I am in receipt of your communication.

Your presence is requested in my quarters at the Bella Union Melodeon tomorrow at 11:00 A.M.

Until then, I am

Yours very truly,
Daniel Webster Wheelock,
Alderman,
City of San Francisco

13

BELLA UNION MELODEON
NIGHTLY
A CONSTANTLY VARIED ENTERTAINMENT
Replete with FUN and FROLIC
Abounding in SONG and DANCE
Unique for GRACE and BEAUTY
And Perfect in Its Object of Affording
LAUGHTER FOR MILLIONS!
A Host of the Best
DRAMATIC, TERPSICHOREAN AND MUSICAL
TALENT WILL APPEAR
Emphatically the
MELODEON OF THE PEOPLE
Unapproachable and Beyond Competition.

The dodger was printed on the kind of paper that could not have associated with The Honorable D. W. Wheelock's personal stationery. Its coarse fibers were tinted an unappetizing shade of apricot and the edges of the dull black letterpress characters had bled, making them muzzy and hard to read. The character who had thrust it into my hand was of a piece with the stock: short and round, buttoned into a loud checkered vest, a morning coat two sizes too small, and loose trousers belted just under his armpits, with yellow gaiters on his black brogans and a deer-stalker cap. He patrolled the boardwalk in front of the theater, accosting passersby with a nasal bray touting the wonders to be found inside and shoving the sheets into their midsections; forced to defend themselves, they grabbed at their bellies and wound up holding a dodger. No one got past him without one while Beecher and I were watching, and the traffic was heavy.

The Bella Union was three stories of frame construction—painted, not whitewashed—on the northeast corner of Portsmouth Square at the foot of Telegraph Hill, with shutters on the windows designed to repel invaders and vigilantes. Its name was painted in neat block letters across the false front, and the structure itself appeared as solid as a bank or a county courthouse. Natives referred to it as "The Ancient," which in a city that burned over every few seasons applied to anything more than ten years old. Neither fire nor scandal nor the cicada-like cycle of Community Cleansing could eradicate it. It kept coming back like a nest of yellow jackets.

We entered a cavernous saloon, whose gaming tables and long bar were already crowded at late morning, drinking under a glittering canopy of upended flutes, snifters, and cordials and waiting their turns at faro, *vingt-et-un,* and a seven-foot-tall Wheel of Fortune, the biggest I'd seen outside Virginia City. The place was a dazzle of gaslight and highly polished surfaces, which made a gaudy setting for the dingy sailors' jerseys, miners' overalls, and dusty town coats that filled it. The bouncer, whose hair slickum and tailored coat did no more than necessary to disguise the fact he was a pugilist, gave us no expression at all from behind his blisters of scar tissue when we asked where Mr. Wheelock might be found until I gave him my name. Someone had prepared him. He ducked his head and directed us to a stairwell half hidden behind a box containing a mechanical man who told fortunes.

On the way past the box, Beecher glared at the painted figure inside. It looked like Judge Blackthorne in a turban. "Reckon he's real?"

"Cost you a nickel to find out," I said.

"I didn't come here to get robbed."

"Try to blend in anyway."

The walls of the stairwell had been freshly painted; not a rare thing to find in a combustible city, but scarce enough in slap-bang Barbary. A floral carpet covered the steps, through which we could feel the buzz of brass from the band tuning up in the theater behind the saloon. That was The Ancient's bread and butter: the little stage where buffoons recited jokes from *Captain Billy's Whiz-Bang* and pretty *danseuses* in tights and short ruffled skirts performed cartwheels to *Parisien* cabaret tunes penned in New York tenement houses, and the curtained booths where breathy Southern belles with granite eyes inveigled inebriated customers to buy champagne and claret. Where the transaction went from there was strictly between the belles and the customers and the little man in the immaculate black cutaway who collected the take at the end of the evening. You could leave your money at the tables all over town, but when it came to staggering home with your pockets hanging out and an idiotic smile pasted to your face, the Bella Union was the spot—along with the Verandah, the El Dorado, the Empire, the Mazourka, the Arcade, the Fontine House, the Alhambra, and the Rendezvous. There was an unending supply of gulls and of sharpers to pluck them.

Beecher, climbing the stairs behind me, must have read my thoughts. "You been here before?"

"Couple of hundred times, from here to St. Louis."

"Me, too. Through the back door."

The stairwell opened onto a corridor with more floral carpeting, ending in a door marked PRIVATE. My knock was answered immediately by a young beanpole in a morning coat and high starched collar, balding in front. Gold-rimmed spectacles pinched his nose, with a ribbon attaching them to his lapel. A pair of watery blue eyes went from my face to Beecher's, registered annoyance there, and returned to me. "Yes?"

"Page Murdock and Edward Anderson Beecher to see Daniel Webster Wheelock."

"Nero."

I was wondering what response to make to this when a man approached the beanpole from behind. He was two inches taller, which made him six inches taller than I was, and his shoulders stuck out several inches on both sides of the other man. He was blacker than Beecher and better dressed than any of us, in a rose-colored Prince Albert cut to his frame and a ruffled white shirt. His face had the thick bone development of a born fighter, but no scars. That made him either very good or very discouraging to a potential opponent.

"I am Roland Quinn, Mr. Wheelock's personal secretary," the beanpole said. "He made no mention of a Mr. Beecher."

"He made no mention of a Mr. Quinn, but here we all are."

He touched the nosepiece of his spectacles. "Nero is Mr. Wheelock's personal bodyguard. He will look after your weapons."

"Nero?" Beecher wore his thin smile.

"My father taught himself to read from Gibbon." The big man's voice was a silky rumble.

I unholstered the Deane-Adams and spun it butt out.

"Not out here." Quinn glanced irritatedly past my shoulder, then stepped aside, holding the door. Nero moved the other direction with a gliding maneuver, as if he were mounted on oiled casters.

We stepped inside and gave him our revolvers. His hickory-colored eyes swept us from head to toe and returned to our hats. We removed them and gave him a look inside the crowns. He nodded, laid our pistols next to some others on the shelf of a massive rack with an oval mirror set in its center, then took our hats and hung them on pegs beside a couple of straw skimmers, several bowlers, and a silk topper. His gliding gait took him from there to a door at the back of the room, where he turned his back to it and became part of the architecture, hands at his sides with his thumbs parallel with the seams of his trousers.

Quinn shut the door and tipped a hand toward a row of shield-back chairs facing a Chippendale writing table.

"Mr. Wheelock is running late this morning. He'll be available presently."

It was a reception room, scattered with chairs and setees and decorated with grim-looking landscapes in heavy gilded frames. Several of the seats were occupied, by as wide a variety of humanity as could be found anywhere outside a train station: gents in morning coats and sidewhiskers, Hoodlums in their trademark motley, a decomposing old salt in his sodden woolens, tying and untying knots in a length of tar-stained hemp with his duffel at his feet, two painted tarts in laddered stockings, and a handsome woman just on the shady side of forty, seated knees together in a modest floor-length dress of costly manufacture with her reticule in her lap and her hair pinned up flawlessly under a becoming hat. What her story might be kept me occupied for much of the long wait.

A Regulator wall clock knocked out the time between chimes, patiently and in spite of one of the sidewhiskered gents, who kept dragging out his pocket winder and confirming the hour. After twenty minutes, he got up, collected his topper and stick from the rack, and pranced out, blowing out his moustaches and muttering something about how folk from the wrong side of the tracks needed taking down a peg. Quinn, seated at the writing table, went on scribbling with a horsehair pen and never glanced up. One of the tarts waited until the door shut, then said something in a low voice to her companion, who cut loose with a short nasal bray and resumed contemplating the tin ceiling. Two Hoodlums came in to take his place. When, five minutes later, the gent returned, he found all the seats taken, and resigned himself to stand next to the hat rack. No other defections were attempted during the time Beecher and I were there.

A third Hoodlum, decked out in a long navy coat with gold frogs over tan trousers, came in and shook hands with one of the pair who'd preceded him. This one wore high-peaked shoulders like Tom Tulip, with a dirty white scarf wound around his neck that only brought out the pits in his pasty complexion. I eavesdropped on their conversation, and wrote down what I remembered of it later on the greasy square of paper that came wrapped around the smoked herring I had for supper. I still have the sheet, in case anyone wants to study the exchange and translate it for later generations:

—Dance at me death if it ain't old Pox. I heard you was polishing iron.

—No, Freddie, that was a whisker. Picaroons what said they was crushers tried to put me up to me armpits, but I seen it was a lay and speeled to me crib.

—You always was a cove on the sharp.

—Well, I ain't puppy. How's Bob your pal?

—I ain't seen her in a stretch. We split out.

—Black-Spy, you say. I thought you was plummy.

—As did I. She stagged me to the tappers. Stunned me clean out of me regulars, she did, and I served her out.

—I'd of staked me intimate she was square as Mary.

—You'd be hicksam if you did. I tell you she's Madam Rhan.

—You must of felt yourself a proper put.

—Stow your wid, Pox. You wouldn't know a punk if she pulled your kick right under your handle.

—Don't take snuff, Scot. If she split on you, why ain't you in the shop?

—I had an old shoe. I was headed for jade sure as Grim, but Cap'n Dan dawbed the beak and bought me the iron doublet.

—Smack the calfskin?

—Twig me flappers. Am I in darbies?

—What's Cap'n Dan's lay?

—That's what's brought me round. If it's tobbing he wants, I'm his rabbit.

—Tobbing's cheap. He'll want more than that for his screaves.

—Old Toast keeps his cues under his top-cheat, that's dead game.

—I'll cap in on that, Freddie, old nug. Flimp me for a finiff if I don't.

I don't know if I got it down exactly as I heard it, and I'm certain—"dead game," as Pox and Freddie would say—that the spelling's wrong (assuming it was a written language at all), but it isn't likely it would read like Fields and Webber if I'd managed to record it verbatim. Most of the other people in the room took no pains to conceal the fact they were listening in, but those who understood what they heard probably wouldn't have betrayed anything incriminating to the authorities. There in Daniel Webster Wheelock's reception room was the one place in San Francisco where the criminal code was superfluous. They could have plotted to kidnap the president in plain English and not a word of it would have gone as far as the ground floor. As for me, for all I knew the two were debating the fishing off the Jones Street pier.

It's a dead language now in any case, buried along with the Bella Union and the Slop Chest and the Devil's Acre and old Chinatown beneath the rubble of the '06 quake and the city they erected on top of it; the current heirs to their underworld territory speak a dreary patois made up of sweepings from moving-picture title cards and cheap novels. In a little while, the last person who ever pattered the flash with a fly cull will be as dead as Barbary. I doubt the city fathers will dedicate a statue to any of them.

There was more to the conversation, but I didn't hear it. The door at the back of the room opened again and a man in a wrinkled suit came out, mopping his red face with a lawn handkerchief. He was either an unsuccessful drummer or the mayor. Quinn peered past him, nodded at someone inside, and looked at me over the tops of his spectacles.

Beecher and I rose and went in, nearly colliding with the impatient fellow in the morning coat, who had started forward from his position beside the hat rack when the secretary nodded. He stopped abruptly, checked at last by a graceful movement from Nero, and pulled at his sidewhiskers.

"Mr. Wheelock will see you next, Congressman," Quinn said as the door closed behind us.

14

"Oh, Lordy."

They were Beecher's first words upon being admitted to Wheelock's private apartment, and nine presidents later I haven't come up with any that serve as well.

After the businesslike reception room I'd expected to find an office, or failing that one of those fussy overstuffed parlors that varied only in minor details from townhouses on Fifth Avenue to ranches in Colorado, and were even mounted on wheels and coupled to trains going forty miles an hour between Dallas and the Black Hills of Dakota. There would be leather and brass and oak, possibly the head of some dead animal hung on the wall like an old master, and the smell of good cigars and whiskey. The lithographs of Prominent New York Homes in *Harper's Weekly* had stamped a sameness of interior furnishing and ornamentation across the most variegated continent on earth.

However, they hadn't crossed the threshold of Wheelock's cloister above the Bella Union Melodeon.

The walls were covered in blue silk, with peacocks and bridges and doves embroidered in silver and scarlet. Paper lanterns had replaced the gas jets in the corners, shedding warm amber light on the scatter of hand-loomed rugs, black lacquer boxes, golden Siamese dancers, rows of silk-bound books in a bamboo press, and the teakwood table at which the master sat carving a grouse. A thread of incense smoke coiled up from the lap of a plaster Buddha at his elbow, spreading sandalwood scent throughout the room.

The chamber was twice the size of the reception area, and yet the only Occidental items that had found their way into it were a framed Certificate of Community Service on one wall, issued to The Honorable D. W. Wheelock, signed by members of the Committee of Vigilance for the Protection of the Lives and Property of the Citizens and Residents of the City of San Francisco, and the serge tunic and cap of a fire captain hanging from a peg. Cap'n Dan himself wore a heavy silk dressing gown covered with golden dragons, and a white scarf of the same material around his neck.

The rest of him might have fallen off the wall of portraits at the Chicago Businessman's Association. His rectangular face was shaven clean and he had white hair fine enough to strain sugar through, brushed back patiently from a sharp widow's peak. There was the suggestion of a beak about the nose, and a thin trap of mouth that looked as if it spent most of its time shut tight while the chilly blue eyes beneath their black brows (touched up, I suspected, by the same gifted barber who scraped his pink chin) measured and dissected the speaker and weighed his bowels on a set of postmortem scales. It was an Anglo-Saxon face with a touch of the Nordic, a ruthlessly well-preserved sixty. I'd never seen one more dangerous; and I'd made the acquaintance of rapists, guerrillas, and multiple murderers from Tombstone to Slaughter Springs.

When we entered, he laid aside his fork and silver-handled carving knife, wiped his hands on a linen napkin, and thrust his right across the table for me to take.

"Deputy Murdock. Two apologies. A matter of some urgency kept you waiting longer than I'd intended."

"What's the other?" I'd encountered stronger grasps, but there was a bit of the show business in them. His was as natural as a panther stretching its limbs.

"For not rising. I have an infirmity which plunders the act of its meaning." He tipped his other hand toward the carved ivory stick that leaned against the table. It was the only reference he ever made to his club foot when I was present.

"I never could see the sense in it." I removed the sack of pennies from my coat pocket and dropped it in front of his plate. "Your man Tulip left this behind."

He smiled. His teeth were as white and even as Axel Hodge's, but it was my bet they fit him better at the end of the day. He looked at Beecher, who stood back out of arm's reach; a habit deeply ingrained, to spare both parties the embarrassment of an omitted handshake. "I don't know this other gentleman's name."

"Beecher."

"A noble one. I've read Mrs. Stowe's book and own a bound

collection of the Reverend Beecher's sermons. Were you named for either of them, by any chance?"

"I was named for my father. I don't know where he got it. He was sold before I was born."

Wheelock was unabashed, or if he was otherwise, he didn't show it. "Please be seated. Have you gentlemen eaten?"

We said we had, although the sight of the grouse with its accompanying plates of green beans and sweet potatoes made poor stuff of the biscuits and gravy in my stomach. We drew up a pair of bamboo chairs and leaned our forearms on the table.

"Forgive me while I continue dining. I neglected to break my fast this morning and I'm under my physician's instructions to maintain a regular diet. Nervous stomachs are as common to my profession as gunshot wounds are to yours. You're both deputies?"

I said, "Only during regular business hours. After sundown, we're road agents."

"I heard something on that order, although I hardly expected you to confess to it. What's your home jurisdiction?"

"United States District Court, Territory of Montana."

"Harlan Blackthorne's bench. He's known even here, where we have no shortage of notorious characters. Is he as hemp-hungry as they say?"

"Only when he neglects to break his fast. He has a nervous stomach."

He showed irritation for the first time. It was probably intended. "I was hoping we could discuss this like gentlemen."

"There are no gentlemen here, Alderman. In Helena, we hang men like Tom Tulip. We hardly ever hire them."

"Well said. However, you cannot fail to have noticed that there is a great deal more difference between Helena and San Francisco than mere distance. When I was still a young man, before there was a Montana Territory, the ship's masters who docked here referred to the place as Port Hazard. They did not mean the treacherous conditions in the harbor. The gold strikes emptied their crews before they could even drop anchor. Once a mutineer, a man hasn't far to fall before he turns thief and killer, particularly after he learns that wealth is not so easy to come by as advertised."

"It's the same story where I come from."

"Only in the beginning." Wheelock forked a piece of bird into his mouth, chewed it thoroughly, and washed it down with water from a cut-glass goblet. "It's the natural order of things that a community is born in blood and pain, passes through an unruly adolescence, and stabilizes in maturity. Abilene and Dodge City have become as safe as houses, and Helena will follow them in time. San Francisco is an exception; the bad element simply will not leave. I blame the mild climate. You will remember that after God banished Adam and Eve from Paradise, the serpent remained.

"The brigands here have had thirty years to establish themselves," he went on. "They've survived fire and vigilantes and their own wicked company. It's been one continuous war for nearly as long as you've been alive, and you know what only four years of fighting did to the men of your generation, filling the frontier with daylight robbers and every other sort of pillaging scum. The sight of a blue helmet holds no terrors for these creatures. They have their own police force and their own system of justice, from which there is no appeal this side of Davy Jones's locker. Is it any wonder our decent citizens have been forced to adopt their methods in order to keep the peace?"

"The nearest Tulip ever got to a decent citizen was close enough to crack his skull and lift his poke."

"You malign him unnecessarily. He lives off his harlot wife, along with the small percentage I pay him to collect the tax from Nan Feeny and her fellow entrepreneurs. The proceeds go into the operating budget. It costs money to prevent anarchy."

"I didn't think the Hoodlums donated their time."

He smiled again, a strictly hydraulic operation. His face wasn't connected to the workings of his brain any more than an alligator's.

"You're not that much less infamous than your employer, Murdock. You've kept the printing presses in New York and Chicago busy recording your exploits. Even allowing for two parts exaggeration to one part truth, you're a prime example of the kind of officer that under other circumstances would decorate the lethal end of the gallows."

"The difference being that I never cracked a skull I thought belonged to an innocent man. It's a slim distinction, but it's what I've got and I'm hanging on to it."

"You're a fortunate young man. One wonders, when you let go, how hard you'll fall."

"I'm not a young man, Alderman. And you're not Abe Lincoln."

"Certainly not. I'm a Democrat."

Beecher had been exploring a flaw in the table's teakwood grain with a forefinger. He looked up. "When you two gentlemans is through scratching dirt, we can get to why we're here. I don't wonder you got so many people waiting outside. You blow more steam than Old Number Ten."

Wheelock, chewing, gave him a look so mild I knew there was murder behind it. Beecher was as good as a barometer for measuring pressure, even in calm weather. A colored man with opinions never failed to turn the tidiest hair.

The Man of the People finished his sweet potatoes and pushed away his plate. "Your friend has a point. You didn't return your plunder just to get into my good graces."

I found the second double eagle from the attack aboard the caboose and slid it across the table with my index finger. He left it where it was.

"That's hardly better. I've been offered bribes many times. The amount is usually more substantial."

"I didn't expect it to surprise you," I said. "It was minted right here in town, and you probably see a lot of them in this condition. By the time they get to Montana, they've usually changed hands a dozen times and banged around inside a herd of pockets alongside the coppers and cartwheels and ore samples and whatever else a man might carry with him from camp to camp. This one made it all the way to Gold Creek without a scratch. Can you explain that?"

"I won't try. I'm a politician, not a detective."

He seemed pleased with this assertion. There's no accounting for pride.

"It makes sense if the coin came straight there from San Francisco in the possession of someone who got it fresh from the mint. Short of a written command from a superior officer, I can't think of a thing that would travel with a man that far that fast. This coin is an order of execution."

"Indeed. Well, you'd know more about that sort of thing than I. Most of the murders here are committed in hot blood."

"Alderman, do you belong to the Sons of the Confederacy?"

"I have a sponsorship. I have one with the Grand Army of the Republic as well." He picked up his goblet and swirled the contents.

"Isn't that a conflict of interest?"

"No. I am not active. I belong to most of the fraternal orders. My constituents are gregarious. There are seven separate delegations among the tong alone, and several splinter societies inside each one."

"Do you have a sponsorship with the tong?"

"The Chinese don't vote. I would accept, however, if they were offered to Occidentals. It might lead to understanding, and prevent another war like the one we had in eighteen seventy-five."

I asked if he contributed to the Sons' treasury.

"No. That's what having a sponsorship means. If I were to start paying dues, I would be ruined in two years. The city pays me only six hundred per annum." He sipped from his twenty-dollar goblet.

"Chester Arthur's an active Freemason. He pays dues."

"Chester Arthur's a Republican."

"Back East they think you're involved somehow."

"I imagine a great deal is said of me back East, and that very little of it is true."

"Not that much is said. I never heard of you before last week."

"I'm not offended. I have no intention of seeking national office."

His burnished impassivity was getting the better of me. I wanted to peel it back the way Beecher had started to do. "I was told the Bella Union is the new rebels' headquarters."

"I understand they rent the theater once or twice a month, purely for socializing. However, you'll have to ask Sam Tetlow for details. He's the owner of the enterprise. I merely lease this floor."

"Where can I reach him?"

"I cannot answer that because I don't know. He's in seclusion, preparing for his defense. He's to be tried next month for murdering his partner, Billy Skeantlebury. They came to a difference of opinion, followed by an exchange of gunfire."

"Who's running the place while he's away?"

He sighed. "That is my privilege. I've assumed interim management at his request, in return for compensation in the amount of one dollar."

"Why didn't you say that before?"

"You would have asked me about Tetlow's arrangement with the Sons of the Confederacy, and you would not have believed me when I expressed ignorance. I'm only a custodian. I've no authority to make changes and I know nothing of any business conducted here before my tenure. That was the condition under which I consented to manage. A man in my position must be cautious."

"Not cautious enough to turn him down," I said.

He smiled his sterile smile. "Tetlow is a major contributor

to the party. He may be acquitted. Stranger things have happened in Barbary."

"You might want to reconsider your arrangement. The San Francisco branch of the Sons of the Confederacy is implicated in more than two dozen murders. They tried to kill me twice, and each of the shooters had a shiny new gold piece in his kick. If this keeps up, they'll make me a rich man."

"Or a dead one."

"None of us is made of boilerplate," I said. "One of the men they killed was a United States senator. I doubt they'd hesitate to snap a cap on a city alderman."

"All the more reason to remain in the dark."

I sat back. "I don't suppose you could tell me who delivers the rent on the theater."

"You'll have to ask Quinn about that. He handles and records all the transactions."

"Can you call him in?"

He drew a thin platinum watch out of a pocket of his dressing gown. It was attached by four inches of plaited hair to a Chinese coin with a square hole in the center. "I would, but as you know, I am running late. You'll have to interview him outside."

"In front of half the Hoodlums in Frisco?"

"San Francisco," he corrected. "The native Spaniards insist upon it."

I rose. I'd broken myself against his wall. There wasn't a crack in it that I could see. Beecher got up, too, and we started out. Wheelock called my name. When I turned, he put a forefinger on the double eagle and scraped it my way.

"Just so there are no misunderstandings," he said. "A man in my position—"

"I heard." I went back and picked up the coin, tossed it back and forth between my hands. "Who set the torch to Nan Feeny's place?"

His smooth brow creased. "That incident is still under investigation. The police suspect a man who calls himself Sid the Spunk. He was a frequent customer at the Red Rooster, but no one has seen him in almost two years."

"Did they drag the harbor?" Beecher asked.

"It's a big harbor, in a bigger bay. Every few years some civic genius proposes bridging it, which would claim the life of every Chinese laborer south of Sacramento Street. Perhaps that explains why the proposal keeps coming up."

We left. The reception room was as crowded as a theater lobby, with the impatient congressman fighting to maintain his position within view of the secretary. Under Nero's close scrutiny, we collected our hats and weapons and went out into the hall. The air was cooler there, away from all those anxious bodies.

Beecher said, "That man sure does use a lot of words just to tell you to go to hell."

"He told us more than that," I said. "He told us who runs the Sons of the Confederacy."

15

Axel Hodge elbowed Billy aside, poured Beecher and me a beer each, and set them down in front of us. This was remarkable enough in view of the fact that twelve hours earlier he'd begged Nan to let him kill us both, and more so when you considered the amount of engineering involved. He had to reach above his head to work the taps, then carry both glasses by their handles in his only hand to the top of his custom-built ladder without gripping the side rails, and he did it all without spilling a drop. He must have been a sight to see clambering up the rigging of a windjammer when he still had ten fingers.

"This one's on Pilgarlic, mates; that's 'Odge and no other, if you ain't fly. You're the first in here what's ogled the cove in his own crib to me knowledge. Was it all sparks and glisten? I've a finiff with Billy says he lives out-and-outer."

"I don't know about that," I said. "He's got the place done up like a Chinese whorehouse."

"Ha!" Billy stood in front of the back bar with his arms folded across his chest. The tattoo on his flabby right forearm was either an anchor or a mermaid.

Hodge turned hopeful eyes on Beecher, who confirmed the information with a nod. The little man's face fell. Then he hoisted it back up through sheer might.

"Well, there's 'orehouses and 'orehouses, even in chinks' alley, some as what the emperor himself wouldn't be peery to drop his galigaskin in. What's got over the devil's back goes under the devil's belly, I say. Cap'n Dan's flush of the balsam. Old Grim take me if he lives like a spung."

There was no reason I should have done Hodge a good turn, but I was too tired for the game. "He makes six hundred a year from the city and he was wearing more than that. Do what you like with it."

He hung half off his ladder and twirled his ball and chain at Billy. "Pony up, you mab's son of a lugger. You said he put on a parson's show."

"I never did. I said he always goes about in them fireman's britches like he hadn't a deuce." But he excavated a crumpled banknote from a pocket and tossed it onto the cracked marble bartop. Hodge swept it up and stuffed it down inside the neck of his jersey.

I asked where Nan was.

"In her doss. The old ewe don't stand the hours she used to. She said to knock her up when you fell in. She wants the hank on you and Cap'n Dan."

Pinholster had come in from wherever he lunched and taken up his post.

"It's not worth waking her up for," I said. "Just tell her the bill's paid through to October." I finished my beer and turned from the bar.

Beecher asked where we were going.

"*I'm* going to study the history of the four kings. Meet me back at the room in an hour."

"Yes, boss."

As I was drawing a chair out from under the gambler's table, Beecher banged down his glass, reclaimed his Le Mat from Billy, and left the saloon.

Pinholster belched into his fist and broke open a fresh deck. "Your pardon. I got hold of a bad oyster, which in its turn has got hold of me. What's the matter with your friend?"

"Long hours, short pay. We can't all be tinhorns."

"*Artist* is the preferred term." He shuffled. The cards were a white blur. "How much would you like to lose today, and how fast?"

I said, "That depends on whether you can tell me where Wheelock's personal secretary spends his time when he isn't working."

He shook his head. "That's too close to the dragon's mouth. I own this concession by the honorable gentleman's sufferance. I own my life by it as well. Peaching on Tom Tulip's one thing; this place is rotten with Tulips. Quinn is Captain Dan's Beelzebub. Harm Buckingham, harm King Richard. Pluck as much as a hair off that fair head and Wheelock would burn down the Coast to find the men responsible. Then he'd pour coal oil on the wretches and make them burn longer. If you lived here as long as I have, you'd be afraid of fire too."

"You're talking as if you had a choice in the matter."

He belched again. He looked a little green, at that. "You're a good gambler," he said. "You should know the odds are always with the house."

"You spread them around when you told me where I could find Tulip. He's common coin like you said, not worth taking the trouble to find out who set me on him. It doesn't mean Wheelock won't send over a squad of Hoodlums if I save him that trouble."

"Is there no Hoyle in your profession?" He dealt himself a hand of whist, a game I hadn't seen since before the war. It wasn't a good hand, but you wouldn't know it by looking at his face.

"Hoyle's dead. So is Sid the Spunk, probably. He fell in the harbor after he set fire to the Slop Chest for Wheelock."

"It's a dangerous waterfront. Men have been known to slip on the wharves and stab themselves in the back."

I waited.

"A last request from the condemned." He gathered in his cards and shuffled again. "Will you play me in earnest, just this once? No stakes. I'd like to see if you can be beaten without any help from you."

I found Beecher stretched out fully clothed on the top berth, smoking a cigarette and blowing clouds at the ceiling six inches in front of his face. The smoke flattened against it, turned down in opposition to all the laws of nature, and tangled with the fog coiling in through the gaps in the siding. "How'd you do?" he asked.

"Lost three hands to two. I couldn't figure out how he was cheating."

"Maybe he wasn't."

"I wouldn't bet on it here."

"You did, though."

"We weren't playing for money." I took off my coat. "Rest is a good idea. We're working late again tonight."

"Doing what?"

I told him. He didn't say anything as I sat down on the bottom berth and pulled off my boots. Then:

"You need another man. I'm shipping east on the last train."

I studied the sole of my left boot. It needed a new heel. Cobblestones and hardpack were tough on shoe leather. I missed riding; and I hate horses.

"Doesn't the railroad take off brownie points or something for leaving a job unfinished?"

"It puts them on. Brownie points is bad. Pile up enough of 'em and they pull your tunic. No separation pay, no pension, just the door. Mr. J. J. Hill's a hard man, but he don't ask you to do work you didn't sign on for. If I wanted to be a highwayman, I'd of looked up Jesse James's brother Frank and asked if he was hiring. He pays better and you don't gots to sit around listening to a politician gas about operating budgets and such."

"Tonight isn't strictly a highway operation. Quinn's poke is safe."

"That ain't what I'm talking about."

"Then talk. You've got three hours before your train pulls out."

"That's the point. I gots to do all the explaining. You just bark orders and I'm supposed to say, 'Yas, suh,' and fall in behind.

Seems to me a parcel of Yanks give up the ghost just to put a stop to that."

"They fought to pay for the privilege. Before that it came free. I thought you liked following orders. That's what parade is all about."

"I never took an order I didn't know the reason for."

That seemed fair enough. "We're after information. It happens you and I are in a line of work where the people who have it don't want to give it up. I can buy it from Pinholster, but I've got to answer to Judge Blackthorne for expenses. He's the man who barks orders at me."

He blew out a lungful of smoke. "Maybe so. I feel less like a nigger stowing white folks's possibles and changing their sheets."

I dropped the boot and stood up, folded my arms on the edge of his berth. In the gloom of the windowless room the scar on his cheek flared white when he drew on his cigarette.

I said, "I don't partner up often. Part of the reason is I move faster alone, and moving fast is why I'm still here to listen to you bellyache. The rest has to do with how many partners I've buried. Don't expect us to go home friends, if we ever see home. When I mustered out of the army, I brought my brother back to Montana in an ammunition crate. His grave was the last thing I ever shed tears over."

"Lots of folks lost folks in the war."

"I seem to keep losing them."

He finished his stub, crushed it out against the ceiling, peeled it, and let the shreds of paper and tobacco flutter over the edge of the berth to the floor. Old cavalry habits die harder than old cavalrymen.

"We've all of us buried our share. I dug a hole for my baby girl and cut her name into a hunk of granite. I wanted it to last longer than she done. Pine would of served."

"Is that why your wife's in Spokane and you're not?"

I wanted to take back the question right away. Violating your own rules leads to other bad habits, and it's the bad habits that kill you.

"That was her notion, not that I didn't see sense in it. Little Lucy had my mouth, and after she left us, her ma couldn't stand watching me pour whiskey into it." He touched his scar. They can start hurting again without warning. "Ask you something?"

"Why stop now?"

"Why'd you pick me?"

"I made a good pick. You saved my hide in Gold Creek."

"I was saving mine, too, don't forget. Them two Copperheads wasn't going to leave me standing to tell that pettifogging town marshal what I seen, even if they could figure out which of us was which in that caboose. And you didn't know I was any good at throwing chairs when you decided on me. Ain't you got no friends in Helena?"

"I just got through telling you I don't make friends."

He aimed his melancholy smile at the ceiling. "Now you sound just like Cap'n Dan. I keep asking why and you keep telling stories."

"Blackthorne asked me who I wanted to stand behind my back and your name came out. I think it's because of the way you handled yourself in that parlor car. I told you to go through a dead man's pockets and you set right to it. Some of those pockets were soaked through with blood."

"That just makes me a good nigger."

"That makes you one man in a hundred. In Murfreesboro I knew a sniper who shot twenty-nine rebels out from under their hats at three hundred yards with a Springfield rifle. He had a shooting stand set up just like a buffalo hunter, with an extra rifle and a man to keep him loaded. A thirteen-year-old Tennessee volunteer broke cover and bayoneted him through the liver before he could switch rifles. He had his own bayonet fixed and time to use it and he didn't lift his arms. He froze because he couldn't kill a man except in cold blood."

"You should of picked the thirteen-year-old."

"I bashed in his skull with the butt of my carbine. Wheelock would say I lacked vision."

"Well, I ain't proved myself yet. For all you know, I'm only good aboard trains."

Not having anything to say to that, I climbed into my berth. Three hours later, the whistle belonging to the last train east drifted in, sounding as lost as the foghorns in the bay. Beecher was snoring smoothly. I doubt I got fifteen minutes' sleep all told. I couldn't get rid of the feeling I'd opened my mouth and lost my luck: which was the only commodity worth hanging on to in Port Hazard.

PART THREE

The White Peacock

16

Quinn—whose Christian name was Wallace—roomed on a narrow side street off Montgomery, above a German restaurant. The way there led past a row of banks and brokerage houses built on interest rates that would have broken the back of a J. P. Morgan; Pinholster had referred to the mutton-chopped dyspeptics who ran them as the boldest thieves in Barbary's history. The restaurant served its *Wienerschnitzel* and *Sauerbraten* in one of the prefabricated buildings that had sailed around the Horn in the middle fifties and been reassembled on site, an instant city. A flight of open-air stairs led from an alley in back to the secretary's quarters.

Before going around back, I peeped through a front window and located the beanpole seated at a corner table with a checked napkin tucked inside the V of his vest. He was slicing an immense sausage amid plates of mashed potatoes, baked beans, assorted relishes, and sauerkraut, with a wheel of cheese in the center of the table and a schooner of beer as big as a punch bowl at his elbow.

Beecher took his turn looking and straightened. "Man must have a tapeworm."

In the alley, the fog reached to the ground-floor windows. I stationed Beecher under the stairs and climbed to the room the gambler had identified as Quinn's. The door had a skeleton lock. I found a key that worked among the little collection I'd assembled over the years, let myself in, and relocked it behind me.

I didn't light any lamps, but a side window faced a corner gas fixture, and in any case there wasn't much to see: a single bed on an iron frame, a washstand, a small writing table laid with all the necessary paraphernalia, a chair set next to a lamp for reading, and a stack of newspapers and books on the floor beside it, including *Wealth of Nations*, Pitman's *Stenographic Shorthand*, and *The Adventures of Tom Sawyer*, a surprise. Stacked untidily under the bed was a number of cheaply printed pamphlets with pornographic illustrations, which wasn't. The room was a fair indication of the man who occupied it. I sat in the reading chair with the Deane-Adams in my lap and made myself comfortable.

It wasn't a long wait. After twenty minutes, the steps outside groaned and a key scraped inside the lock. I let him open the door and step inside before I called out.

"Quinn, this is Deputy Marshal Murdock. Stand where you are."

For a man who spent most of his time bent over a desk, he had sound reflexes. He jerked at the elk's-tooth fob dangling from a vest pocket and had an over-and-under derringer in his hand.

I cocked the five-shot. Quinn stiffened; not so much because of this as at the echoing click behind him. Beecher stood on the staircase landing with his Le Mat pointed at the secretary's back.

"We're not here to rob you or arrest you," I said. "We want to ask you some questions."

His spectacles made blank circles in the gaslight coming through the window. The narrow face behind them was a cypher. Wheelock hadn't chosen him for his penmanship. After a long moment, he returned the derringer to his pocket. "May I light a lamp?"

I said, "As long as a match is the only thing that comes out of your pocket."

"I'm not a Hoodlum. One pistol has always proven sufficient." He produced a box from an inside breast pocket. A moment later, warm yellow light glowed through the glass hobnail globe on the writing table. Beecher came in behind him and closed the door. At a nod from me he returned the pistol to his belt. I laid mine on my thigh and rested my hand on top of it. "How was supper?"

"Adequate to sustain life. I'm not partial to German food, but it's included in the price of the room." He seated himself on the edge of the mattress, feet together, hands folded in his lap.

"You sure can put it away," I said. "A man with a clear conscience has a good appetite."

"I have a condition that requires frequent feeding."

"Told you," Beecher said.

"Please ask your questions. I'm sure my eating habits are not what you came here to find out."

Beecher said, "He ain't such of a much when it comes to being a good host. You want me to instruct him on the finer points of etiquette?"

"Not yet." I smiled at Quinn. "Beecher's new to law enforcement. He's full of ideas about how to make it work faster."

The secretary said nothing.

I said, "Your employer told us you're the one who collects the rent on the Bella Union theater from the Sons of the Confederacy. He said you could tell us who pays it."

"I doubt he used those words. Private transactions are matters of confidence. I could only discuss them under the terms of a formal written directive, signed by a judge."

"That's inconvenient. The judge in this case is eight hundred miles away."

"I'm afraid that isn't my concern."

Beecher tipped over the washstand. The pitcher and bowl shattered on the floor. Quinn started, but left his hands in his lap.

"Beecher was a buffalo soldier," I said. "Sometimes he takes it literally. What's your landlord's position on disturbances in the night?"

"Don't forget damages." A pair of muslin curtains framed the side window. Beecher took one in his fist and tore it off the rod with a violent jerk. Quinn winced, but kept silent.

I looked at Beecher and lifted a shoulder. He went to the writing table, pulled the stopper out of a square bottle of ink, and tilted it over the sheets of closely written foolscap spread out on top.

"Stop!" said Quinn. "You make a convincing point."

Beecher righted the bottle. A single drop had spotted the corner of one page.

"Letter home?" I asked.

Color stained Quinn's sallow cheeks. "I'm composing a novel. I don't intend to remain a secretary my entire life."

I nodded at Beecher. He resealed the bottle and returned it to its brass stand.

Quinn said, "The man's name is Flinders. Horatio Flinders. He was one of the first Forty-Niners to strike it rich, but he lost it all in the Panic."

"Copperhead?"

"There are rumors about his activities during the war. I don't think a case was ever made against him."

"The Bella Union can't come cheap. Whose money is he using?"

"I don't know."

I signaled to Beecher, who reached for the ink bottle.

"It's the truth! He pays in cash and I enter it to the Sons of the Confederacy. He's a foul-mouthed old tramp, filthy in his habits. One is hardly tempted to engage him in conversation."

"Where does he live?"

"I doubt he has a home. He sleeps in doorways."

"Not good enough."

Quinn kneaded his hands. "He's a slave to the pipe. He spends most of his time in an opium den on Sacramento Street. The White Peacock. It's a tong place, run by a man they call Fat John. I don't know any more than that."

"Chinatown?"

"Yes. You'll want to bring your man."

"He isn't my man," I said, before Beecher could open his mouth. "Give him your belly gun. We'll leave it outside."

He dangled it by its fob. "It isn't loaded. I'm not skilled with firearms."

Beecher took it and broke it open. He nodded.

I said, "You must be the only unarmed man in Barbary."

"There's one other. Mr. Wheelock."

Beecher returned the weapon. I stood and holstered the Deane-Adams. I asked Quinn where he was from.

"New Jersey. I came out here to apprentice in a law office. It burned down before I got here."

"What made you hire on with Captain Dan?"

"I thought it might lead to public office. I'm too good at what I do, evidently. If I quit, he won't write a reference, and he refuses to sack me."

"I'm indispensable myself. I haven't had a holiday since the last time I got shot."

"I hate it here. I hope to sell the rights to my novel for enough money to set myself up back home. Horace Greeley was a charlatan."

"What's the book about?"

He colored again. "It's a romance. It's about a charmaid who falls in love with a mining magnate."

"What are you calling it?"

"*Nancy's Knickers, or the Amorous Adventures of a Girl of the Serving Class.*"

I looked at him.

"It's a working title," he said.

We left. Out on the landing, I grinned at Beecher. "The ink

bottle was a good idea. There's no quicker way to a secretary's heart."

"You be the renegade next time. If this gets back to Mr. Hill, he'll have me throwing tramps off freight cars." He started down.

17

The old-timers called them "Forty-Eighters."

There weren't many left to call them that, the first wave having either made its fortune and built marble mansions on Nob Hill or gone bust and drifted on, and those who were still stuck in shanty San Francisco were hard put to find anyone who would listen to what they had to say. Those who managed to attract an audience recalled aloud that the first three Chinese to land at California walked down the gangplank of a brig called the *Eagle* a scant five months after the first cry of gold rose at Sutter's Fort, well before the true horde of bearded western prospectors took to the hills with their picks and pans in '49.

What happened to those three adventurous celestials—two men and one woman—was unknown even to the old-timers, but officials counted ten thousand the next year, and by 1870, the census reported that the Chinese population of California had exceeded seventy thousand, with half that number settled in San

Francisco. Dreams of wealth had forsaken them. They operated laundries—more than a thousand were going full steam during my visit—worked construction projects, performed domestic chores for well-to-do whites, made cigars, sewed in sweatshops, and peddled opium in an area three blocks wide and seven blocks long, known intermittently as Little China, Chinatown, and Chink's Alley. They were governed by a merchants' association called the Six Companies, which in return for paying their passage from the land of their ancestors claimed a percentage of their income from the jobs it obtained for them upon arrival. But a government was a poor thing without the means to enforce its rules of conduct; hence the tongs, about which more later.

In the beginning, the immigrants were herded into bungalows manufactured in China and assembled by the workers who had accompanied them. Tiny and crowded, they were by all accounts comfortable for the coolies who had known worse conditions back home; but they were gone, gone. Fire had devoured them, and the survivors and their descendants now lived in board-and-batten shacks, tumbledown lean-tos, and rat-infested cellars, the last entered by means of ladders and filled with poisonous smoke when flames raged, and plague when they didn't. These billets were rented, not owned, by their inhabitants, most were anonymous, and those that had names did not advertise with even so much as a sign with crudely painted Chinese characters. There was no reason for that, with hundreds more Chinese looking for lodging than there were lodgings, and still more every day. Such names as they had were given them by wags and journalists, and were far more colorful than the dreary reality inside: Devil's Kitchen, Ragpicker's Alley, the Dog Kennel, the Palace Hotel.

The streets were narrow and twisting and made of the same soup of mud and excrement, animal and human, that visited raw boomtowns everywhere, but which in this case had not changed in thirty years. Planks were provided here and there for crossing, but Beecher and I had barely stepped over the invisible line that separated Chinatown from Barbary proper when we saw an ancient woman, indescribably wrinkled, hoist her skirts and wade across Dupont in the middle of the block, up to her knees in muck.

We made our way by moonlight and such illumination as spilled out through the cracks of shanties on either side; there were few windows and no gas lamps this side of Portsmouth Square. At corners, we took turns shinnying up posts and striking matches to read the signs. We got lost twice—several streets were unmarked, the posts fallen over or chopped down for kindling and never replaced—and we walked with pistols in hand. I'd felt more secure patrolling wide-open cowtowns on the wrong side of the deadline with a reward on my head, posted by the local association of Regulators.

In those places I was most vulnerable in the deserted sections. In Chinatown, the busy boardwalks in front of the laundries left me feeling open and unprotected. Even at that hour the better-lit streets were alive with pedestrians, male mostly, hurrying along in their plain tunics and pillbox hats, carrying baskets of sodden clothing or firewood and elaborately paying no attention to the only two Occidentals in sight. I'd put in my time among Indians and Mexicans and immigrant settlers and had sacrificed most of my ingrained opinions of people who didn't look like me or speak my language, but in that alien country buttoned into the middle of a sprawling American city, I was grateful for the extra pair of eyes I'd brought along. How Beecher felt, I couldn't tell, but he made no attempt at conversation and his face was so taut the scar stood out as if it were fresh.

As anticipated, the White Peacock was not as grand as its name. Like the crowded rooming houses that bordered it, it bore no sign, and like them, it didn't need to; its smell was apparent before the building came into sight. Opium had had its fashion in mining camps and ends-of-track I'd visited, and I recognized the odor, not unpleasant, of pills softening in the flame and of the prepared substance converting to smoke. It was like baked poppy seeds.

Beecher sniffed. "Don't need directions from here."

"You know the smell?"

"From the other side. It was the only place in Spokane where I dreamed about anything but little Lucy. I didn't take the habit, though. It felt bad, not feeling bad. You ever chase the dragon?"

"Once. I threw up."

The building itself might have been another rooming house except for the smell and a number of soporific Chinese sprawled inside the sheltered entrance, oblivious to the two Westerners who stepped over them to knock on the door. It had no windows, and the flat roof, which smelled of fresh tar, was low enough for a man to reach up and grasp the edge without straining.

I had the advantage of the Chinese who opened the door. He didn't know me, but I recognized him.

He looked from white face to black and back to white and made no sign of either familiarity or surprise.

"Chinee papah, mistuh man?" I said.

His expression went even flatter. He knew me then. He started to close the door, but I leaned my shoulder against it. I showed him the star.

"Horatio Flinders," I said. "He's a regular customer. Five minutes."

He shook his head. "No unnerstan."

I grinned. " 'Stubble your red rag, Jack Sprat!' "

He considered this direct quote. Then he smiled, and I wished he'd go back to deadpan. His teeth were a uniform shade of amber and filed to razor points. He flung the door wide.

We entered a low room, smelling of fust and the odor already described, lit only by the small flame in an incense burner in the center of the floor. It was as dark as a cellar. As I stood waiting for my eyes to adjust, my right hand began to ache, and I realized I was squeezing the butt of my pistol in its holster hard enough to crack the gutta-percha grips. I relaxed my grasp, but only to restore circulation. I'd spent time in black alleys that felt more friendly.

The Chinese closed the door. The current of stirred air made the flame wobble and nearly go out. My hand began aching again. I was as afraid of the dark as any small boy.

Clothing rustled nearby. A moment later, sudden as lightning, a T-square of yellow light cracked the blackness at the opposite end of the room. A shadow fluttered inside it, then the light vanished. A door had opened, then closed, swallowing the Chinese and leaving us in greater darkness than we'd known.

"I'd rather be dragging a drunk through a day-coach than here," Beecher said.

In a little while I realized we weren't alone in the room.

Customers lay like piles of clothes on wide upholstered benches—*divans,* they were called, lending the name to the dens they furnished, which then was shortened to *dives* by addicts whose tongues were too thickened by smoke to manage two syllables—and an old Chinese with a corn-silk beard and owlish turtle-shell spectacles sat cross-legged on a cushion on the floor, turning a bead of opium on the end of a long needle over the incense flame. Pipes, made of cheap bamboo, ornate jade, and everything that came between, lay about on the floor and on the divans where they'd slid from the smokers' hands. No one appeared to be paying us any attention, although I was sure the old Chinese was aware of us and every movement we made. He looked the part of a tong leader and I wondered if he was the proprietor Quinn had told us about.

The door opened again, and this time it didn't shut. The young Chinese stood in the opening. "F'an Chu'an say he see you."

I asked who F'an Chu'an might be. He showed his pointed teeth.

"Some white men call him Fat John."

"Horatio Flinders is the man we came to see. Does F'an Chu'an sound like Horatio Flinders?"

"He see you."

I looked at Beecher, who shrugged. We followed the man through the door.

It opened onto a flight of steep narrow steps leading into a shallow cellar, lighted by a paper lantern on a hook screwed into the sloping plank ceiling. The steps were blackened at the edges from an old fire and the stairwell smelled of char.

The cellar was indistinguishable from the ground floor,

except for the absence of the old Chinese. In his place, a man half his age sat at an identical incense burner, stirring a thick brown syrup in a tiny crock with a needle. This was the raw opium, from which a dollop would be extracted and allowed to crystallize into a bead suitable for burning. More customers sprawled on divans and pallets, smoking, dreaming, and waiting for their next pipe. The atmosphere was thicker here, where decades of smoke had had nowhere to go but deep into the earthen walls and floor joists inches above our heads. A man had only to lick any surface to enter the astral plane.

We passed through another door and found ourselves in a room ten feet square, hung with faded tapestries. In them I recognized the same designs I'd seen on Daniel Webster Wheelock's silk walls, only much, much older, embroidered by hands long since gone to earthly corruption. Oriental rugs, nearly as ancient, covered the floor three deep, obscuring the chamber's subterranean nature; it could have been a tearoom in any of the Chinese hospitality houses in the larger Western cities. In the center stood a small square table draped in black velvet, behind which a young Chinese stood pouring what looked like very strong tea—if it wasn't axle grease—into a tiny, handleless porcelain cup from a proportionately small pot. A gold-hilted sword in an ornate sheath studded with jewels, older than California, lay across the backs of a pair of ruby-colored china figures made to represent pug dogs, the table's only decoration. More paper lanterns, perched in niches hewn into portions of wall not covered by tapestries, shed light adequate to what looked like a delicate and possibly ceremonial decanting operation. It was enough to dazzle those of us who had just come in from the cave outside.

Our escort bowed and said something in Chinese to the man behind the table, who responded with one syllable. The other man bowed again and turned to face us.

"F'an Chu'an asks his visitors to seat themselves."

We hesitated. The man pouring tea was, if anything, younger than the man who had brought us, thirty at the oldest. Small and slender—"Fat John" was obviously as close as most Western tongues could come to pronouncing F'an Chu'an—he wore a yellow robe of plain silk, washed so many times I could make out the lean musculature of his arms and chest, and a black silk mandarin's cap with a jade button on top. His queue was black and glossy, carefully plaited, and hung nearly to his waist. His upper lip was cleft, a deformity of birth rather than the result of an injury sustained later in life. It affected his speech, so far as I could determine, not knowing the language, and reminded me of the infernal smile of a cat.

Finally we selected a pair of painted wooden stools from a collection of them scattered about and drew them up to the table. The two Chinese remained standing. The man behind the table finished filling the cup and started on another. He said something in a low, pleasant voice that suggested he was accustomed to speaking aloud without interruption. His impediment failed to embarrass him.

"F'an Chu'an apologizes for his inexcusable ignorance of English and asks me to translate. My name is Lee Yung Hay. He invites you to sample his disappointing tea."

I noticed that Lee Yung Hay had abandoned his pidgin dialect, which was not to be confused with his command of the local gutter slang. I said we'd be honored. I didn't add that since he'd already started pouring I wasn't in a position to decline. F'an Chu'an spoke again.

"You are the men called Mur Dok and Bee Chu'r. You way-laid the man called Tom Too Lip and gained an audience with Captain Dan Wee Lok. Both these things have impressed him."

I said, "Tell him I admire his intelligence system, as well as his hospitality. Wheelock took away our weapons."

The answer came almost before Lee Yung Hay finished translating. In response, the subordinate raised his right hand as if in greeting. It was holding a short-handled hatchet. He moved again and it was gone. I suspected he wore some kind of belt rig under his smock.

"F'an Chu'an is aware of the white man's reliance upon percussion weapons and that he would not presume to deprive you of their succor. He is grieved to add that I am capable of separating your hands from your wrists before you can cock your hammers."

I smiled. "Mine's a self-cocker."

"Thank you. I should be honored to begin with you."

F'an Chu'an finished filling a third cup and spoke.

"While you share his roof you are under the protection of the Suey Sing Tong. No harm shall come to you if you respect the customs of his house."

"We appreciate that. If he'll let us see Flinders, we'll be on our way and he can drink his tea in peace."

I heard Flinders's name in the translation and in the answer.

"You honor him with your association. The man Flin Dur is a guest as well and entitled to his protection also."

Beecher spoke up. "Fat John likes to hear himself talk, don't he?"

Lee Yung Hay interpreted this before I could break in. Our host smiled his cat's smile and set a cup in front of Beecher.

"F'an Chu'an apologizes for his disagreeable chatter. He is a man who enjoys conversation for its own sake."

I said, "Tell him it's a quality he shares with a number of Indian chiefs I've met. Good tea should be sipped slowly." I lifted my cup; apparently an unfamiliar custom, since the toast was not returned.

Our host was encouraged, however, and for the next twenty minutes entertained us with a history of the tong, a society that did not exist in China, but had been organized to protect immigrants from American oppression, and incidentally to ensure that the Six Companies were not forgotten by the laborers they'd brought over come payday. He did not explain why seven separate tong affiliations were necessary, nor why they occasionally went to war with one another, and no mention was made of the fees the expatriates were forced to pay to protect themselves and their property from the tong.

F'an Chu'an was a fugitive himself, having been compelled to abandon the study of medicine in Hong Kong when his father was unmasked as one of the chief conspirators in the Taiping Rebellion. While in hiding, the young student grew a queue, then took ship disguised as a common coolie. He'd sweated in a laundry on Dupont Street for two years, at the end of which his education, native intelligence, and the combat lessons taught him by his rebel father had secured him a position with the Suey

Sing Tong as a leader among the *boo how doy,* or fighting men. His cool head under fire spared his sect from humiliation in a pitched battle with the Kwong Dok Tong in 1875, when he was barely twenty, which ended in a bloody draw, and when the Suey Sing leader died several days later of injuries sustained in the fight, F'an Chu'an was elected to replace him. He'd spent the last eight years maintaining his position against challenges from below and without.

Beecher and I sipped tea and listened to the young gang leader enumerate his accomplishments in modest tones, translated with sneering bombast by Lee Yung Hay, for whom all other victories, including Yorktown and Waterloo, paled to insignificance. He was as hard to take as the tea, which was strong enough to bounce a cartwheel dollar off the surface. I broke in while he was trumpeting the Suey Sings' role in defending the Chinese population against bullying by Hoodlums, and the historic pact, supervised by Wheelock, that kept the Hoodlums in check in return for an agreement to confine the city's opium traffic to Chinatown.

"What can F'an Chu'an tell us of the Sons of the Confederacy?"

The subordinate twisted his lip, but put the question to his superior.

"Your civil war is of no interest to F'an Chu'an. China's most recent rebellion claimed fourteen years and twenty million lives."

"That isn't the question I asked."

"I did not finish. These fellows who cannot unshackle themselves from things gone are as jabbering women, to whom he turns an unhearing ear. As Confucious says, 'Things that are done, it is needless to speak about. Things that are past, it is needless to blame.' "

I'd had enough of Lee Yung Hay. "Does he feel that way about you peddling dope in Barbary?"

The whites of Lee Yung Hay's eyes showed. His upper lip curled back from his picket-shaped teeth, his arm jerked. Beecher and I both clawed at our revolvers, but the hatchet was out and sweeping in a horizontal circle toward me. Then something flashed and Lee Yung Hay's head tipped off his shoulders. A gout of blood made a roostertail in the air and splattered a tapestry. His headless trunk was falling, but the arm swinging the hatchet continued its arc, driven purely by reflex and momentum. My gun hand was in the blade's path. Something flashed again and the hatchet dropped to the floor, its handle still gripped in a hand that was no longer attached to its wrist.

F'an Chu'an stood holding the gold-hilted sword in both hands, his inferior's blood sliding down the vane and dripping off the point. He'd snaked it out of its jewel-studded sheath and swung it twice in less time than it takes to describe.

"I hnought tho," he said. His English was good for a man with a cleft lip.

18

It was a situation I'd been in before—three armed men facing off across a few tense feet of floor—but this one offered some unique features, including a grinning severed head bleeding into a valuable rug, a disconnected hand lying nearby, its fingers still tightly wrapped around the handle of a hatchet, and the body that belonged to the head and the hand sprawled between them on its back, one leg bending and straightening spasmodically as if it were trying to climb to its feet.

Oh, and a young Chinese with a visionary expression on his face, gripping a three-hundred-year-old sword.

I pictured the pensive look on Judge Blackthorne's face when I reported what had happened, heard his likely response:

Really, Deputy, the hand alone would have been sufficient. What is the nature of this obsession you have with melodrama?

At the moment, though, I was concentrating on F'an Chu'an. China's history—and what he had told Beecher and me of the tong—suggested that once one begins lopping off parts of the anatomy it's difficult to stop. I wasn't sure, once he resumed swinging, whether the two of us together could weight him down with enough lead to slow his hand before our heads joined Lee Yung Hay's on the floor of the White Peacock. He looked like a crazed butcher with the blade standing straight out from his body and a spray of blood staining his yellow robe.

The sound that brought him out of his trance might have been water dripping from the spout of a pump. The first gusher of blood that had struck the tapestry on the wall had saturated the venerable fabric, run down, and begun pattering off the bottom edge onto the floor.

His shoulders relaxed. He let go with one hand and lowered the sword until its point rested on the rug at his feet. We let our pistols fall to our sides, but we didn't put them away. He was still armed.

F'an Chu'an's vocabulary wasn't as broad as the dead man's and his pronunciation suffered because of his impediment, which may have explained why he kept his knowledge of English a secret from his followers. He groped for words, and a number of times we had to ask him to repeat a sentence we found unintelligible. He'd known for some time that a member of the Suey Sing Tong was selling opium outside Chinatown in violation of the agreement Wheelock had engineered between Barbary and the tongs, and had suspected that Lee Yung Hay was involved. All he'd lacked was proof, which the other man had provided by attacking me when I'd accused him. The sword was the only artifact he owned that had belonged to his father, who traced his ancestry back to a philosopher in the imperial court of Wan Li, and who had been arrested and executed by the current emperor for his part in the rebellion that had driven his son to emigrate to America; F'an Chu'an had smuggled in the sword inside a rolled rug containing the rest of his possessions, maintained the weapon in its original condition, and practiced daily the centuries-old warrior exercises for which it was intended. Lee Yung Hay's was the first human blood it had spilled since its first owner used it to commit suicide in 1579.

My responsibility as an officer of Blackthorne's court was to arrest him, and give testimony at the inquest. Chances were no charges would be brought against him, acting as he had in the defense of a deputy federal marshal. It seemed like a lot of trouble to go to just to get back to where we stood at that moment, so I did nothing. I admit that my decision was affected by the facts that he was the leader of an armed gang whose number I could only guess at, and that most of Chinatown and all of Barbary lay between us and the city jail. I watched him wipe the blade on the table's velvet cloth and put it back in its sheath and returned the Deane-Adams to leather. Beecher put away the Le Mat. His scar had lost some of its contrast, but he was the same man who had handed me a telegram across a fresh corpse on the train to Garrison. I imagine I was pale, too.

Our host bowed and apologized for the poor manners of the devil's son who now lay in pieces at our feet. He said he was in my debt for helping him to prevent another opium war. Then he excused himself, pulled aside a tapestry that masked an opening into another chamber behind the tearoom, and let it fall behind him. We were alone with what remained of Lee Yung Hay.

Beecher said, "Should we go?"

"Not without what we came for."

"What kind of place *is* this?"

"I don't know. Hell maybe."

The Chinese came back in wearing a different robe, this one faded green and if anything worn thinner than the one he'd had on before. Whatever the tongs spent their tribute money on, it wasn't their wardrobe.

We followed him into the cellar room where opium was prepared and consumed. He bent and whispered something to the man seated at the incense burner, who looked around through the gloom and shook his head. F'an Chu'an whispered again. The man was still for a moment; then he nodded. He got up and let himself into the room we'd just left. That made him the cleaning crew.

F'an Chu'an said Horatio Flinders was not in the cellar. He started toward the stairs. As he ascended, the hem of his robe made a serpentine hiss sliding off the heels of his slippers, which were made of fine paper with gilded dragons on the toes. Once again we fell in behind him.

The old man upstairs rose as his employer approached. He was tall for a Chinese, with the high brow and rounded shoulders of a scholar; the image of the Oriental ascetic that advertisers used to sell tarot cards and books of conjuring tricks. One of the eyes behind the huge, round spectacles was glistening white. He was half blind. When F'an Chu'an whispered, the old man bowed deeply from the waist and shuffled from divan to divan, bending over each one and examining the face of the man who lay upon it. Most of the faces were Chinese, but I thought I recognized one of the sailors I'd seen sprawled on Nan Feeny's front porch the day we'd arrived at the Slop Chest. High tide hadn't taken him very far.

I was thinking this when the old man returned. He bowed again and pointed to a divan in a corner that was almost enveloped in shadow.

Our host led the way. He stood aside as I bent over the man spreadeagled on his stomach. He stank of raw whiskey, rotten teeth, unwashed flesh, urine, and excrement. The overcoat he had on was rent up the back, darned all over with thread as old and brittle as self-respect, and filthy beyond description. It was of that color, neither brown nor green, common to the clothing given out at missions.

Horatio Flinders, one of the millionaires of '49.

I put a hand on his shoulder and shook him. His mouth dropped open with a wet smacking sound, informing me immediately of the decay that was going on inside, but apart from that, he didn't stir. I braved lice, grabbed a fistful of his dirty gray hair, and lifted his head. A thread of drool spilled out one corner of his mouth and made a glistening mercury pool on the divan.

"Slap him," Beecher said.

I slapped his cheek with my free hand. I didn't like the way his skin felt. Chances were I wouldn't have anyway.

I called for a match.

Beecher found one, struck a flame off the seat of his pants, and held it out. I took it and passed it back and forth in front of Flinders's eyes. I shook it out and lowered his head to the divan.

"Dead."

Beecher said, "One pipe too many."

F'an Chu'an grunted assent.

I set my jaw and made an examination. The body felt cool. A man could be dead a long time in a place like the White Peacock before anyone came to check on him. My hand touched something wet on his rib cage that was as familiar as it was unpleasant. I drew out my palm.

This time Beecher didn't wait to be asked. He struck a match and held it close.

"That's two in one night," he said. "I don't reckon the odds are high against it here."

I wanted to agree with him, even if it made my job harder. There is something inevitable and comforting about unthinking evil. It's like a natural disaster no one can do anything about. But the words stuck in my throat.

"Pinholster was right: Never bet against the house." I wiped the blood off on Flinders's coat.

19

Horatio Octavius Flinders, it turned out, was one of San Francisco's most beloved characters; the *Call* said so in as many words in a black-bordered editorial lamenting his loss. I saw no reason to question the statement. Newspapers are infallible in matters related to the community.

Comparisons were made between the "vagabond forty-niner" and the Emperor Norton, an addle-brained tramp who'd strutted the streets of the city for twenty years, claiming to be the ruler of America and dining on the cuff in local restaurants, until he left this world in 1880. That Flinders had slept in doorways, panhandled for opium money, and only forgot the hunger that was eating him from inside when he was dreaming black dreams didn't make it into the editorial, possibly because it would have confused the analogy. When his claim was paying off, he'd tipped waiters twenty dollars, thrown champagne parties at the Astor House that lasted three days, and sailed back and forth across the

bay aboard his custom-built steam-powered yacht; that was the
H. O. Flinders the *Call* mourned. He sold more papers than the
emaciated, vermin-infested wretch the coroner's men dragged
out of the White Peacock, or the bitter rabble-rouser who advo-
cated armed insurrection against the United States government
the day Lincoln was inaugurated. Death and baptism will work
miracles upon the soiled soul.

An inquest convened two days later found that the deceased
had been stabbed through the heart by a person or persons
unknown, armed with a blade that penetrated eight inches. I was
in the gallery in the county courthouse, and I thought immediately of F'an Chu'an's ancient ceremonial sword. I also remembered the sword-cane carried by the Hoodlum who'd accosted
Beecher and me on the train platform the day we arrived, and of
the assorted knives we'd taken off Tom Tulip: Break one, confis-
cate the rest, it didn't matter. Replacements were everywhere.
Everything that moved in Barbary and Chinatown could skewer
or shoot or bludgeon at the drop of a handkerchief. Any experienced investigator would begin by eliminating those citizens
who *didn't* arm themselves first thing after rising.

That was my opinion, in any case, but I wasn't asked. For
some reason, the coroner's court judge didn't call me to the
stand, even though I was the one who'd discovered the corpse
and was the senior officer on the scene.

The reason sat in the front row of the gallery, wearing the
dress uniform, navy festooned with gold braid, of a captain in
the San Francisco Fire Department.

Wheelock had entered shortly before the court came to order,
leaning on his carved ivory stick and swinging his club foot in its

specially built-up shoe in a practiced circle that nearly disguised his limp. He'd taken a seat directly in the judge's line of sight and remained silent and motionless throughout, hands folded on top of the stick, while the party in gray dundrearies behind the bench shot him frequent glances during the coroner's testimony. No other witnesses were summoned. From gavel to gavel the proceedings took twenty minutes out of the county's time.

There was no uproar. Half the seats were vacant, and most of those that weren't contained curious spectators drawn there by the editorial in the *Call*. That publication attended in the person of a scarecrow in frayed cuffs with an angry boil on the back of his neck, scribbling ferociously on folded sheets of newsprint with a stump of yellow pencil. Captain Dan put on his visored cap and limped out immediately upon adjournment. I tried to catch up with him, but got snared in a crowd in the hallway that was waiting to get into a more popular proceeding in criminal court. I apologized to a small, elderly gent in white handlebars for bumping into him; when he reached up to tip his bowler and tell me it was quite all right, I saw that he was handcuffed to an officer in uniform, who glowered and told me to move on. Afterward, I realized the polite little man was Charles E. Bolton, awaiting arraignment on a series of stagecoach robberies he'd committed single-handed under the name Black Bart. That made two prominent figures I'd almost knocked over during my visit to the City of the Golden Gate.

Wheelock had buttoned down the investigation into Flinders's murder, and for the time being, there was no approaching him about it. The pug who kept the peace at the Bella Union barred me from the stairwell to Captain Dan's quarters, and although Beecher suggested we try manhandling another Hoodlum, I was dead certain Wheelock wouldn't rise to that bait a second time. Truth to tell, I wasn't all that determined to question him. It was clear to me the old forty-niner had been killed to seal the identity of whoever was paying the rent on the use of the Bella Union theater for the Sons of the Confederacy to meet, and the honorable gentleman had tipped that secret by showing up at the courthouse and directing the inquest from his seat in the gallery.

"Ain't that all you need?" Beecher asked.

"Judge Blackthorne will want more."

"What do we do to get it?"

"We're doing it."

He grunted and drank his beer. We'd had this conversation before.

"This time the wait should be more entertaining." I folded the edition of the *Call* I'd had spread out on the ruined bar and showed him the cartoon on page three.

It was an old-fashioned rendering of leering Death, looming in his black robes like a dark cloud over ramshackle Barbary with his scythe raised in both skeletal fists high above his head. At the bottom of the panel lay a jumble of skulls, human rib cages, and other assorted bones, superscribed by numbers representing the murder toll to date, the numerals dripping black ink like the blood pattering off the tapestry in F'an Chu'an's tearoom. The artwork was realistic enough to rear nightmares in a generation of children.

"Looks like a ten-cent shocker," Beecher said. "There anything there folks don't know already?"

"Knowing isn't seeing." I read him the editorial that covered two columns beside the cartoon. It was headed THE CARNIVAL OF CRIME.

> *The Barbary Coast! That mysterious region so much talked of, so seldom visited! Of which so much is heard, but little seen! That sink of moral pollution, whose reefs are strewn with human wrecks, and into whose vortex is constantly drifting barks of moral life, while swiftly down the whirlpool of death go the sinking hulks of the murdered and the suicide! The Barbary Coast! The home of vice and harbor of destruction! The coast on which no gentle breezes blow, but where rages one wild sirocco of sin! In the daytime it is dull and unattractive, seeming but a cesspool of rottenness, the air impregnated with smells more pungent than polite; but when night lets fall its dusky curtain, the Coast brightens into life, and becomes the wild carnival of crime that has lain in lethargy during the sunny hours of the day, and now bursts forth with energy renewed by its siesta.*

"*Sounds* like a ten-cent shocker. You reckon the places around here paid for the advertisement?"

"There's more."

The article went on to rehash the details of Horatio Flinders's untimely expiration—"the wreckage of the once-gallant *Forty-Niner*, pulled from the stinking heap of lost souls in the worst dungeon in Little China" and of the court action that had disposed of the tragedy in less time than required for the mayor to take tea with the governor, and called for "no less than the intervention of the U.S. Army, or, failing that, determined action by decent San Franciscans to eradicate this blight for once and all."

It was signed by Fremont Older, Editor-in-Chief; and unlike the earlier dirge for Flinders it carried no black border. The effect was that of a robust gentleman of the old school stripping off his pigskin gloves for a rough-and-tumble behind the club.

Beecher finished his beer and signaled Billy for a refill. " 'Eradicate this blight.' That mean what I think?"

"It happened before," I said.

"What'll that do to the Sons of the Confederacy, you reckon?"

"Nothing, maybe. Everything if they forget to step out of the way."

"What about Wheelock?"

"Wheelock's got no place to step. The only thing he has going for him is there's no one else to keep Barbary from blowing sky-high. If it blows anyway, he's just an alderman."

He smiled. "And a fire captain, too, don't forget. He sure does like to put on that uniform."

"A fire captain is only worth having as long as there's something to burn."

Wheelock had the Flinders investigation buttoned down so far as the legal and political system went in San Francisco, but he hadn't counted on Fremont Older. The editor-in-chief of the *Call* had started at the top of the journalistic pay scale as a forty-dollar-a-week compositor with the *Territorial Enterprise* in Virginia City, Nevada, lost that position during the 1873 Panic, and freelanced for grubstake pay writing obituaries and editing agony columns throughout California before taking a steady job as a reporter with a paper in Redwood City for twelve dollars a week. That rose to eighteen when he fell into a part ownership. Upon taking the helm of the *Call,* he'd set up office in the same building that housed the United States Mint, where he'd spent much of his time coining purple phrases about conditions in shantytown, which for reasons best known to him he had chosen as the target of his personal mission for destruction. There were readers who insisted that Older was the man responsible for naming the region the Barbary Coast, after the den of depravity of that name in Africa, but that was more likely the inspiration of some anonymous sailor who had visited both places.

No matter. In that quarter, Older marked the sparrow's fall, whether it was the death of a coolie left to starve in an alley because he couldn't afford to pay the fees demanded by the Six Companies or the fate of the wandering daughter of a well-placed Philadelphia family kidnapped and sold into slavery on Pacific Street or the robbery and murder of a sailor in a house of pleasure in the neighborhood engagingly known as the Devil's Acre. He was there to report the facts when three young Chinese were hacked to death in a tong skirmish, and when there was nothing more scarlet to cover than a drunken derelict stumbling and falling under the wheels of a brewer's dray, he was there, too. On those rare occasions when a week passed quietly, he dressed an adventurous staff member in rags and sent him to live in a lodging house in Dead Man's Alley for three days, at the end of which he was expected to set down all the lurid details in type, and if he didn't have any, to make some up. I couldn't figure out why Older wasn't as successful as Joseph Pulitzer.

Whatever his complaint was with Barbary, he seemed to have found his handle with Flinders and had no intention of letting go. In the issue that followed "the carnival of crime," he surrendered his editorial slot to a long letter by someone who signed himself "Owen Goodhue, D.D., Maj., S.A. (ret'd)," offering to take Older up on his invitation and pledging the support, "spiritual and physical," of a Citizens' New Vigilance Committee, "with which I have the honor to consider myself a person of some small influence." The letter proposed that "one hundred substantial citizens of the City and County of San Francisco" be deputized by the sheriff's office, "with all due entitlement and authority to enter the area known as the Barbary Coast, not excluding Chinatown, and employ all means necessary to restore law and order." It added, in terms not too subtle for the more rudimentary subscribers, that if such deputization, entitlement, and authority were not forthcoming, it was the Christian duty of all respectable persons who agreed with the conclusions of the messrs. Older and Goodhue that civilization had broken down in the area referred to previously, "to seize, wrest, and arrogate the instruments of justice and force and visit punishment upon offenders, without regard to rank, gender, nationality, or property, public or private, at such time and on such a date as will be announced presently."

This compost heap of redundancy, tub-thumping rhetoric, and overripe declension took up a quarter of a page that might otherwise have been dedicated to enlightenment. It was answered the next day in the lead column on the front page by statements attributed to C. T. Warburton, Sheriff of San Francisco County, to the effect that the situation in Barbary was in hand and that he had no intention of cloaking "a collection of cranks and malcontents" in the authority of his office. Older made no comment, apart from a sly reference to the fact that Warburton was not facing re-election this year.

There was no hope from the military, either: A laconic item at the bottom of the second column reported that a wire sent to President Arthur asking for a declaration of martial law and dispatch of troops to San Francisco had received no response thus far.

I didn't see Wheelock's hand in any of this. Neither Warburton nor Arthur held jurisdiction inside the city limits, and both were old enough to remember the draft riots in New York City and the damages to life and property that resulted when civilians took up arms to no specific purpose. The sheriff may have witnessed the last time vigilantes set out to restore order in Barbary and made only chaos. In any case they could both claim that the affairs of their offices lay elsewhere.

On the following day appeared a full-page advertisement, with flags unfurling in the corners and a flaring eagle with arrows in its talons at the top, opposite the usual endorsements for Tutt's Pills, men's woolen drawers, improved harrows,

St. Jacob's Oil, and the New Line of Fancy Goods obtainable at Clemson's Emporium on Market Street:

SUMMONED!

100 SUBSTANTIAL CITIZENS 100

To the Southeast Corner of Portsmouth Square

at 8:00 P.M.

on Friday, September 28th

Whence the Party will Proceed

Through the Area Known as the Barbary Coast

and Chinatown

to Arrest, Detain, and Discipline

Brothel-Keepers, Opium Peddlers, Pickpockets,

Assassins, Harlots, Procurers,

White Slavers, Pan-Handlers, Vagrants,

Burglars, Sneak Thieves, Confidence Men,

Burkes, Bludgeoners, Blacklegs,

Swindlers, Gamblers, Smugglers,

and Uncertified Celestials

100 SUBSTANTIAL CITIZENS 100

GATHER YE SONS OF FREEDOM

"I didn't see no niggers on the list." Beecher folded and returned the newspaper to me. "Reckon I'm safe. What's an 'uncertified celestial'?"

"Any Chinese without identification."

"Hell you say. When it's done there won't be a yellow face left 'twixt here and Seattle."

"I wonder who's this fellow Owen Goodhue."

We both looked toward Pinholster's table. The gambler had left for supper.

Billy the bartender spat on a glass and polished it with his bar rag. "Nan's the one to ask about Doctor Major Goodhue. She's had personal experience."

I asked what kind.

"Close as you can get with your duds on. She shot him once."

20

"That Billy would hang whiskers on a goat," Nan Feeny said. "I never shot Goodhue. The pepperbox misfired."

We were gathered in her quarters behind the saloon. Beecher and I were seated, he enjoying one of the late Commodore's well-preserved cigars. Our hostess wore a ditch in the floor between her bed and the decanter filled with peach brandy. She had on one of her long, high-collared dresses, topped off by the ribbon she tied around her neck to remind her how close she'd come to hanging for shooting a square citizen to death in that room. She'd have saved shoe leather if she didn't insist upon drinking from a tiny cordial glass like a woman of gentle breeding, but the trips back and forth didn't slow down her consumption. A miner would have been pressed hard to keep up with her with a tankard. All this vigilante talk had her more on edge than even the previous transaction with Wheelock's man Tom Tulip. Her speech had reverted to the broad accents of Boston and she kept abandoning the local vernacular for the variety practiced on the Eastern seaboard; which was a little easier to comprehend, if it didn't come at you like Confederate grapeshot.

Outside, Barbary continued unbowed. Eight or nine tin-tack pianos were clattering like steam pistons with not ten fingers of recognizable talent anywhere in evidence, the one-armed concertina player at the Pacific Club was homing in on "Jack o' Diamonds," a sailor's leather lungs let fly with a deep bass whoop, expressing either boundless joy or black anguish, a harlot or one of the sweet young *danseuses* at the Belle Union countered with a thin soprano shriek like crystal shattering. A shotgun barrel emptied with a deep round roar; a bartender punching a hole in the ceiling to break up a brawl, or in a customer to defend the cash-box, or maybe it was just a part-time rat-catcher paying for his drinks the easy way. The resident rodents were running as big as bobcats that season and paid more bounty than renegade Mexicans. If Owen Goodhue and his one hundred substantial citizens expected the advertisement in the *Call* to have a sobering effect on vice, they were in for disappointment. Somehow I thought the reverse would be true. They had hemp fever and would enjoy nothing better than to catch the pack in full howl.

"Why'd you try to shoot him in the first place?" I asked Nan. "And who is he?"

"The first answers the second. To look at the Sailor's Rest now, you'd not guess what it was at high tide, before Wheelock's slubbers put the spunk to it; glass all round, with curtained boxes for the fish to have their fancy and pretty waiter girls in short smickets and silk vampers hoof to hip. One night there's this row out front. I hooked my little barking-iron and legged it

there and laid my lamps on that scrub parson Goodhue duck-
ing one of my girls in the trough where they sluice the prads.
Holding her under by the neck, he was, and her flapping her
mawleys and trotters like a snaggled hen. I says, 'Here, what you
think you're about, drownding that little molly?' He says, 'Tain't
drownding her a-tall, harlot. I'm baptizing this child in the
name of the Lord and the Salvation Army.'

"White of him to put the Lord at the top of the bill," said
Beecher.

She stabbed him with her eyes, gulped peach brandy, and
lifted the decanter. Telling a story uninterrupted was one of the
privileges of the mistress of the establishment.

" 'Baptizing be damned,' I says. 'Stand away or I'll let California climate through your bread-bag.'

"Well, he just showed me his tombstones and went on a-
baptizing. The girl ain't fighting so hard by this time.

" 'Cock your toes up, then, you jack cove,' says I, 'and take
your lump of lead.'

"Well, I shot the blighter; or would of, if the fog hadn't got
to the powder. As it was, the cap snapped, and he heard it and
left off his lay there and then. I pulled back the hammer again
and he tucked tail and trotted, spitting Scripture over his shoulder and calling me whore and I don't know what else, except
that there's none of it I ain't been called before, and by better
scrubs than him."

"What about the girl?" I asked.

"She swallowed half the trough, but I got her on her back
and pumped her out the way the Commodore showed me.
Venus' Curse croaked her at the finish, up on Broadway after she

left the Rest. Maybe it wasn't such a good turn I done her after all, though she was grateful enough at the time, and still more so not a month later, when Goodhue baptized another girl clear to Glory in a rain barrel in the alley back of the Fandango."

I asked if he'd stood trial. She laughed and shot brandy down her throat.

"Cove behind the bench was a Christian man; fined him twelve dollars for breaching the public peace and made him pay fifty to the girl's family for compensation. The Salvation Army took a rustier view of the whole transaction and told him to pad the hoof."

That explained the "Maj., S.A. (ret'd)." I'd wondered if he'd been any kind of real major. "Who does he work for now?"

"Owen Goodhue. He'd say God like as not, but with him they're one and the same." She set down her glass and bent over the packing crate she kept next to the barrel stove, filled with old numbers of the *Call* and other paper scraps suitable for lighting fires. After rummaging for a minute, she came up with a crumple of heavy stock, which she brought over to me.

It looked like a wanted circular, complete with a full-face photograph of an old road agent with broom whiskers chopped off square across his collar and a coarse wool coat buttoned to the neck like a military tunic. The base of his beard and the broad, flat brim of a campaign hat with dimples in the crown like the Canadian Mounties wore drew two parallel lines, with the fierce face framed between like a hermit's peering through a window. The eyes beneath their drawn brows were set close above an S-shaped nose, broken several times and never reset.

I didn't like the fact that I couldn't see his mouth through the coarse growth that covered the bottom half of his face. It reminded me of something I'd read in a book in Judge Blackthorne's personal library, now destroyed by fire, about creatures on the floor of the ocean that disguised themselves as heaps of moss in order to lure curious small fish into the hungry maws hidden beneath the tendrils.

Bold black capitals printed across the top of the sheet read:

**LECTURE
AT THE EAST STREET MISSION
WEDNESDAY, APRIL 4th
7:30 P.M.**

There followed the picture, captioned: "Owen Goodhue, D.D., Maj., S.A. (ret'd); Founder of the First Eden Infantry, Army of the River Jordan." Beneath that, again in large capitals:

"WHEN GABRIEL BLOWS 'ASSEMBLY,' WILL YOU ANSWER?"

"Clever," Beecher said, when I'd read it aloud. "I always thought the army would be a lot more like hell."

A dense paragraph appeared under that heading, full of biblical quotations with chapters and verses. I noticed they were all from the Old Testament, always the most popular with the kind of devout party who liked to use words such as "seize," "wrest," "arrogate," and "punish."

I reread the caption. "D.D.," I said. "Is he a dentist?"

"Doctor of Divinity." Nan pursed her lips above her cordial. "If he got it from anyplace but the College of Queen Dick, I'm a sister of charity. His joskins hand out that scrip every couple of months all over Barbary. I wouldn't of took it this time except we had a cold snap and I was low on kindling."

"I'm glad it warmed up before you burned it. I always like to know what the devil looks like this visit."

"He ain't Old Nick, though he'd welcome the kick upstairs. Or downstairs, seeing as how it's the Pit we're talking about. He's just another black imp. The town's flush with 'em, and I ain't just referring to the picaroons round here. You'll find 'em in case lots on Nob Hill as like as down Murder Point."

She started to drink, then lowered the glass. "Don't think from that he ain't a cove to be ware hawk of. He was with the vigilantes what strung up Jim Casey and Charlie Cora at Fort Gunnybags in fifty-six."

"I don't suppose he stood trial for that either," I said.

"Nary a one of 'em did. The governor called in the U.S. Army, and dance at my death if the vigilantes didn't give them a proper caning and sent them slanching back to Sacramento. Goodhue was just a squeaker then. He's near thirty years meaner, and has got the Rapture to boot. He and his hundred substantial citizens'll go through Barbary like salt through a hired girl. This time I'm keeping my powder dry for when that Friday face of his shows up here three days from now."

"That pepperbox only fires six. Vigilantes travel in bigger packs than that. Why not just close up and leave town till it blows past?"

"I never thought of that. I'll take a parlor car to Chicago and crib up in a suite at the Palmer House." She drained her glass.

It was the tot that broke the camel's back. Her speech slurred and gradually became incoherent—even more so than when she was speaking the Barbary dialect—and when she tried to get up from the bed for another trip to the decanter she fell over on her face and began snoring into the mattress. Beecher helped me rearrange her into a position less likely to suffocate her. As we were leaving, she started talking in her sleep, blubbering endearments to the Commodore.

Wednesday morning's *Call* carried another full-page advertisement, bordered once again by flags and the ferocious eagle:

WARNING!

This was followed by the same list of miscreants that had appeared in the previous call to arms, beginning with brothel keepers and ending with uncertified celestials. This time a roster of specific names had been added:

"Little Dick" Dugan, Murderer;

Tom Tulip, Procurer;

Ole Anderson, Shylock;

"Hugger-Mugger" Charlie, Counterfeiter;

Fat John, Chinaman;

Axel Hodge, Procurer;

Nan Feeny, Harlot.

If Seen within the Limits of the City of San Francisco after 8:00 P.M. on Friday, September 28th, you will be Arrested

and Detained for Trial by the Citizens' New Vigilance
Committee, and if found Guilty of Presenting an Endangerment
to the Civil and Moral Welfare of this Community, will be
Dealt With in the same Manner as Those who in the Past have
ignored this Warning; and if Acquitted, will be Escorted
beyond the City Limits by such Means as will be explained
directly the Verdict is Rendered; and should you attempt to
Return, will be Dealt With as the Rest.

Arrangements to be Made by

100 SUBSTANTIAL CITIZENS 100
Of the City and County of San Francisco.

I'd gone out early after a night of little sleep and many bed-bugs, and came back to show the page to Beecher, who paused in the midst of pulling on his boots to read it. He handed it back.

"Fat John's going to have a hard time beating that China-man charge," he said.

"He's no worse off than the rest. The only reason Goodhue didn't come out and say he'd lynch them all is Older wouldn't print it. What did Nan ever do to endanger the civil and moral welfare of the community?"

"Forget to check her powder before she shot at Goodhue."

I threw the paper into a corner. "Put on that other boot. We're going to the post office."

"Expecting a letter?"

"Sending a wire. Maybe Judge Blackthorne knows someone in Sacramento."

21

DEPUTY U S MARSHAL PAGE MURDOCK
SAILORS REST
SAN FRANCISCO

CANNOT INTERFERE CIVIL MATTER STOP
BARBARY WILL HAVE TO TAKE ITS BITTERS AS
BEFORE STOP IF YOU HAVE FORGOTTEN
YOUR ORIGINAL MISSION ADVISE AND I WILL
REFRESH YOUR MEMORY

                                    H A BLACKTHORNE

I gave the boy who brought the telegram an extra quarter to
make up for snapping at him for the delay. He explained he'd
had to stop and ask several people where to find a place called
the Sailor's Rest before he found someone who could tell him it
was the Slop Chest he was looking for. To save time on both

ends I'd sent my long wire to Helena without coding it, then had wasted a precious hour by respecting Nan Feeny's sensibilities when I told Blackthorne where to send his reply.

I crumpled the flimsy and threw it into a spitoon. It was full, and brackish water slopped out onto the floor.

"'ey!" Axel Hodge smacked the bar with his iron ball. Billy was in back using the outhouse.

I told Hodge to go to hell.

His white porcelains flashed in his beard. "That top don't scare me, mate. I been to Brisbane."

"Why is it necessary to tell everyone you meet you're from Brisbane? It's obvious every time you open your mouth."

He stopped smiling. "It wasn't for Nan, you'd be togged out in a pine shirt."

I let him have that as a gift. He was on Goodhue's list.

I couldn't decide what irked me more: the judge's refusal to bend federal regulations he'd already bent so many times they looked like pump handles, his little barb about forgetting the reason I'd come to San Francisco, or that annoying "H. A." at the end. In composing telegrams he generally signed himself "Blackthorne," nothing else. The showy use of initials warned me he might be considering another run for Congress.

I looked around the room, at the bottles on the shelves, refilled so many times with liquor inferior to their labels that the labels themselves were blurred and peeling at the edges; at the pickled eggs in the mammoth jar at the end of the bar, with pickled flies floating on top of the brine; at the glum sailors perched on the footrail and the even glummer creature slumped in her faded satin and wilted feathers at Pinholster's table, taking advantage of the gambler's absence to rest her feet in their broken high-topped shoes. I wouldn't have given a cartwheel dollar for the lot, but it had been home for two weeks, and in less than sixty hours a mob of angry townies stoked up on rotgut and Revelations was due to storm through with axes and truncheons and flaming pitch and reduce it to smoking rubble for the second time. It wouldn't rise again from its ashes, because the woman who had rebuilt it the first time would be strung by her neck from the nearest structure left standing.

Hodge had been right. Nan Feeny had spared Beecher and me both from his portable cannonball after the business with Tom Tulip, and whatever good turn the vigilantes might perform for the Union by destroying Wheelock's base of power, and with it the Sons of the Confederacy, I had to stop them for her sake.

I slung my empty glass down the bar, hard enough to send it aloft when it hit the first dent if Hodge hadn't scooped it up on the fly with his one hand. I'd wanted to break something. I'd violated the only rule I ever bothered to keep, and I'd done it twice, making friends with my partner and a woman I barely knew.

Pinholster came in carrying a thick white mug of steaming coffee from the restaurant down the street where he took breakfast, shooed out the bedraggled boardwalk queen, who snatched up her reticule, snarled something at him that even he didn't seem to understand, and hobbled out into the street. For the first time since we'd met, he gave me an eager glance and shoved the chair opposite away from the table with his foot. I was curious enough to take it.

"I'm a condemned man," he said brightly, removing a fresh pack of cards from his inside breast pocket. "Did you see the paper this morning?"

"I didn't see your name on Goodhue's list."

"Yes, I was a bit disappointed. It's stellar company. Little Dick Dugan's done more to support the employees at the city mortuary than the last three fires combined. Ole Anderson's a bigger crook than Jay Gould, and Hugger-Mugger Charlie hung out so much bad paper the first month after he got his printing press up and running, you couldn't pass a good banknote anywhere in town. Even a trusting soul like Nan wouldn't take anything lighter than government silver. It's the more general list I'm talking about. Gamblers and blacklegs are the same thing and they both found a place. How about a quick game of three-card monte before Friday? That's the traditional hangman's day, you know. Leave it to Old River Jordan to come up with that. It saved him having to spell it out and getting his advertisement rejected." He broke the seal on the deck and shuffled.

"I can see why it would cheer you up."

"In this work, the ace of spades can be the next card you turn. If you hit a losing streak and it lasts long enough you can starve, or freeze to death sleeping in an alley. If, on the other hand, you buck the tiger too long, someone's bound to think you're shaving the odds and blow a hole through you on a busted flush. Stay in one place past your time and the city fathers think you're driving down property values and deal a wild card to the legal firm of Tar and Feather, which isn't nearly as funny as the cartoons in the *Call* make out. I've seen it; I know what boiling tar can do to a man's complexion, not to mention the effect of twenty pounds of goose feathers on the function of breathing.

"Oh, the silk hats will make noise afterward, arrest some of the buggers, and maybe send three or four of the loudest to San Quentin for a year; they can make it fifty, and you're just as dead when they come out as when they went in. Let's say you survive all that. The smoky saloons get to your lungs or one day the barkeep miscalculates the ratio of branchwater to wood alcohol and you drop dead in the middle of the biggest pot you ever had going. Just plain living kills you at the end of the day. Why *not* a rope? Cut it." He smacked down the deck.

I held up a palm. He shrugged and cut three cards off the top.

"Don't mistake me for Jesus," he said. "It's a good life and I don't intend to let go of it at Goodhue's price. The first wave of Substantial Citizens through the door of my room above the Golden Dawn Laundry will come away with a bellyful of buckshot for their eagerness. After that I'll choose my targets. My little Colt derringer holds two. Maybe they'll even give me the chance to reload. That ought to put a hole in the One Hundred. Find the three of hearts." He laid the cards facedown side by side on the table, sat back, and lifted his mug.

I left them there. "Doesn't anybody run anymore?"

"That's an alternative I hadn't considered. I'll think about it while you're picking."

"The only reason Nan is on Goodhue's list is she stopped him from drowning one of her waiter girls. He'll have a hard time working that into his campaign for the public good."

"Granted, he went too far there. The State of California may even issue a bill of indictment before someone gets around to cutting her down. The good founder of the First Eden Infantry was among the conspirators named in the general arrest warrant after Casey and Cora were lynched at Fort Gunnybags. The charges lifted like morning fog. The cards are getting stale."

"What's the bet?"

"There isn't one. I'm just warming up the deck."

I watched him pulling at his shaggy moustache. "Where are you from?"

"I was born in Chicago and spent my life there, excluding my time in the navy. I'd flattered myself I'd lost the accent."

"You still lean a little heavy on your *R*'s. How long have you been here?"

"Six months."

I must have lost my poker face. He did, too; his eyes glittered like a greenhorn's over a king-high straight.

"How does a man who spends all his time at this table find out so much about Barbary in six months?"

"I listen. I watch. You know the process as well as I do. You can't talk all the time and concentrate on the game, and you can't win if you never raise your eyes from your hand. Three of hearts." He tapped the table.

"I don't feel like playing."

"Do me a favor. If you like, you can call it the pathetic request of a doomed fellow traveler."

"You're forgetting I can't be bluffed. You don't have any intention of letting Goodhue's men drag you out and string you up, with or without the shotgun and derringer."

"I wasn't referring to that. I have a lesion. Four doctors have told me I have a year left. Three, if I stay out of saloons. Which means I'll be gone with next year's leaves. Four of a kind beats a full house."

I studied his long, unshaven face for tells. Nothing there. "I'm still waiting for my answer," I said. "A man doesn't pick up as much as you in so short a time without asking a lot of questions of a lot of people. I've known gamblers to be many things, but curious isn't one. Who are you?"

"Pick a card. Please."

I grabbed one without looking at it and turned it over. It was the three of hearts. There was something underneath it. I turned over the other two. They were each the three of hearts, and each had concealed something. I looked at Pinholster.

He made an apologetic shrug. "I couldn't be sure you'd pick the right one."

I looked down again to see if anything had changed. Nothing had. Three pasteboard rectangles lay in a row on the table, much smaller than the playing cards he'd placed atop them. Each was engraved with the all-seeing eye of the Pinkerton National Detective Agency.

PART FOUR

The Vigilantes

22

"What's your real name?" I asked.

"Pinholster. Chicago discourages agents from using pseudonyms during undercover work. Answering to an invented name takes practice, and there's always the chance someone who knows you will see you and call out your name in public. As a matter of fact, I haven't told anyone a thing that wasn't true since I've been here. We're instructed not to unless absolutely necessary. If, for example, someone asks me if I work for Pinkerton, I'm permitted to dissemble."

We were speaking low and playing blackjack for the benefit of anyone watching. I said, "What about that lesion?"

"True as well, unfortunately. It's the reason I volunteered for this assignment. For obvious reasons, the local office didn't want to use one of its own operatives, and no less an authority than Oscar Wilde has declared that San Francisco has all the attractions of the next world. It seemed an excellent opportunity to find out what's in store for me."

"Who taught you to gamble?"

"My sainted father. He threw in his hand when a boiler blew up on the Ohio River near Evansville in eighteen sixty. Surviving passengers swore he was holding three aces with the likelihood of another bullet in the hole. The agency favors employing people from a variety of backgrounds. Who better to burrow his way into Barbary than a fellow who knows the history of the four kings?" He dealt himself twenty-one and scooped up the ante.

"What's the assignment?"

"A soap manufacturer in Exeter, England, died late last year, leaving an estate of seven hundred fifty thousand pounds, with a thousand set aside for an illegitimate son whom no one else in the family was aware existed. The young man was the product of a dalliance with a bookkeeper, who took ship to America with the infant twenty-seven years ago. The fare was a gift from the soap tycoon in return for the woman's discretion. The family cannot claim its inheritance until the bastard surfaces for his part, or until evidence of a good faith effort to locate him is submitted to Her Majesty's court.

"The New York office traced the mother to the charity ward of a hospital in Brooklyn, where she died of an indelicate disease in sixty-three. Circumstances had evidently obliged her to walk the Streets of Gold for victuals and lodging for her and her son. The child was placed in an orphanage, whose records were spotty, but agents managed to find a woman named Cruddup, who with her late husband had adopted the boy. She was uncooperative, but persistence and the bribe of a ton of coal—the

interview took place in February—persuaded her to report that
the boy, whose name was Seymour, had run away at age fourteen, after attempting to burn down the flat where the family
lived. It was not his first attempt. Mr. Cruddup had been driven
to flog him with his belt when he caught him pouring kerosene
on a pile of clothes and old newspapers in the middle of the
kitchen."

"Did she say what he looked like?"

"She said he was a 'funny-looking little monkey.' It wasn't
helpful, and the inducement of another ton of coal did not suc-
ceed in prolonging the interview. I could have told them that.
What possible use could one widow have for two tons of coal?
One is sufficient to see the average household through an Eastern winter." He paused to rake in another pot; talking and concentrating on the cards seemed to present no difficulty.

He went on. "County records list a Seymour Cruddup, six-
teen, in juvenile detention for nine months ending in sixty-six on
two counts of arson, but none of the officials currently serving
were there at the time, and there was no description on file. We
have no description to date. He vanishes then, possibly commit-
ting additional conflagratory depredations under an assumed
name, until Seymour Cruddup resurfaces on the employee man-
ifest of the cargo ship *Bertha Day*, which left New York Harbor in
eighty-one, rounded the Horn, and docked in San Francisco in
January of last year."

"The ship's officers must have been able to give you a
description."

"One would think that would be the case, but we shall never
know. The *Bertha Day* went down somewhere in the Horse

Latitudes during a storm last November with all aboard, including the officers who had served with her captain for two years. The rest of Cruddup's shipmates are scattered throughout both hemispheres."

"And so the trail ends there."

"So far as can be documented. However, I have a theory, which I've been working on, apart from the occasional inside straight, since March."

I let him take another hand while I waited. Figuring out what all this had to do with me helped kill time while Barbary was getting ready to blow itself apart.

"Criminals rarely change their lays," he said. "They're simple animals, and once they manage to work out a system that entertains and supports them, they tend to cleave to it unto death or the penitentiary. Fire appears to be young Mr. Cruddup's vehicle of choice, and an inflammable city like San Francisco is the ideal place in which to pedal it. The leap from there is not too great to the one man who can claim responsibility for most of the celebrated fires not attributable to chance."

"Sid the Spunk."

He nodded; the tutor abundantly pleased with his charge. "The young man has something of the poet in him. 'Spunk,' you cannot have failed to determine, is the popular argot for 'match' on the streets hereabouts, and 'Seymour the Spunk,' while equally alliterative, doesn't quite answer. With all these Sydney Ducks about, a fellow with origins in working-class England, reared by a cockney mother, would slide quite nicely in among the many transplanted Brits in this exotic place. Whether he christened himself or the monager was visited upon him by his admiring colleagues is beside the point. Admittedly, it's a long guess, but I'm convinced it's the right one. A good gambler plays the percentages; a great gambler proceeds upon instinct. As does a great detective. I'm a twenty-year man with Pinkerton. The old man is capricious, but he doesn't hold with deadwood."

"Congratulations. Why aren't you on your way back to Chicago? Sid the Spunk is dead."

"It's a point, and the conventional wisdom supports it. In the absence of a corpse, I'm not prepared to enter the conspiracy. Which brings me to why I'm taking your money. Blackjack again, old fellow. You must have angered the lords of chance today." He laid down two tens and an ace.

"I'll get it back when my luck changes."

"I shan't live that long. I hardly need explain that playing cards is a skill. You're good, but you haven't had my opportunity for practice. When I order breakfast, I am calculating the odds against having my eggs prepared precisely the way I request; and so the day goes, until I retire and dream of percentages. Just now, the law of averages supports Sid the Spunk's extinction, either on the night the Slop Chest burned down by his hand or shortly thereafter. Before that he was a legendary character in a place that does not want for them; a mysterious figure whom no one I've interviewed admits to having met face to face. An example is to be made through a destruction of property; the word reaches Sid; and the thing is done, after which the Spunk is doused and gone, to flare up again elsewhere when another example is required. The steep decline in the arson statistics directly the Slop Chest was put to the torch strongly suggests the Spunk was spent, possibly to prevent him from peaching to the authorities should he be apprehended later."

"It's a sound bet," I said. "I wouldn't take it up."

"You'd be wise not to. However, I'm persuaded to do so, by a piece of intelligence that recently came my way from the direction of Captain Dan's own firehouse."

He'd dealt me two cards, one up, one down. I left them.

"Since you're not a blind better, I'll assume the game is finished." He gathered it in, shuffled the deck, and placed it on his side of the table. "The alarm was delayed going into the firehouse. That was what was reported in the *Call*, and the veracity of a free press is above question. In any case, by the time the brigade reached the scene, the building was engulfed, and there was no help for it but to extinguish the blaze before it spread through the neighborhood. The volunteer I spoke to was not in the firehouse when the alarm came in, but came running toward the flames and smoke from the establishment across the street, where he had been taking his leisure with a woman of flexible reputation. I don't mind telling you I lost a substantial amount of money to the fellow in the course of winning his confidence, nor that it was the hardest work I've ever done, because he was an abomination with cards in his hands. You aren't the only man in this city who has cheated against himself, though I'll take an oath there aren't three."

"Play your card." I was losing patience with him, lesion or no.

"The young man swore he saw two men carrying a body away from the blazing building; which would signify nothing, except no casualties were reported in the fire, in the columns of the *Call* or anywhere else. I quite believed the fellow, for what would he gain from a lie? He already had most of my money."

"You think Sid died in the fire?"

"With the possible exceptions of a cannon loose aboard a ship at sea and the heart of a woman, nothing is less predictable nor more capricious than a fire in full blossom. Even an experienced arsonist, lingering to ensure the success of his enterprise, can find himself standing in the wrong place when a beam falls or a chimney collapses. Do I think Sid died in the fire? I have serious doubts. Why should anyone risk the victim's fate removing a corpse from the scene? Even money says he survived; or in any event that he did not expire on the site. He was injured, possibly fatally, but if so his condition was not so obvious his rescuers didn't think him worth saving. Was it Sid the Spunk? A steeper bet, perhaps, but not so steep I wouldn't hazard the odds. The man's very existence is a secret. Life is cheap in Barbary; one more struck down is unworthy of even a paragraph on the same page with the ships' arrivals. A life *saved* is a rarer thing altogether, and even a naysayer like Fremont Older could hardly be expected not to keep the details alive through three editions. Who but the man responsible for the fire could expect to remain invisible under the circumstances? Will you take the bet?"

I said, "I haven't seen your hole card."

"It's a common one hereabouts; but even a deuce can claim a pot if you know how to play it. My fire volunteer insisted the two men he saw carrying away the injured party were Chinese."

I don't know how long I sat there without moving or speaking. It was long enough I thought I might be attracting the attention of others, who would wonder why two men were sitting at a gaming table with a deck of cards sitting between them undisturbed. Pinholster thought so, too. He swept up the deck and began shuffling.

I anted, not bothering to look whether I was laying down a dollar chip or a twenty. "Your man could have misinterpreted what he saw. For all he knows, he was looking at two men carrying away a drunken friend."

"It's possible. It's probable." He dealt. "It's probable I don't have blackjack on this ten-spot. The hole card would have to be an ace, which is a chance of one in forty-six. What would you bet?"

I folded my hands on top of my cards. I hadn't even looked at what I had in the hole.

He turned his up. It was a seven.

"Too bad," he said, gathering in the chips. "However, cards are not life; and life in Barbary is not life anywhere else on earth. Sid the Spunk lives, and may even now be mastering the mystery of chopsticks in Chinatown."

"What if he does? That's good for you, but nothing to me. Why even bring it up?"

"It's nothing to me as the situation stands. I'm an undercover man, the hole card in this game, and as we've just seen, the hole does not always conceal the solution. I'm nailed to this table, whereas a face card such as yourself is free to act. I can't go haring into Little China, demanding answers and evidence. You can; you have, and the fact that you're here now proves you're the straight flush in this game."

"You don't have the bank to offer. Why should I sit in for you?"

"I can see you've never played bridge. No patience with

partners." He fanned the cards out in a straight line, flicked one with a glossy nail, and flipped them all back the other way so that the suits showed. "You haven't seen my bank. I know where the Sons of the Confederacy are holding their next meeting."

"So does everyone in town. No one knows when."

He looked at me. His face didn't slip.

I sat back. "Oh."

He swept up the cards, reshuffled, and laid out two hands of bridge. "I'll teach you the basics. It's a civilized game, unknown in Barbary. Keep your cards high and your voice low."

23

The fog was rolling out to sea at midmorning, swept as by a broom made entirely of sunshine. An old man, his face burned red over several sandy layers of brown, paused in the midst of slitting open the silver belly of a fish to point with his serrated knife toward the end of the pier, where even as I looked the fog slid away from the figure standing with arms folded atop a piling. I went out there and stuck my hands in my pockets.

"Busy harbor," I said.

Beecher kept his eyes on the horizon, which was a spired scape of masts and complex rigging, overhung by smudges of black smoke from the stacks of the steamers, of which there were getting to be more than square-riggers. In a few years there wouldn't be a sail visible between Japan and the California coast.

"This ain't nothing," he said. "You ought to see Galveston when the cotton's in."

"I didn't know you got down that far."

He looked up at me from under the brim of his hat and smiled. The smile wasn't for me.

"I worked on a packet boat one whole summer. Left home in Louisiana at twelve and didn't look back. Looking forward, that's the spooky part."

"How'd you end up in Washington?"

"Plenty of sail and not much draw. The wind blowed north after I mustered out of the Tenth. I was headed for Vancouver, but I dropped anchor when I met Belinda. That's when I went to work for Mr. J. J. Hill."

"Belinda, that's your wife?"

"Was last time I seen her. I can't answer as to now."

"Ever think about going back?"

"Only every day." He seemed to remember he had a cigarette smoldering between his fingers. He drew on it and snapped it out over the water. "How'd you find me?"

"Nan said you like to stroll down this way. I didn't know you two had gotten so close."

"Someone's got to smoke them cigars. They won't last forever."

A seagull landed on the next piling and began cleaning itself with its hooked beak. Beecher lit another cigarette and snapped the match at the bird, which flapped its wings but didn't take off. It resumed its search for lice.

"Bastards ain't afraid of man or fish," he said. "Feed on garbage and carcasses. I reckon they find their share here."

"Of what, garbage or carcasses?"

"Both. Any animal that won't run or fly from a man is just

waiting its time till it can pick at his flesh. I seen 'em crawling like rats all over a dead Mexican in Galveston. Even a buzzard kills sometimes, just to keep its hand in. Not these bastards. They even stink like bad meat."

He straightened suddenly, drew the Le Mat, and fired a shotgun round at the gull. It exploded in a cloud of feathers and fell over the side of the pier.

My ears rang. "I see you've been taking practice. That why you come down here?"

"I come for the air." He plucked out the spent shell and replaced it with a loaded one from his coat pocket. His fingers shook a little. "Where there's sea air, there's gulls. You can take ship clear out into the middle of the ocean and there they are. Where do they roost?"

I changed the subject. I didn't think we were talking about seagulls anyway. "I just played a few hands with Pinholster."

"How much you lose this time?" He belted the pistol.

"I broke even."

I told him about Sid the Spunk and the next meeting of the Sons of the Confederacy. He refolded his arms on top of the piling.

"That's tomorrow night. They're carving it close with Owen Goodhue." He drew on the cigarette. "You reckon he's still in Chinatown?"

"Sid? He's that or dead, if he didn't quit town altogether. According to Pinholster there hasn't been a suspicious fire in Barbary since he put the match to the Slop Chest."

"Well, I doubt he left town. You heard what Wheelock said. They keep coming back."

"I wouldn't set much store by anything Captain Dan says."

"He's a politician through and through. You wonder why he bothers with the baby rebels."

"Barbary's a cesspool. All the scum in the country drains into it sooner or later. That's his power base. He'll do what he can to protect it."

"Reckon he'll send his Hoodlums after Goodhue?"

I shook my head. "Vigilantes aren't cattle, for all they look it when they're in full stampede. You can't turn them by just picking off the leaders. Some other fool with more sand than sense will step in and plug the hole. Same thing with gulls." I jerked my chin toward a piling farther down, where a fresh bird had just landed.

He glared at it. "What you fixing to do about Sid the Spunk?"

"Well, I'm not 'haring into Chinatown, demanding answers and evidence.' Pinholster's been reading dime novels. Luck's the only reason you and I didn't come out carrying our heads the first time. I came down here hoping you'd have an idea."

He pushed himself away from the piling and took out the pistol. I stepped back automatically, removing myself from the line of fire. He wasn't looking at the seagull, however. He was facing the opposite end of the pier.

I drew the Deane-Adams as I turned. Three Chinese were standing at the end, dressed identically in long dark coats, with slouch hats drawn down over their foreheads. When they saw our weapons, the two on the ends threw open their coats and raised a pair of shotguns with the barrels cut back almost as far as the forepieces. The hammers clicked sharply in the damp air.

"Steady." I almost whispered.

There wasn't another human in sight on one of the busiest waterfronts in the world. The windows of the brick warehouses looming behind the Chinese were blank and blind. Even the fisherman who had pointed Beecher out to me had slipped away, as quietly as the tide. The gull made a noise like a rusty shutter and flapped away.

Only the lower halves of the three Asiatic faces were visible beneath the shadows of their hat brims. The sharp cheekbones, pointed chins, and straight mouths of the armed pair looked as much alike as Orientals were said to by Occidentals who never bothered to look twice. I was pretty sure they were brothers, maybe twins. The shotguns looked as if the recoil would shatter the fine bones in their slender wrists when the triggers were tripped. Of course it wouldn't. It hadn't all the other times, and the way the men held them said there had been plenty of those.

Beecher and I were standing at the end of the pier, with nothing behind us but the Pacific Ocean and nothing below us but undertow and the bones of others who had stood there before us. The only way off was through the three men standing on the landward end. I cocked the five-shot. Beecher had already drawn back the hammer on his Confederate piece.

"The harmbor is a dangerous mplace."

The Chinese who spoke stood in the center, a step back from his companions. He was taller and thinner, and his speech was impaired by a deep cleft in his upper lip. In Western dress he looked more like a rangy alley cat than the pampered, well-brushed variety he had resembled inside his tearoom at the White Peacock. He stood with his hands at his sides.

I wet my lips. The moisture evaporated from them as soon

as I finished. "Yes. Men have been known to slip and stab themselves to death."

F'an Chu'an—I still couldn't think of him as "Fat John," even in those clothes and this far outside Chinatown—reached up and pinched his upper lip between thumb and forefinger. I'd seen him do that before, to aid him in his English pronunciation.

"I'm told you seek the man called Sid the Spunk."

He made a slight motion with his other hand. The shotguns vanished beneath the long coats.

We lowered our revolvers. Beecher spat out his cigarette. It hissed when it struck the wet boards at our feet.

24

We can talk in here," F'an Chu'an said. "I have an arrangement with the Six Companies."

We had walked from the pier to one of the brick-box warehouses that faced the harbor like a medieval redoubt, where he'd produced a ring of keys from a coat pocket, sprung a padlock, and let us in through a side door. Inside, sunlight fell in through high windows and lay dustily on rolls of material wrapped in brown burlap and stacked to the rafters thirty feet above our heads. The air was a haze of moth powder. From here, the bolts of silk, broadcloth, wool flannel, jute, and damask would be carried by wagon to dozens of basements where Chinese immigrants bent over needles and treadle sewing machines, making dresses and suits of clothes for catalogue merchants to sell to bookkeepers in New York, shopgirls in Chicago, and farm wives in Lincoln, Nebraska: more than a million dollars' of dry goods in that one building, and not a watchman in sight. That would have taken some arranging. There were birds' nests in the rafters, and probably a couple of dozen bats suspended beneath, waiting to unfold themselves at nightfall and thread their way outside through gaps no bigger around than a man's finger. Our footsteps rang on the broad floor planks running the length of the broad aisles that separated the stacks. F'an Chu'an's bodyguards had lowered the hammers on their shotguns and Beecher and I had put away our pistols.

"I apologize for the detestable presence of my escort," he said, pinching his lip. "Their protection is necessary whenever I venture beyond Sacramento Street."

Beecher said, "They look like knickknacks."

"They are my cousins, Shau Wing and Shau Chan. They have been with me since Hong Kong."

"Did you smuggle them in wrapped in a rug?" I asked.

He didn't answer. He might not have understood. I wouldn't have taken Pinholster's odds he hadn't.

"The Suey Sing Tong is one of the oldest in America," F'an Chu'an said. "It was organized in the gold fields in order to protect Chinese mine workers from resentful Westerners. It soon became necessary to protect them from other Chinese as well. The bandit tradition in the country of my birth extends back to before the first dynasty.

"From there our numbers spread to railroad camps, laundries, and cigar manufactories. The tong is young, but it is schooled in the ancient ways of combat. They include rules of behavior, which were regrettably ignored by the late Yee Yung Hay when his perfidy was exposed. Once again I ask your forgiveness." He bowed. The two Shaus bracing him remained as motionless as porcelain figures; Beecher had a good eye, as well as a gift for description.

I said, "Your father's sword took care of that. What became of the body, by the way? Being accessories after the fact, we ought to know."

"Your curiosity is perhaps reckless. Knowledge is often fatal here. There is a storm drain beneath the White Peacock, which leads to the bay. It was Shau Wing's idea to construct a shaft connecting to it, shortly after we opened for business. Waste disposal is a problem in Chinatown, but not at the White Peacock."

"If you'd used it to get rid of Horatio Flinders, today's situation might be different."

He bowed again. "With respect, Deputy Mur Dok, it was you who sent Deputy Bee Chu'r for the police."

"I know. Every now and then that star gets heavy in my pocket. Two unreported killings in one night and I wouldn't have been able to lift it."

"Yin and Yang."

That was one I didn't understand, but I let it float past. "How did you find out I'm looking for Sid the Spunk?"

"I have ears in many places."

I tried to remember who was in the saloon when I was talking with Pinholster. Most of them were strangers. You can lower your voice almost to a thought and still be overheard by an experienced eavesdropper.

I said, "I thought of you right off, when I heard a man who might have been Sid was carried away from the fire at the Slop Chest by two Chinese. How many people in Barbary know you studied medicine in Hong Kong?"

"There are few secrets here. Even death cannot conceal them utterly. It grieves me to report that Sid the Spunk is dead."

"You're not the first who's told me that. A lot of people seem to want to think he's a corpse. I wouldn't have expected a common Hoodlum to attract so much interest."

"I wish they were wrong. Everything possible was done to deliver him from his fate. I am a deplorable novice, and what skills I once had have withered through disuse. The injury was too great, and there was not time to put him in more competent hands."

Beecher spoke up. "The storm drain?"

F'an Chu'an affected to have noticed him for the first time. The class system that had produced the tong leader was older than ours by a thousand years.

"It was unfortunately the only recourse. The bay accepts without judging."

"I got to wonder how the ships make it in and out for all them bones."

"Who brought him to you?" I asked. "The Shaus?"

"They are never far from my side. I will not profane your ears with the names of the two wretches who came upon him and sought to win my favor by taking him to the White Peacock. They are filth beneath your feet."

He might have meant that literally.

"Why would they think you'd be happy to treat him? One Spunk more or less wouldn't make much difference here."

F'an Chu'an stopped pinching his lip. He was thinking. "What I say next must not leave this mbuild"—he pinched—"this building. Even the tong is only permitted to exist under certain conditions."

"Should I swear on my life?"

He might have smiled. It was hard to tell with his hand in front of his mouth. He said something in Chinese to the men at his side. One of them made a noise like a terrier barking and replied.

"Shau Chan says, 'The white devil is not without humor.' That is an unsatisfactory translation. I speak Mandarin, Szechuan, and Cantonese, but the delicate points of English are as a dragon."

I said his English was fine. It had improved since our last meeting. Judge Blackthorne had told me never to trust a man who pretended to be more ignorant than he was.

"I am a wicked man," he said. "I have slain innocent men, I have stolen bread from the starving, I have lain with women who were the property of other men. I poison my people for money. I offer no apologies for the path I have chosen. I submit, however, that I am not the tenth part of the nameless ogre who led the Hop Sing Tong since before I came. This beast of whom I speak lay with the virgin sister of Lem Tin, my most loyal lieutenant, and sold her into slavery, under whose torment she sickened and died. When Lem Tin went to him for vengeance, the ogre had his heart cut out of his living breast and sent to me wrapped with silk in a jade box. This was an intolerable insult.

"I requested a meeting with the leaders of all the tongs to protest the ogre's action and to call for his trial and punishment. I told them Lem Tin was my friend, closer to me than a brother, that he had been disgraced, and was within his rights under tong law to challenge the ogre. The other leaders conferred and reached the decision that the ogre behaved permissibly in the interest of preserving his life. I was asked to accept this conclusion and to offer the ogre my friendship. This I did, along with a pledge upon the bones of my father that I would not be the one to violate the accord. Fifteen minutes after it began, the meeting was adjourned, and the leaders went to the Rising Star Club to celebrate the peace they had made. The ogre was among them. I was not. That decision is the reason I stand before you this day."

The air in the warehouse felt clammy, in spite of the strong sunlight. I fought off a shudder. The men flanking F'an Chu'an would no doubt have interpreted it as a sign of weakness.

"There was a fire," F'an Chu'an said. "Most regrettable in this fragile place. It started, said the men who fought it, in the cellar, upon the ground floor, and atop the roof of the Rising Star Club, within minutes. The leaders of the Gee Kung and the Kwong Dock Tongs burned to death on their divans, unable to stir from their black dreams. Fong Jung of the Soo Yop escaped the flames, but the smoke destroyed his lungs and he returned to China to die in the land of his ancestors. The ogre who led the Hop Sings, Lem Tin's assassin and the defiler of his sister, was driven by the smoke and heat to leap from a window upon the second story. He shattered his spine and has not left his bed from that day to this.

"The gods are often indiscriminate. Three other leaders survived without injury. They joined the others' successors in accusing me of starting the fire. I was tried and would have been executed under tong law but for fifteen men of respect who came forward to swear that from the time I left the meeting until the alarm was raised, I could be seen casting lots in the White Peacock. I was exonerated."

At this point F'an Chu'an made a little bow, as if Beecher and I were the ones who'd acquitted him. The cat's smile was in place.

I said, "Did anyone happen to ask where Sid the Spunk was when the fire broke out?"

"His name was not mentioned during the proceedings. Chinatown is a country apart from greater San Francisco. He is not widely known within its boundaries. I remind you that we converse in confidence. It is not necessary to explain by what avenue we found each other. Perhaps you will think of him with charity when I say that he would not accept payment for his services. When I declared that I had no wish to chain myself in his debt, he said that the obligation was his, to one who had been close to him and who had been forced into degradation also. He would say nothing else beyond the fact that Lem Tin's sister was not unique in her experience. He would not abandon this position, and having come but recently from that infamous meeting, I lacked the strength of will to turn aside his offer. Do you wonder still why I did not hesitate to exhaust my poor skills on his behalf when he was brought to me later, broken and burned?"

I shook my head. "What about the bones of your father?"

"It is my belief they lay where they were buried."

I searched his face for amusement, or contempt, or some other sign that the words he spoke were connected to what he was thinking. I gave it up as a bad job. "Why risk leaving Chinatown to tell me, with your name on Owen Goodhue's list?"

"For that, you have Lee Yung Hay to thank. You cannot know the extent of the catastrophe had his activities in Barbary become known generally."

"I'd have thought saving our lives discharged that debt," I said.

"You force me to contradict you; a necessity I find most painful. My debt was increased by the act. In the country of my birth, to spare a man's life is to make that life one's own, with all the responsibilities that entails. When I learned of your interest in Sid the Spunk, I saw the opportunity to relieve myself of the burden. I could not guarantee your safety should your natural instincts lead you across Sacramento Street. That you did so once and survived was more fortunate than you know. I consider that you and I stand upon equal ground when I warn you that to venture again into Chinatown will be to resign yourself to merciless fate."

This time I said it. "The storm drain?"

"The bay accepts," he repeated, "without judging."

Beecher said, "I reckon we're even."

"That is my belief."

F'an Chu'an glanced from side to side. The Shaus stirred and the three of them headed toward the door. Beecher and I followed them out. F'an Chu'an fixed the padlock in place and left us without a word. Seconds later he and his companions disappeared around the corner of the warehouse. Later I wasn't sure I hadn't dreamed the whole thing.

25

On the last night but one for Barbary, Beecher and I set out with determination to get as drunk as we could and still find our way home to the Slop Chest.

Although the second part was problematic, the first was a dream easily obtainable anywhere within thirty blocks of our bug-infested berths. There were upwards of three thousand aboveboard drinking establishments in the City of San Francisco, most of them on the shady side of Nob Hill, and Nan Feeny estimated that an additional two thousand operated without licenses. These "blind tigers" sold home-brewed beer, whiskey cut with creek water—Beecher found part of a crawdad floating in his glass the first place we stopped—and turpentine laced with brown sugar to give it the color and approximate flavor of rye; the sightless beggars who tapped their way along the boardwalks and sat in doorways rattling the coins in their cups hadn't all lost their eyes at Shiloh,

despite the signs around their necks identifying them as crip-
pled veterans. An article in Fremont Older's *Call* placed the
annual income from the local sale of intoxicants above ten
million dollars, roughly three times what Congress shelled out
to outfit the U.S. Army. Witnessed at first hand, it looked like
more.

"I forget." Beecher looked up blearily from a glass recently
evacuated of freshwater life. "Is this a dive, a bagnio, or a dead-
fall?"

I looked around. We were in the cellar of a warehouse stacked
with barrels of sorghum, with greenwood tables and benches
crowded to one side to make room for dancing. A glum-faced
fiddler and a pianist with an eyepatch made a respectable job out
of "Cotton-Eyed Joe" for the benefit of sailors, miners, and probable Hoodlums who were stepping on the toes of female employees of the establishment in short skirts and provocative blouses.
I'd heard the blouses were a suggestion contributed by the police,
who had raided the cellar a month or two earlier for parading the
women around with nothing above the waist. I tried to remember where I'd been a month or two earlier and decided that wherever it was, it didn't compare.

"I think it's a dance hall," I said.

There was a brief interlude when one of a pair of customers
who had each seized an arm of the same hostess smashed a bottle on the edge of the bar and threatenened his rival with the
jagged end. A bartender resolved the situation by slamming two
feet of loaded billiard cue across the skull of the unarmed man,
who then dropped out of the competition. The man with the
broken bottle blinked, then discarded his weapon and dragged

the young lady out onto the dance floor as the musicians struck up something lively.

"Reckon I'm drunker than I knew," Beecher said. "Looked to me like the barkeep hit the wrong man."

"He was closer. It came out the same either way."

"Everything's backwards here. I don't get out soon I'm going to start thinking this is the way the world works."

"It *is* the way the world works. You and I get paid to spin it the other way."

"Speak for yourself. I ain't seen so much as a nickel since we left Gold Creek."

I got out my poke, opened it under the table, and passed a few banknotes across his knees. "That's as much as I can spare. I wired Judge Blackthorne for expenses, but the hinges on his safe need oiling. You'd think it came out of his own pocket."

"It did, if he owns property."

"He owns twenty linen shirts, a dozen frock coats, and a bunch of books by a fellow named Blackstone. Whatever else he had burned with his chambers. It wasn't much. The grateful citizens of Helena gave him the house he lives in with his wife in return for defending civilization. I don't know how much the federals pay him, but he doesn't spend any of it. He's the property of the U.S. government, just like that monument they're building to George Washington."

"You feel that way, why don't you quit?"

"He's the best man I ever worked for."

"That's the way I feel about Mr. Hill; not that we ever met or that he wouldn't throw me downstairs if I showed up in his office." He gave me one of his rare grins with the cigarette he was lighting stuck between his teeth. Then he looked troubled. "Ain't one of us ought to stay sober? How we going to stand behind each other's back if we can't tell it from the front?"

"Take a look around. Shantytown's got a death sentence hanging over it. All the Hoodlums and cutthroats are too busy trying to have a good time while they still can to bother with two law dogs from out of town. I don't know about you, but I think we've earned a holiday."

"This got anything to do with Sid the Spunk being dead?"

"Don't be a jackass. Sid isn't dead."

Just then one of the dancing girls let out a stream of language that would have curled the edges of a slate roof and swung into a pirouette with nine inches of curved steel sticking out of her dainty fist. The brute she was dancing with saved his throat by stumbling and falling. As it was, the blade took off the top of his right ear. Bright blood arced out, ruining the costumes of two other dancers who were trying to get out of the way. The bouncer, a short, stocky albino with too much muscle bunched around his neck to accommodate a collar, sprang away from the wall, got hold of the woman's knife arm, twisted it behind her back, and hauled her off the floor with both satin-shod feet kicking. The bartender who had broken up the other fight threw a towel at the man on the floor, who jammed it against his lacerated ear. The other bartender, small and wiry in an apron that brushed his shoe tops, came out from behind the bar with a mop to clean up the carnage. Another brute built along the same lines as his friend helped the injured man to his feet and escorted him outside, the towel still held in place and staining bright maroon.

All this took place in about twenty seconds. The staff had rehearsed all the actions many times before, and even the two civilians had been through enough similar scrapes to take themselves out of the action without stopping to file a protest.

"Let's move on." I got up and slapped a dollar on the table to take care of the drinks. Beecher followed.

On the boardwalk in front of the dance hall, I put a hand on his arm. "Wait a minute."

The bleeding brute and his companion were standing in the middle of the street, sunk in mud to their insteps. The man holding the towel to the side of his head made a violent gesture with his free hand. They were shouting over each other's words. Other pedestrians, accustomed to such scenes, crossed the street on either side of the pair without pausing or even turning their heads. In Barbary, non-involvement wasn't just a policy; it was a law of survival.

The two men closed suddenly, as if embracing. They parted, and the man holding the bloody towel turned and came back toward the dance hall, leaving his friend standing in the street with his hands hanging empty at his sides. He looked after his departing companion, then shook his head, turned, and waded off through the mud toward the other side of the street.

I saw the squat-barreled pistol in the other man's hand as he mounted the boardwalk. I nudged Beecher and we parted to clear his path to the door. I let him pass, then drew the Deane-Adams, spun it butt-forward, and tapped him firmly on the back of the head with the backstrap. His knees bent, the short pistol clunked to the boardwalk, and I kicked it into the street, where the mud sucked it under in less than a second. It was out of sight before the man hit the ground.

"Slicker'n snot," said Beecher as we walked away. "I thought you was fixing to put a hole in him."

"It seemed drastic just for stepping on a girl's foot." I inspected the revolver for damage to the frame and stuck it back in its holster.

"How'd you know he'd come back heeled?"

"Wouldn't you, for an ear?"

Gunshots rattled a street or two over, traveling swiftly on the fog drifting in from the harbor.

Beecher said, "You're dead on about this place. Like a kid getting in his licks before someone boxes his ears."

"I saw it in Abilene, just before the city fathers voted to ban the cattle outfits from town. It's like a fever."

"You deputied Wild Bill?"

"It was after his time. Part of the hell being raised was mine. I was punching cows then. I hadn't got the call yet."

He shook his head. "We ain't the same, you and me. I'll have had my life's portion of hell after we leave here. From here on in, I'm polishing spitoons and liking it."

"Who for, J. J. Hill?"

"No, sir. For the first hotel or saloon I come to in Spokane that's hiring. Or some other town, if Belinda won't have me. I've had itchy feet since I left Louisiana. I want to see what it's like to stay put for forty or fifty years."

"You're a smart man. I wasn't too sure when you took me up on this offer."

"I didn't exactly have a choice."

"You could have left that chair standing where it was in that caboose."

He said nothing for several yards. I had the impression he was wishing he'd chosen differently.

When he spoke, however, it was to introduce a different subject. "You really think Sid the Spunk's alive?"

"Whenever someone goes out of his way to tell me something, my policy is it's a lie. F'an Chu'an owes Sid more than he owes me, and a debt to a dead man isn't worth paying. Also, a corpse doesn't need protecting."

"What about Pinholster? He lie, too?"

"No reason. His man saw what he said. Our Chinese friend is modest. He's a better doctor than he made out. He pulled Sid through, and he's either hiding him in Chinatown or covering up his tracks."

"Sid might of quit Frisco."

"Then there'd be no reason to convince us he's dead."

"We fixing to go on looking for him?"

"That's Pinholster's cradle. Let him rock it. Judge Blackthorne already thinks we're off chasing rabbits."

"Not tonight, though."

"Not tonight. Tonight we're getting drunk."

We entered a place called the Slaughterhouse, on the southern end of Battle Row. There, the patrons were gathered around a little platform built for musicians, where a red-bearded Irishman with leather lungs was auctioning off a drunken naked girl. Her ribs showed and she had tiny breasts, but there were no visible scars and the bidding was up to fifty dollars. Each new bid was louder than the one before.

Beecher leaned in close and shouted in my ear. "I thought this ended in sixty-three."

"I don't think it's a full sale," I shouted back. "Just an overnight rental."

The whiskey was a little better than turpentine, although it might have been useful in loosening rusty bolts. It burned furrows down our throats and boiled in our stomachs. A balloon opened in my head, making sounds echo and multiplying everything I looked at. The skinny girl went to a sailor for sixty-two-fifty and was replaced on the platform by three fat girls, or maybe it was just one, who was quickly stripped with some assistance on her part, and upon whom the bidding soared rapidly; the air outside was nippy and there's nothing like cuddling up to a heap of naked flesh on a cold night. A couple of sailors got into a fistfight over a fifty-cent raise, and part of the audience peeled away to form a circle around the brawlers. No attempt was made on the part of the establishment to separate them.

"Should we take a hand?" Beecher asked.

"I'll put a dollar on the little fellow."

I didn't see how the fight came out. Things and people were losing shape and time passed on a sliding scale. Two other customers argued over a spilled drink; one smashed the other in the mouth, and I thought I was only a witness until I woke up the next morning with my right hand swollen and throbbing and extracted a shard of broken tooth from the third knuckle. In order to examine the hand, I had to pull it out from under the naked woman who was lying on top of it, and half on top of me in my narrow berth at the Slop Chest. I extricated myself from the snoring creature, dressed, and wobbled out into the saloon, where Beecher grinned at me from the end of the bar.

"Sixty-five even," he said. "You beat out the nearest man by a dollar. You fixing to charge it to expenses?"

26

"Long live the emperor," Nan Feeny said. "Sluice your gob with this. It'll draw the sting from that rotten swig what they pour at the Slaughterhouse."

I watched her fill a glass with something orange and yellow from a canning jar. It glopped twice and she stirred it with a spoon until it assumed a uniform consistency as thick as sausage gravy.

"Should I ask what's in it?" I picked it up and sniffed at it. It had a familiar smell I remembered from childhood, mixed with something never before encountered. It wasn't entirely unpleasant.

"Buttermilk and grenadine, to start. I'm sworn to family secrecy as to the rest. My grandfather in Limerick died with a glass in his hand. Don't let it funk you," she said, when I set it down untasted. "He was shot by a vicar."

I picked it up again. "What's it do?"

"Well, it won't get rid of that baggage in your room. I ought to charge you extra rent."

"I packed her off with two dollars for her time. When was the last time something happened in the Sailor's Rest you didn't know about?"

She touched the ribbon at her throat, thinking. "Christmas Day, eighteen seventy-nine. I was down with the Grippe. Tip it down, and don't leave off till you can see me through the bottom. It won't work took in pieces."

I drank it in one long draught. It tasted the way marigolds smelled rotting. She saw on my face what was going on in my stomach and pointed at the spitoon in front of the footrail. I bent and scooped it up in both hands. It was a near enough thing even then. When I came up, wiping my mouth with the back of a hand, she was unstopping a bottle of ginger beer. "That should cut the copper."

I took two swigs. The metallic taste began to recede, and with it the pounding in my skull. My legs were still weak. I leaned on the bar for support.

"I'd of warned you away of the Slaughterhouse if you asked," she said. "The bilge they use to cut the squail's worse than the squail itself."

I'd wearied of the conversation, which I'd only half understood anyway.

"Where are Billy and Hodge? This is the first time I've seen you behind the bar." I was the only customer apart from a sailor losing steadily to Pinholster. Beecher, who recovered from the effects of strong spirits as quickly as he succumbed to them, had gone out in search of breakfast.

"It's Billy's morning out. He spends every rag he makes on a mollisher up on Telegraph Hill. Axel's down with a worse case than you, right along with the rest of Barbary. Come this time next week, they'll all be smacking the calfskin in Goodhue's congregation; them what ain't dancing at their death from the gas lamps."

"And where will you be?"

"Well, Goodhue's calfskin ain't mine, for all the words are the same. I ain't touched a drop of the peach since night before last, nor will I through tomorrow night, when I'll sit on the bed the Commodore bought, with my pepperbox close to hand and loads enough to see me through Gabriel's blast. I don't intend to sail to Hell unescorted."

"If that's Barbary's philosophy, Goodhue's Hundred are in for subtraction."

"A properly raptured Christian ain't so easy to kill as all that; ask Caesar. And a hundred has a way of becoming a thousand once they're kindled."

I couldn't argue with her arithmetic. I'd seen it put to the test in too many towns.

"What's Goodhue's draw? Bible slappers don't kick up much dust most places."

"Most places ain't Frisco. Every few years the swells get their crops full of Barbary and they don't look too hard at whoever steps up to the mark. After it's done they call in the army, hang the loudest, and dress for dinner. In the old country, we lit a candle. Here they light Barbary."

"Where does Goodhue hang his hat?"

She pursed her lips. She had something of the school matron

in her. I remembered she'd been a governess in Boston before circumstances drove her West.

"He's got him a crib on Mission Street, courtesy of the God-fearing folk of San Francisco. It's a sin to own things if you can trade Paradise Everlasting for bed and board." She mopped the bartop, sweeping away marble splinters along with the spills. "I wouldn't aim for his heart, if that's where you're bound. The ball would pass through empty air and hit a soul worth saving on the other side as like as not."

"Don't believe what you read in the dime novels. I haven't shot anyone in weeks."

She stopped mopping. Her face went blank. "Steer clear of the Major Doctor. He's Black Spy in a collar."

"If he's human and speaks English, I've got nothing to lose by seeking him out."

"That's your second mistake. Your first is wanting to seek him out to begin with. He was a barrel-maker before he took to the cloth, and age ain't weakened him nor piety gentled his nature. He's throwed more than one poor sinner down the steps of the East Street Mission just for questioning his interpretation of the Word."

"I'll stay away from stairs."

"You'd profit higher staying away from Goodhue."

"Now I'm curious. I've never locked horns with the clergy."

"What's the percentage? I thought it was the Sons of the Confederacy you was after."

"I'm not forgetting that. I'm not forgetting I'm sworn to keep the peace, either."

"You got to have peace to keep it."

I smiled. I was feeling better by the minute, thanks to either the conversation or Nan Feeny's orange elixir. It put me in mind of the wisdom of a deputy marshal, dead these five years, who'd told me he couldn't understand people who never drank hard liquor, rising each morning knowing that's as good as they would feel all day long. He'd been stone-cold sober the day he was killed.

"Peace is just a time to reload."

She swept up the ginger beer bottle and clunked it into the ash can behind the bar. "I'll see they cut that into your stone," she said. "If I live through tomorrow night."

The sailor threw down his cards, scraped back his chair, and wove an unsteady pattern toward the bar. I slid into his place.

Pinholster, stacking his chips, shook his head. "If you ever decide to change professions, I don't recommend mine. When people win, they crow at you, and when they lose, they bring your parentage into question. You never see them at their best."

"I'm short of sympathy. You could have posed as a priest."

"Even worse. I'd have to listen to them complain about their losses in confession. I assume, since you've cleaned me out of both cash and intelligence, that you come with news."

"Sid the Spunk is dead."

He shuffled the deck. "May I inquire as to your source?"

"Let's just say I got it from the mysterious East."

"You surprise me. Celestials are renowned for their wisdom

and their unwillingness to share it with the uncivilized West. Obfuscation is the one dialect common to all the provinces of China."

"Corroboration is a dangerous business in Chinatown. I'm expected to take a hatchet for the United States of America, not for Allan Pinkerton."

"It's Fat John, then?"

I said nothing. I'd forgotten how good he was at spotting tells.

He shrugged and set down the deck. "That's that, I suppose. My last assignment."

"Don't look so funereal. Now you can go back to Chicago before all hell busts loose."

"I'm haunted by the suspicion that Sid the Spunk will show up to see me off. I wouldn't care to go to my reward knowing I'd failed at the finish."

"Your reward may come as early as tomorrow night."

He scratched his ragged beard.

"I've never seen a lynching, though I've heard it described. I'd still take the rope over what's in store. Is it your conviction our yellow friend has told you the truth?"

I shook my head. "You didn't pay to see my hand."

"Nevertheless, I believe you've shown it to me." He picked up the cards. "One last friendly game? Just to determine which of us is the better gambler."

"It wouldn't prove anything. You've got nothing to lose."

"I believe the condemned is entitled to a boon."

"How many last requests do you have coming?"

We played, however. The game ended in a draw.

Minutes later, standing on the boardwalk, I looked up at the slanted roof of the Slop Chest, my home away from the home I didn't have. A seagull, red-eyed and fat with carrion, was roosting on the peak of the stovepipe. That was an omen I scarcely needed on my way to see Owen Goodhue, founder of the First Eden Infantry, Army of the River Jordan.

27

eecher caught up with me three blocks away from the Slop Chest. "What we doing today?"

I'd grown tired of the question.

"I'm headed to Mission Street. You can come along if you want. I don't need anyone to stand behind me this trip."

"I hear different, if it's Goodhue you're going to see. He broke a deacon's neck on East Street fighting over Jesus."

"I heard something along those lines. I don't intend to argue Scripture."

"Reckon I'll tag along. I ain't tried riding one of them cable cars."

"One streetcar's pretty much like all the rest."

"You shamed to be seen with me, boss?"

"Stop drawing lines in the dirt. This is a friendly visit. The reverend gentleman might not take kindly to two deputies dropping in."

"I'll wait outside."

"You're coming inside if you're coming with me. You're no good to me with a wall between."

"That's what I been saying."

The conductor, a sidewhiskered Scot with a short clay pipe screwed into the middle of his face, scowled at Beecher, but he took our money. We shared the car with some laborers traveling with their lunch buckets and a ladies' maid with a basket of knitting in her lap; the gentry were wedded to their private carriages and the conductor was adept at blocking access to the steps whenever someone of doubtful character tried to board. We alighted a block short of Mission and walked the rest of the way. Here the buildings were made of proper planed siding and brick, with flower boxes and well-tended gardens fenced off behind wrought iron. Five minutes from Barbary and we might have been separated from it by a thousand miles. The sight of a white man and a Negro walking together drew passing interest from the occasional pedestrian, no more. The Civil War and Emancipation were remote things to genteel San Francisco, like a revolution in Singapore. The male strollers wore brushed bowlers and silk tiles and swung ebony sticks with gold and silver tops. All the women were escorted. Policemen in leather helmets and blue serge congregated on street corners, twirling their sticks. We saw more officers in ten minutes than we'd seen in three weeks. The city had managed to pen up the bad element like Indians on a reservation. I saw then why respectable San Franciscans had little interest in closing down the whorehouses, deadfalls, and opium dens operating within walking distance of their townhouses and colonial palaces; they were protected by a trellis wall, and behaved as if it were made of iron. The place was a powder keg, but they were too busy walking their dogs and raising money to rescue someone else's wayward daughters to look down at the sparking fuse.

The address given to us by a policeman belonged to a modest two-story house with green shutters and a boot scraper shaped like a porcupine on the tiny front porch. I turned a handle that operated a jangling bell on the other side of the painted door.

"Yes?"

We took off our hats in front of an old woman in a floor-length dress with her gray hair in a bun. I inquired if this was the home of Mr. Goodhue.

"*Doctor* Goodhue," she corrected gently. "He is in his devotions at present."

I introduced myself and Beecher. "We're deputy federal marshals. We don't require much of his time."

She took in this information as if I'd told her we'd come to sweep the chimney and let us into a small front parlor containing some mohair furniture and what looked like a complete set of Bowdler's Gibbon next to *The Bible Lover's Illustrated Library* in a small-book press. "Please wait here."

She went out through a curtained doorway, leaving us alone with the smells of melted wax and walnut stain.

"Smells like church," Beecher whispered. It was a room designed for whispering.

I made a tour of the papered walls. Carved mahogany framed a series of Renaissance prints of the Annunciation, the

Crucifixion, the Sermon on the Mount, and the usual Montgomery Ward's run of secular subjects: Cornwallis's surrender, the signing of the Declaration of Independence, fairies, a beefy tenor stuffed into Hamlet's tights. With a few variations, it was the same parlor visitors waited in fron New Hampshire to Seattle, a disappointment after what I'd been told by Nan Feeny. There wasn't a flaming sword or a scrap of brimstone in evidence. I began to wonder if anything she'd said was true, from Goodhue's participation in the violent uprising of '56 to the soiled dove she'd saved from drowning at his hands. Tall tales were a staple on the frontier and it looked as if Barbary was no exception.

"Dr. Goodhue asks that you join him in his cabinet."

We followed her down a short hallway with tall wainscoting, at the end of which she opened a door and stood aside to let us pass through. This room was scarcely larger than the parlor and unfinished. Plaster had squeezed out between the laths of the walls and frozen like meringue, the naked ceiling hung six inches above our heads, and the floor was made of unplaned pine, laid green so that the planks had warped and drawn apart; they bent beneath our weight, sprang back into shape when it was released, and invited drafts from the crawl space underneath. The addition of a rolltop desk, a wooden chair mounted on a swivel, and a low, plain table supporting a stack of books with burst and shredded bindings had done nothing to convince me we weren't standing in an unconverted lumber room. There was no window, just a copper lamp with a smudged glass chimney burning on the desk.

Our host sat on the swivel with his elbows on the desk and

his head propped between his hands, studying a book that lay open and flat on the blotter. He was too big for the chair— nearly too big for the room—and at first glance resembled nothing so much as a tame ape perched on a child's chair for the entertainment of an audience. His shoulders strained the seams of a homespun shirt, his broadcloth trousers, held up by leather galluses, fell short of his ankles, and his feet were shod in farmer's brogans, either one of which was big enough to hang outside a cobbler's shop for advertising. At length he finished the paragraph he was reading, laid an attached ribbon between the pages to mark his place, closed the book, and rotated to face us with his hands on his thighs and his elbows turned out. The book was bound in green cloth, with the legend stamped in gold: *The Fairest Cargo, or The Christian Legions' Crusade Against the White Slave Trade in the New World,* by the Reverend Hobart Thorpe Forrestal. Just in case the point was missed, an illustration inlaid on the cover portrayed a female beauty with an hourglass figure and unfettered hair, clasping her hands to Heaven behind iron bars. No room in the clutter for trumpets and cherubim.

It all seemed like a theater set. I looked around, but couldn't tell for certain if he'd swept a copy of the *Police Gazette* into a drawer when he'd heard us coming. There is no showman like a minister, and no minister quite so authentic in appearance as one who is self-ordained.

"Welcome, gentlemen," rumbled Owen Goodhue. "I had scarcely hoped that our little campaign would draw the attention of Washington City."

His likeness on his flyers didn't do him justice. His head was the size of a medicine ball, with iron gray hair parted in the center and plastered into curls like a Roman emperor's ahead of his temples. Purple lesions traced the S-shaped path of his broken nose, and his close-set eyes burned deep in their sockets. The coarse beard began just below the ridge of his cheekbones and plummeted to its abrupt terminus across his collar, sliced off in a straight line as if with a dressmaker's shears. Here was yet another dangerous face to hang in my ever-expanding black gallery.

I said, "We haven't come that far, and we didn't hear about your crusade until we read the *Call*. However, it's what we're here to discuss."

"And which one are you, Deputy Murdock or Deputy Beecher?"

He had a powerful voice, shaped by the pulpit, and it required control to keep from shaking plaster loose from the laths. He might have trained it by shouting into the barrels he'd made, tuning it by the sound of the echo.

"Page Murdock. This is Edward Anderson Beecher. We represent the United States District Court of the Territory of Montana, presided over by Judge Harlan A. Blackthorne."

"I've heard of the man. Presbyterian, is he not?"

I said he was. "We're investigating an organization that calls itself the Sons of the Confederacy."

"A wicked lot. I supported Abolition in eighteen hundred and fifty-one, when it was far less popular than it became later. Are you familiar with the work of the Reverend Forrestal?" Without turning, he reached back and thumped the cover of *The Fairest Cargo* with a forefinger the size of a pinecone.

"I've neglected my reading these past few weeks, apart from the *Call*." I was trying to steer the conversation back to his pet crusade. He seemed to have a habit of following up each statement with a question that diverted the course.

"You would find it illuminating. The conventional wisdom is that the surrender of that godless man Lee put the period to slavery in these United States. Meanwhile, chaste young white women are being exchanged like currency in broad daylight on the streets of our greatest cities, and forced into degradation which to describe would bring a blush to the cheek of a base pagan. Are you aware of the threat posed by the nation's ice-cream parlors?"

Beecher laughed. Goodhue turned the full heat of his gaze upon him.

"You are amused, my Ethiopian friend; as well you may be, until I explain that most of these establishments are owned and operated by foreigners; Jews and papists, turned in the lathes of Mediterranean seaports where girls are auctioned off in public and conducted in chains to workhouses and brothels, never to be seen again by decent society. These scoundrels ply them with sweets and flattery, and when the tender creatures are sufficiently befogged, offer them employment—stressing that the work is undemanding and respectable—and by these lights lead them down the garden path toward the burning pit. One moment of feminine weakness, and someone's cherished daughter delivers herself to a lifetime of debauchery and an eternity of damnation. I would no sooner allow a child of mine to enter the polished whiteness of one of these emporia than I would escort her into a saloon. Ice cream, you say? The serpent's fruit, *I* say."

As he spoke, his volume rose, until the room shook with thunder. Just hearing it made me feel hoarse. I cleared my throat.

"I haven't seen any ice-cream parlors in Barbary."

"There is no reason why you should, since by the time this poor baggage arrives their purpose is done. Hell's broad avenue begins in New York and Boston and Chicago and ends in Portsmouth Square. Stare deeply into the eyes of the next harlot you see; disregard the painted features and tinted hair, the hollow cheeks and lying lips, and you will discern the frail, faded glimmer of the trusting girl who turned her back on church and home, never suspecting it was for the last time."

Beecher said, "You feel that way, you ought to set up shop in New York or Boston or Chicago. By the time they get here, they're gone for good."

"That is the crossroads at which the Reverend Forrestal and I part ways. He counsels eradicating this pernicious growth at the point where it blossoms, whereas I am in favor of burning it out at its root. Close an ice-cream parlor, incarcerate its proprietor, and two more will spring up in their place, so long as there is profit to be made. It is simple economics. Destroy the houses of sin, and with them the source of income, and there will be no need for the parlors. Smite the sinners, burn their tabernacles to the ground, baptize them in the blood of the lamb. Sacrifice the sheep that are lost along with those who led them astray, and spare those who may yet be folded back into the flock. In order to rebuild, one must first destroy."

The walls were still ringing when the door opened from the hallway. The gray-haired woman's face was stoic. "Owen, I have loaves in the oven."

His voice dropped six feet. "I'm sorry, my dear."

She drew the door shut. The exchange was the first indication I'd had that she was his wife and not just his housekeeper.

I said, "It's the destruction we've come to talk about. We want to ask you to postpone Judgment Day until we lay this Sons of the Confederacy business to rest."

"I am far more concerned with the daughters than I am with the Sons. I care not whether they prosper or perish."

"Some of the names on your list are no threat to anyone's daughter," I said.

"Infamous assassins, harlots, and thieves! Slay the hosts and the parasites will wither. These targets were not chosen arbitrarily. David declared war upon the Philistines, but he joined battle with Goliath, and thereby claimed victory with but a single stone. I wish you gentlemen well upon your mission, but your objectives are not mine."

"You won't reconsider?"

"I will not. Indeed, I cannot. Immortal souls are at risk."

I drew the Deane-Adams.

"That being the case, you're under arrest for obstruction of justice."

Beecher unbelted his Le Mat and cocked it.

Goodhue's brow darkened. The muscles bunched in his arms and thighs. He looked ready to pounce. Then he smirked in his beard. It wasn't a pretty sight, but I preferred it to Goodhue rampant on a field of hellfire. When he spoke, his tone was level.

"Are you so certain that placing a spiritual leader in a cage will postpone the event you fear, rather than accelerate it?"

I was still thinking about that when the door opened again. Mrs. Goodhue took in the pistols without expression. "A man to see you. He wouldn't give his name."

The smoldering eyes remained on me. I returned the five-shot to its holster. Beecher lowered his hammer and put up the Confederate pistol.

"Ask him to wait in the parlor," Goodhue said.

The door closed.

I said, "Whorehouses are like ice-cream stores. There are two or three waiting to take the place of every one you burn to the ground."

"Work worthy of the effort is worthy of repeating. Always and again, until the mortal shells rise and the sorting begins. The price of salvation is patience and persistence."

"You're not the first man who tried to raise a private army for his own ends. They always come to grief at the finish."

"You've forgotten the late Mr. Lincoln. General McClellan was in favor of suing for peace. Lincoln answered him by inventing the draft. But for his interest in his own ends, the war would have ended three years earlier. History is written by the victors."

"He paid for it with his life," I said. "His and three hundred thousand others."

"I am prepared to answer to that account. Are you?"

"I swore an oath to that effect."

He smirked again. "I'm aware of the reading habits of my parishioners. I regret to say it is not confined to Holy Writ. Your exploits have not escaped the notice of the vulgar penny press, and I dare say they do not in all ways conform to the spirit of your oath. I judge not lest I be judged. My own methods are not always those of the Redeemer and His apostles, but I live in the modern world. Mark and Matthew could not have anticipated Barbary any more than the hedonistic Greeks could have foreseen Sodom and Gomorrah. Although Samson found the jawbone of an ass sufficient for slaughtering infidels and idolators, I find that a powder charge is far more appropriate when transacting business with Daniel Webster Wheelock's Hoodlums."

The atmosphere in that raw room was noxious. It might have been the lingering effects of last night or the smoky lamp on the desk, but there was hardly enough air to fill Owen Goodhue's lungs, let alone three sets at once. I wanted out of there, but I needed one more answer.

"I notice you didn't include Wheelock's name on your list."

"God has use for Satan, or He would have smote him centuries ago. In any case, Captain Dan is nothing without Barbary. He will shrivel and drift before the first clean draught that blows unhampered across the ruins."

"You keep talking about Barbary as if it's just a bunch of buildings," I said. "They have people in them."

"What is flesh? We leave it behind when we stand before our Creator."

"Lying or hanging?"

"I do not propose to say. Joshua did not discuss his strategy before Jericho."

"But who will be left to write the Book of Owen?" I asked.

"I am a humble man. If in the outcome of this event my name should be erased from human memory, I hold the matter in no great regard. It is already written in the book of St. Peter.

If I manage to spare even one young woman from the clutches of Demon Lust, I need not fear what is recorded beneath. Gentlemen." He rose, dwarfing the room further. He had to stoop to avoid colliding with the ceiling. It made you want to step back.

Beecher held his ground. "What's white slaving got to do with Horatio Flinders?"

Goodhue hoisted his shaggy brows. "Who?"

We left him. Entering the parlor on our way out, I stopped. Beecher bumped against me from behind.

Daniel Webster Wheelock used his ivory stick to push himself up from one of the upholstered chairs. He had on his fire captain's uniform, and he looked as surprised as I felt.

"Deputy."

"Alderman."

Mrs. Goodhue came in and led him out.

Nero, Wheelock's Negro bodyguard, stood smoking a cigar on the boardwalk in front of the house. He wore a tall gray hat and a full-skirted overcoat to match over checked trousers and gleaming Wellingtons. He lowered the hand holding the cigar and tipped his hat as we walked past.

PART FIVE

The Bonnie-Blue Flag

28

"That man Goodhue's crazier'n ten crazy men," Beecher said.

I nodded. "I can't figure out why he isn't famous."

"Well, he'll be plenty famous after tomorrow night."

We were sitting on a public bench at the top of Telegraph Hill, passing a bottle of Old Gideon back and forth; I'd made the mistake of swearing off liquor before making the acquaintance of the madman of Mission Street. The saloon-keeper in the stained-glass place where we'd stopped for a drink wouldn't serve us on the premises on account of Beecher, but he'd agreed to sell us the bottle when I showed him my star and asked when was the last time his gas line had been inspected.

The view was impressive, even for a native of the High Plains. It extended all the way down to the ships in the harbor and across the bay where houses were going up, so rapidly we could track their progress between swigs. Cable cars screeched down the slope and rattled back up, taking on and disgorging passengers on the fly. I saw my first omnibus. The place was busier than an antheap.

Both sides of San Francisco displayed themselves simultaneously, the stately homes on Nob Hill and the tumbledown shacks on Pacific Street; parasols blossoming to our left like desert blooms after a rain, pushcart peddlers crawling along like caterpillars to our right, hawking rags and cans of coal oil recovered from the dregs of lamps rescued from trash bins. We saw a liveried groom helping a lady in a bustle into a brougham and the assault and battery of an unsteady pedestrian, both at the same time. It was like looking through a stereoscope whose pictures had gotten mixed up back at the factory.

Beecher shared my thoughts. "What you reckon is holding this place together?"

"The same thing that keeps it apart. If it weren't for Barbary, the swells would have to pick fights with each other. Look what's happening on the frontier. We threw out the Indians and let in the lawyers and politicians."

"What makes you so smart?"

"I'm not smart. I'm just alive."

"You fought Indians?"

"I've fought Indians."

"And I know you shot it out with outlaws."

"Outlaws and lawmen."

"How old are you?"

"Forty-two."

"You're smart."

"Not smart enough to quit."

"Maybe you're smart enough to tell me what Cap'n Dan's doing paying a call on Goodhue."

"We'll ask Wheelock tonight at the Bella Union."

He drank, held the liquor in his mouth a moment, then swallowed. "I clean forgot about that meeting of the Sons of the Confederacy. You done any thinking as to how we're getting in?"

"I've been working on it. I still am. I don't figure that punch-simple bouncer from the saloon to set much of a challenge, but if Wheelock shows, he's bound to bring along that bodyguard of his. He knows us by sight, and Wheelock didn't strike me as the kind of politician who keeps anyone on his payroll just because he looks well in a stiff collar."

"Nero's colored. You leave him to me."

"Matching skin won't get you past him. I doubt he concerns himself with brotherhood."

"It ain't getting past him I'm talking about. Some men you just got to go through." He offered me the bottle.

I shook my head. It was already beginning to slosh. My stomach was empty. I'd held my own against dog soldiers and brute killers, but that morning I hadn't been stout enough to face breakfast. "We can't risk shooting. The noise would raise the South and it would be Bull Run all over again."

He raised the bottle to his lips, then thought better of it and thumped in the cork. "I ever tell you about the fight at Buffalo Creek?"

"You scalped a young brave and stayed behind to burn the lodges and shoot the ponies."

"No, the young brave was another fight, and I didn't tell you how Buffalo Creek got won. We was climbing a hill to attack the village. It was first light, and we was walking the horses with gunnysacks tied on their hooves so as not to alert the sentries; cupping their snouts with one hand so's they wouldn't blow when they smelled Indian ponies. We was halfway up when a hunting party come over the hill and spotted us.

"They was just as surprised as we was, and drawed rein just to make certain they wasn't seeing spirits. They was mounted, we was afoot, and if you tell me you ever seen a good organized Arapaho charge you're a liar, on account of you wouldn't be sitting here with hair under your hat. I only heard about them myself, and hearing was enough to satisfy my curiosity."

He grinned his sunrise grin. He was seeing something other than the metropolis at our feet.

"We had this white lieutenant, Brigham was his name, only he sure wasn't no Mormon. When he broke wind, you thought it was the regimental band. I seen men who'd gut you with a bayonet turn green and spew up their rations when they caught the scent. Well, he got so scared he let one fly, loud enough to spook the horses, and you know something? That hunting party was so insulted they lost their manners and galloped down that hill all in a bunch, whooping like drunken cowboys, running right over each other, bumping lances and getting their bows all tangled. Meanwhile, Lieutenant Brigham remembered his training and got us into formation, front rank standing and firing, then kneeling to reload while the second rank stood and fired, and so on. We shot that hunting party to pieces and swung into leather and took out after the turntails and right on over the crest and down into the village. All on account of one man couldn't hold his beans."

He drew the cork, drank, and restopped the bottle.

"We called it the Battle of Brigham's Bowels."

I watched a wedding let out of a church on Stockton, men in morning coats and women in frilled capes spilling down the steps to see off the bride and groom in a phaeton tied all over with white ribbons.

"I don't remember reading about that one in *Harper's Weekly*," I said.

"Well, it wasn't Custer's Last Fight. The point is, you can train a man to overcome everything but his own bad temper. If them braves wasn't so concerned with their dignity, that village might still be standing." He stuck the bottle in a coat pocket. "You let me worry about Nero."

"You aren't going to break wind, are you?"

"That was just an example. I wouldn't never enter into a contest with Lieutenant Brigham. One time—"

"Save it for later. You don't want to use up all your best stories at once." I stood and grasped the back of the bench for balance. Old Gideon needed a four-course meal to tie it down. "Let's get something to eat. We might not find time for supper."

He got up. "What you in the mood for?"

"Anything but beans."

The Ancient rose from a blanket of fog that swathed the gas lamps almost to their orange globes, pale and shimmering under a rustler's moon. It was as solid and yet as otherworldly as the Sphinx, and it seemed to say, *I am the Bella Union, I am Barbary. I was here before the Chinese, before the Sydney Ducks, and I will stand when all the lesser establishments about me have burned or fallen into splinters. Worship me with cheap champagne and expensive women.* We sidestepped a pool of steaming urine at the base of the foundation and went inside. We were met by the bouncer, none of whose scars had faded since the last time. His head belonged on a hunched figure in trunks and a tight jersey in a sporting print, not a thickening body in a black frock coat and white shirtboard.

"Sorry, gents. The place is closed tonight for a private party. Come back tomorrow."

We were alone in the foyer that opened into the saloon, but I didn't know for how long. The auditorium door was drifting shut behind the last body to pass through. I started to turn away, then pivoted on my heel and hit the bouncer square on the chin with all my weight behind my fist. I felt the impact to my shoulder.

He took a step back, then lowered his head between his shoulders and raised a pair of small, hard fists with ridges across the knuckles where they'd broken and healed several times. He took a step forward. Beecher planted the muzzle of his Le Mat against the bouncer's right temple and rolled back the hammer. The bouncer stiffened, then lowered his fists to his sides.

I held my star in front of his face. "We're here on federal business. Take a walk down to the harbor. Have a cigar. Have several. In San Quentin, they don't let you smoke in the cells."

"I don't use tobacco."

"Have a drink, then. Kill the bottle."

"I don't drink, either. I don't hold with most of the vices."

"Which ones do you hold with?" I kept my temper in check. I didn't know when someone might come in from the street or the theater. I didn't want to buffalo him. You can take only so many cracks to the skull, and the bumps and furrows showing through his close-cropped hair went the limit.

"I got a girl up at the Brass Check."

"Go see her. You've got to tend a romance if you want it to grow."

"I'll lose my job."

"There's plenty of work in San Quentin."

After a moment he nodded. Beecher withdrew the pistol and the bouncer walked past us and out the door. He didn't stop for a hat and coat.

"Thought you said he wouldn't set much challenge," Beecher said.

I shushed him, strode to the auditorium door, and cracked it. It opened into a carpeted alcove with stairs to the right and left, which I guessed led to the curtained boxes where the gentry plied Owen Goodhue's lost daughters with drink and pressed their affections in private. I hoped they'd be vacant that night. I drew the Deane-Adams and led the way upstairs. Voices buzzed in the orchestra. The place sounded like opening night for a revue from New York.

"Sir, I'm afraid you've lost your way."

I recognized the deep silken voice before I saw its owner. Wheelock's bodyguard stood in the center of the floral carpet that ran past the entrance to the boxes, his feet spread in patent-leather boots. Tonight he had on plum-colored plush, ruffled white linen, and black broadcloth, tailored to within a quarter-inch of his measurements. It made him look almost normal size until you realized that what appeared to be a ladies' pocket pistol in his right hand was a full-size Colt Peacemaker, with the barrel shortened to accommodate a concealed holster. It was steadied against his hip.

I said, "Nero, this isn't your affair. I represent the law."

I might as well have been throwing pebbles at a statue. The fact that I had a revolver in my hand as well meant no more to him than the color of my eyes. We'd neither of us miss the mark at that distance.

"Nero."

I twitched. Nero didn't. I hadn't realized Beecher wasn't behind me until he stepped around the corner behind the body-guard and called his name. He held the Le Mat straight out from his shoulder with the muzzle aimed at the back of the big man's head. He'd climbed the other set of stairs and followed the carpeted walk all the way around the auditorium.

"That's Beecher," I said. "You met him the other day in your boss's reception room."

That bounced off him. He was a fixture. They'd built the Bella Union around him and he'd be the last thing to go come the next big fire. The Colt didn't move. Judge Blackthorne's deputies were trained in that situation to fire at their primary target, then if they were still standing, turn and try for the men behind them. In that moment I knew Nero had been taught the same thing. We were going to burn each other down, and God couldn't stop it. He'd turned His back on Barbary. My finger tightened on the trigger of the Deane-Adams.

"He won't remember," Beecher said. "We're all the same to him, a pat on the head and a scratch behind the ears. He'll wag his tail and lick the face of whoever comes around to see his master. Ain't that right, nigger-oh?"

He licked his lips. "Nero."

I couldn't fathom it. If Beecher had told me what he'd had in mind, I'd have refused to go along. You could see through it from a hundred yards, and the bodyguard wasn't a fool. But Beecher had known something I hadn't, something I never would. I relaxed my finger just a little.

"That ain't what I asked, you dumb coon. You must have cotton in your ears."

Nero didn't move. A vein I hadn't noticed before rose like a blister on his left temple. I saw it pulse.

"Let's us go," Beecher said to me. "This boy's got spitoons to empty out."

Nero twisted suddenly, bringing the Colt around with him. I made two long strides and swept the barrel of the five-shot across the bulge of his skull. His knees buckled. I reached past him, closing my hand over the Colt and jamming the base of my thumb between the hammer and the chamber. I sucked air when the hammer pinched flesh, but the cartridge didn't fire and I twisted the weapon out of his grip as he fell.

We gagged him with his cravat, used his belt and Beecher's to bind his arms and legs, and dragged him through a door into one of the boxes overlooking the auditorium. I told Beecher to watch him.

"What about you?"

"I came to see the show."

29

It was my first time in the Bella Union's melodeon section, and if it weren't for what had brought me there, I might have been entranced. Tombstone's celebrated Birdcage and the candied theaters of St. Louis and Virginia City could boast of no features not in place in the Ancient. The curtained boxes where customers could sip brandy or sherry or Tennessee Thunder in comfort while watching the show, or draw the curtains and enjoy a show of their own with one of the *danseuses* from the saloon, were stacked three high all around the orchestra, whose seats were upholstered in green plush piped with gold braid. Gas globes were stacked like eggs atop corner fixtures, and the stage glowed between mahogany columns carved into towering shocks of wheat. Cabbage roses exploded on burgundy runners in the aisles. Laurels of gold leaf encircled a coffered ceiling with a Greek Bacchanal enshrined in stained glass in the center, lighted from above so that the chubby nymphs' nipples and the blubbery lips of the bloated male gods and demigods glittered like rubies. It was as decadent as anything in that vicinity. A Christian soldier like Owen Goodhue would shinny up one of the wheat shocks to smash it bare-handed.

There was a particularly lecherous glint in the eye of one deity, busy feeding pomegranate seeds from a cupped palm to a hefty nude sprawled across his lap: a round hole with yellow light glaring through. I was pretty sure it was a bullet hole, possibly a practice round fired by Samuel Tetlow, the Ancient's absentee owner, before he shot his partner.

The place dripped dissipation. Like most of its neighbors, it had burned several times during the tender years of the Gold Rush, and according to Pinholster it had reincarnated itself each time in a shape more lewd than the one before. There were old stains on the velvet seats and carpeting in the box I was in that I didn't think were made by spilled liquor, or even blood, and there was a smell of disinfectant that no cologne, no matter how liberally sprayed about, could disguise completely. Just being there made me feel like a dirty little boy, and I was on U.S. business. I could only imagine what it was like in the company of a young creature with soft flesh and hard eyes while ballet girls performed splits onstage.

A low groaning made me jump. It sounded as if whatever wounded animal had made it was in the box with me. I thought of checking on Beecher, who was in the next box, keeping an eye on Nero. Then came another groan, shorter and ending on a higher note. Someone was sawing at a cello.

Carefully I drew aside one of the swagged curtains and peered around it down onto the stage. The musician, a scrawny old fellow with white hair parted in the center and extravagant handlebars, squatted in evening dress on a low stool with the cello between his knees, searching for the scales with his bow. At last he found them, and as he neared the middle register, a violinist standing next to him joined in with what sounded like the first strains of "Turkey in the Straw," although it was more likely something by Bach or Vivaldi or some other wicked European whose music I couldn't hum no matter how recently I'd heard it. A third musician slid a chair across the stage, perched on its edge, and started tuning a guitar. He spent a lot of time between strums twisting the frets or whatever they were called, and each time when he tried it he seemed to find the same note. I have no ear for music.

A third of the seats in front of the stage were filled, with more visitors shuffling down the aisles. All were men. Some wore black swallowtails, others town suits and old overalls. A large number wore Confederate gray. The uniforms appeared tailored to fit, from far better material than the old shoddy, and were certainly in too good a condition to have gone through combat, or even hung in some cedar closet for eighteen years. There were chevrons and bars, some clusters, but no stars as yet. I had an idea the Sons of the Confederacy hadn't room for more than one general; or two, if Blackthorne and Marshal Spilsbury were right about the rift in the ranks.

The men in uniform were young, by and large; at the most, they looked to be in their late thirties, scarcely old enough to have exposed their regimentals to enemy fire. A few were barely out of their teens, with pimples on their foreheads and public first attempts at moustaches and imperials. Some of the officers wore sabers, and from the way they clanked against their heels when they walked, it seemed obvious they wouldn't know how to handle them when they were out of their scabbards either. If I were casting a play set at Gettysburg, I'd have called off the audition based on those who had responded.

I began to wonder if this was the same organization that had tried twice to kill me and had committed some two dozen murders for the cause of Southern liberty. But then I'd been all wrong about Owen Goodhue, on the evidence of his ordinary-looking parlor; caught up in the fire of his faith, he was a guerrilla, cut from the same vengeful cloth as Bloody Bill and Clay Allison. They don't always oblige you with horns and a forked tail.

Applause burst, making me jump yet again. The trio onstage had stopped tuning their instruments and hurled themselves into a lilting, pastoral ballad, no great success when it was first played in public, but which events had made something else of altogether. The older men in the audience recognized it first, started singing on the third note, and caught up with the melody by the fourth bar. By that time, the younger men had begun to join in:

> O, I wish I was in the land of cotton;
> Old times there are not forgotten.
> Look away . . .

As the second chorus started, the instruments got louder, the tempo increased, and the deep purple velvet curtain glided silently upward, revealing at last the Confederate Stars and Bars, twelve feet by eight, strung by its corners from rigging suspended from the flies far above the stage. The flag was made of paper-thin silk that rippled in the air currents stirred by clapping hands. The applause rose volcanically, pulling the men in the audience to their feet and tearing cheers from two hundred pairs of lungs; for the theater was crowded now, without a vacant seat in sight. I felt my own heart lifting, and I'd fought the bloody rag for four years, burying close friends slain in its shadow.

That's how it's done. They snare you with bands and bright colors, and six months later you're sleeping with lice in a muddy hole, half-starved and scared half out of your mind.

The spell broke when a shrill cry rose above the cheering, high and thin and breaking at its peak, like a bullwhacker's whip. It froze my spine. I hadn't heard an authentic rebel yell since Petersburg, where Beauregard's men hung their naked backsides over the top of the redoubt and dared us to storm it. A wild boar shrieks like that when it knows it's beaten but won't die without taking some of the hounds along for company. I'd hoped I'd never hear it again. It was an even worse omen than the seagull roosting on Nan Feeny's roof.

I leaned out to see who was responsible for it, but I had to hold back to avoid being spotted, so I couldn't pick him out. The yell took me too far into the past to have belonged to someone who hadn't seared his lungs with cannon smoke, or slipped in blood and spilled entrails, fighting bayonet to bayonet with his enemy's sweat stinging his eyes. There was a real live big cat down there among the tin tigers. I had that feeling, like a falling sensation in a nightmare, that we would meet. Like attracts like.

When they finished playing, the musicians rose. Hands were still pounding, and I thought they'd take a bow, or follow up with "I'm a Good Old Rebel"; but they merely picked up their chairs and carried them and their instruments offstage. I credited them for maintaining perspective. A monkey with a tambourine would have gotten an ovation playing "Dixie" for that crowd.

The stage was empty for a minute, perhaps longer; long enough anyway for the spectators to reseat themselves, begin to fidget, and crack a nervous cough or two. Just about the time they would have started murmuring, a lone figure emerged from the wings, walked to the center, limping a little despite the aid of a stick, and turned to face the seats, holding the stick across his thighs like an officer's riding crop.

Polite applause started, then died. The audience seemed eager to clear space for the man's first words.

Daniel Webster Wheelock had traded his fire captain's uniform for the butternut tunic and military-striped trousers of a Confederate general. Knee-high riding boots engineered to draw attention from his club foot glistened like black satin and the tiny star on either side of his collar clasp winked golden in the footlights. Modestly, he'd chosen a simple uniform design and had resisted promoting himself higher than brigadier. Even in warrior dress he was a politician to the core.

Another minute crawled past on its belly. Wheelock's head turned slowly, as if to study each face in the orchestra. I withdrew deeper into the shadows, but he never raised his eyes toward the boxes. His head stopped turning.

"Bull Run," he said.

Applause, nearly as loud as for the opening of "Dixie."

"Wilson's Creek."

A louder burst still, accompanied by a shrill whistle.

"Ball's Bluff!"

With the name of each Confederate victory, Wheelock's voice rose, and with it the volume of approval from the audience. Cedar Mountain, less well-known, drew an uneven response, strongest from among those old enough to have read about it in the newspapers, been told about it by veterans, and in one case at least, experienced it at firsthand; that rebel howl managed to raise the hairs on my neck once again. Fredericksburg met unanimous appreciation, as did Chancellorsville and Cold Harbor, the last unequivocal success for the Old Dominion; Wheelock's listeners rose as one, feet thundering on the floorboards, shaking Barbary's oldest continuing house of pleasure to its foundation. A number of hats flew ceilingward and drifted back down. I hadn't seen so many gray kepis in one place since Lee's lost legions lined up to stack their long guns and swear an oath to the Union.

On "Cold Harbor," Wheelock had raised his stick above his head, striking a pose similar to Custer's with his saber in a thousand lithographs, framed and hung behind the bars of saloons from Concord to Cripple Creek. His face was flushed, his gray eyes glittered. If I weren't sure he prepared himself for these things in cold blood and absolute sobriety, I'd have thought he'd helped himself to a pull from the bottle that had begun to make the rounds of the men sitting in the first two rows. Who needs whiskey when you can draw fire from the blood of a couple of hundred fellow fanatics?

When the swell subsided and everyone was back in his seat,

Captain Dan lowered his stick to its former position. Now he spoke low, allowing the melodeon's acoustics to carry his words to the back.

"I have never owned a slave," he said. "I daresay none of these presents have. Some of us are too young ever to have seen a Negro in chains. Fort Sumter was not fired upon in order to secure the fetters of a misguided past, but to ensure States' Rights, that the fates of our farms and shops and hearths would not drift before the capricious current of Washington politics." (Applause.) "The two hundred fifty thousand who died in the field at Gettysburg, Chickamauga, and the Shenandoah Valley, among so many others, who succumbed to infection and fever in hospital tents at Mechanicsville and Pea Richmond, among so many others, did not give their lives to keep men in shackles, but to free them from tyranny." (Applause and shouting.) "For nearly twenty years, we have eaten the lies of our conquerors in place of bread, drunk the vinegar of their insults in place of water, and for this bitter sustenance we have been expected to pull our forelocks and give thanks. The time has come for us to rise from our knees and smite them to theirs; if not in ranks, as at Bull Run and Fredericksburg, then one by one, all across North America."

Once again the house was on its feet. The great flag rippled fiercely as in a storm. I wondered if the Ancient could withstand the foot-stamping; all it had had to face before was fire and vigilantes.

During this reception, Wheelock half turned and raised his stick, signaling toward the wings. The man who came out wearing the uniform of a sergeant and carrying a battered gray campaign hat looked familiar. He'd handed the hat to the alderman and struck a modest pose beside him, hands folded behind his back in parade rest, before I recognized Tom Tulip, the Hoodlum Beecher and I had robbed in order to arrange an audience with Captain Dan. I hoped he'd be given a chance to speak. I'd have paid admission to hear his cockney gibberish coming from a man fitted out as a volunteer with the 17th Mississippi.

I was even more curious about that hat. The brim was tattered, the crown stained through with grease or old sweat, the band was missing. It looked as if it had seen more combat than all the spectators combined. It was a long way from delicate, and carrying it upside down with the crown cupped in two hands as if it were some fragile vessel filled with rubies and sapphires, seemed unnecessary. Wheelock handled it the same way, clamping his stick under one arm so he could engage both hands and waiting for the noise to die down.

When it did and all were sitting, he continued in the same low tones as before. "I purchased this hat at no small expense from a dealer in curiosities in Richmond, Virginia, who had acquired it from a veteran who needed the money to support his family. The veteran picked it up from the ground where it had fallen when General James Elwell Brown Stuart was struck down at Yellow Tavern. This is Jeb Stuart's hat."

Awed silence greeted this intelligence, broken momentarily by a hushed murmur. Owen Goodhue might have gotten the same reaction from his congregation by displaying a splinter from the True Cross. Finally, applause crackled gently, so as not to disturb the spirit of the head that had worn the hat.

"I will ask Sergeant Tulip to place General Stuart's hat in the hands of the first gentleman to my right seated in the front row. Without looking inside, that gentleman will remove one of the coins I have placed in the crown and pass the hat to the gentleman to *his* right, who will do the same. The hat will continue to pass among you until it is empty. It will then be returned to Sergeant Tulip. I ask that you do not look at the coin you have drawn, nor show it to anyone else, until I instruct you to do so. Although I state this as a request, you will consider it an order from your commanding officer. Sergeant Tulip?"

Tulip accepted the hat from Wheelock and carried it into the wings. A moment later, he reappeared in the far left aisle and held out the hat, which was taken reverently by the man seated nearest him, who reached inside without lowering his head, rummaged about, and withdrew his closed fist. During the ten minutes it took for the hat to make the rounds, Wheelock entertained his listeners with an account of Jeb Stuart's activities during the war that stirred even me, ending with the general's own delirious refighting of all his old battles during his last moments and his one-sided conversation with his eldest daughter, who had died at the very moment he was deploying his troops on the Rappahannock.

"I offer this epitaph, spoken from the heart by General Lee upon learning of his old friend's death," the alderman concluded: " 'I can scarcely think of him without weeping.' "

Someone in the audience sobbed for the fate of a man who had died when he himself was too young to lift a rifle. Wheelock was a first-rate political hack, there was no doubt about that. He could wring tears from a doorknob.

When Tulip had finished his errand and returned the hat to its owner, Wheelock dismissed him to the wings. Wheelock cradled the hat in one arm, gripping his stick in his other hand, and called for more light. The gas globes in the corners must have been fed from a central pipe; they glowed more brightly, illuminating the orchestra as if the sun had rolled out from behind a cloud.

"Please oblige me by holding aloft the coins you selected so that I may see them."

Clothing rustled. The light found dull silver in most of the upraised hands; the hat had contained forty or fifty cartwheel dollars. However, even at that distance I could pick out the gold double eagles glittering among them. I counted eight.

30

"Will the gentlemen who drew the gold pieces join me?"

Some toes were stepped on and a couple of forage caps dislodged from a couple of heads, but the eight men found their way to the aisles and proceeded up the stairs that led to the wings and onto the stage. Most of them appeared to be in their twenties, self-conscious in their uniforms. One was nearly my age, wearing a corduroy coat rubbed shiny at the elbows over civilian trousers reinforced with leather and custom-made boots, the last worth more than everything else he had on put together. His sandy hair spilled to his collar and he wore a Custer moustache that concealed his mouth and most of his chin. There was something about his pigeon-toed walk, his backward-leaning posture, that suggested a lifetime in the saddle, and not necessarily with a lasso in his hand pursuing stray calves. I knew a guerrilla when I saw one; and I knew without having to think hard on the subject that here was the source of that bone-chilling rebel yell.

Wheelock made a show of examining each coin, as if looking for signs of counterfeiting, then returned it to its owner, leaning forward as he did so to whisper something. Some of the faces paled. In these cases, he stared at them until they nodded, then turned to the next man. When he was finished, he raised his voice to address the audience. The men with the double eagles stood strung out on either side of him like an unrehearsed chorus. A number of them were still shaken.

"I will not announce the names of the loyal members of the Sons of the Confederacy who stand before you," Wheelock said. "This is a precaution, and I trust an unnecessary one, as you have all sworn an oath of secrecy concerning what takes place beneath this roof, as well as to come to the assistance of a brother of the order under any and all circumstances. I remind those of you who know their names of the penalty of violating that pledge. We are at war, gentlemen. Make no mistake on that point."

A murmur thrummed through the orchestra. He raised his stick and it trailed off into silence.

"As each of these soldiers presented himself, I spoke a name in his ear. I did not speak the same name twice, and all will be known to the membership presently. Each man has committed the information to memory.

"At this time I ask Sergeant Tulip to return to the stage."

The Hoodlum came out from the wings with a hesitating step. He looked puzzled. This wasn't in the programme.

Skin prickled on my back. I wasn't sure why. My hand closed around the grip of the Deane-Adams in its holster. I hadn't willed it to.

Wheelock placed a hand on Tom Tulip's shoulder. "Sergeant, this meeting is about to adjourn. I ask you to lead the membership in singing 'The Bonnie Blue Flag.'"

Tulip appeared relieved and nervous at the same time. He probably hadn't sung in public since the last time he'd been drunk in a saloon, and from his unease it was clear he was as sober as a parson. However, he stepped forward, removed his cap, held it over his left breast, and raised his voice in an uncertain tenor:

> We are a band of brothers, and native to the soil,
> Fighting for the property we gained by honest toil;
> And when our rights was threatened, the cry rose near
>   and far,
> 'urrah for the Bonnie Blue Flag that bears a single star!

When the song began, a few voices joined in from the audience, but the spirit didn't spread, and by the end of the second line Tulip was singing alone. He noticed it; his voice broke on "threatened." But he continued in a wavering tone. The first "hurrah" came out as a sob. He knew what was coming before I did.

> 'urrah! 'urrah! For Southern Rights, 'urrah!
> 'urrah—

The long-haired guerrilla stepped up behind him, hauled a Navy Colt from beneath his belt, and shot him through the head.

Tom Tulip's chin snapped down as if he were taking a bow, then jerked back up. He sank to his knees and fell on his face. The powder-flare had set his hair on fire, but it smoldered out quickly. Almost immediately the entire theater stank of sulfur and scorched hair and flesh.

The echo of the report rang through dead silence. Most of the faces onstage were pale now to the point of translucence. One of the younger men turned and vomited. A new stench joined the others.

The Deane-Adams was in my hand. I took a step back into the shadows of the box and drew a bead on Wheelock's chest. Then on the guerrilla's. I couldn't decide where to begin.

Wheelock was speaking again. I held off.

"Shed no tears for Sergeant Tulip. He was an opportunist, who joined the Sons merely to curry my favor and advance his own larcenous interests. However, that is not why he died.

"War is not won on the field of battle alone. The tragedy of Appomattox Courthouse taught us that, if it taught us nothing else. Diplomacy is a weapon as powerful as steel and shot. The Confederacy failed the first time because it had no allies in this hemisphere.

"This morning, I met with Owen Goodhue. You cannot fail to have heard the name. He has posted his vigilante manifesto throughout San Francisco, along with a list of the names of those whom he believes must die if the city is to live. To carry out this sentence of death, he was prepared to put the entire Barbary Coast to the torch, and to slay as many as attempt to stand between him and the condemned. Tom Tulip's name was near the top of that list."

I lowered the revolver. This was one political speech I wanted to hear to the end.

"The Reverend Goodhue has agreed to call off his crusade if the Sons of the Confederacy will carry out the sentence he has imposed. With Barbary at peace, we will be able to wage our war against the Union without interference from the vigilantes."

He passed his stick along the line of men standing beside him. All were rapt, except the guerrilla. He was busy replacing the charge he'd fired from the Navy.

"Each of these men has drawn a gold coin issued by the United States Mint here in San Francisco," Wheelock said. "It is symbolic of the enemy we have sworn to oppose, as well as the individual he has by his acceptance of the token agreed to destroy by his own hand. The names are as follows:

" 'Little Dick' Dugan, murderer;

"Tom Tulip, procurer;

"Ole Anderson, shylock;

" 'Hugger-Mugger' Charlie, counterfeiter;

"Fat John, Chinaman;

"Axel Hodge, procurer;

"Nan Feeny, harlot.

"One of these has fallen. The others must die by sunset tomorrow.

"You will, of course, have noted that there are seven names on this list, and that eight gold coins were drawn. I have added one more; a redundancy, I must confess, because his death was ordained two months ago, but he has thus far eluded his fate. He is in Barbary at present. His name is Page Murdock. He is a deputy United States marshal, and he is a dangerous man. The soldier who slays him will rise far in the ranks."

More murmurs. Under other circumstances I'd have felt the compliment.

"General, sir, I volunteer for that there duty."

The guerrilla had a Missouri accent, no surprise. He had Centralia and Lone Jack written all over his lean sunburned face.

"That won't be necessary, Lieutenant. You've discharged your responsibility. Your brothers have not yet tasted blood."

"I'll do it for one of them plug dollars. It wasn't Lieutenant when I rid with Arch Clements. I finished out a captain. I won't hide from my name, neither. It's Frank Hennessey, and I cracked a cap on my first bluebelly before most of these here children was borned."

"Your former rank is irrelevant. The order stands."

The way Hennessey rolled his pistol before he put it away spoke pages about what he thought of Wheelock's order.

That made up my mind. I took aim on Hennessey's broad chest.

A hand closed around the revolver. I nearly tripped the trigger from shock.

Beecher's voice was harsh in my ear. "We'll be up to our chins in baby rebels."

"Did you see it?" I said.

"I seen it. I heard what came after, too. Now ain't the time. Let me work around to the other side. After you take your shot I'll pin 'em down while you hit the stairs."

"What about you?"

"I started out a brakeman. I've clumb up and down freight cars and hot boilers going seventy. I reckon I can find my way down a building standing still."

"Where's Nero?"

"He's out like the cat. I give him another tap just to make sure. Count to thirty."

"Twenty's all you get," I said. "My aim's better when I'm mad. And I don't intend to stop with that shaggy bushwhacker."

"I never thought you would." He slipped out of the box.

31

While counting to twenty, I set up my shooting stand.

I tugged the Peacemaker I'd taken away from Nero out from under my belt, where the curved walnut grip had been digging a hole in the small of my back, inspected the chambers, and laid it on the polished mahogany of the box's railing. That made it handy in the unlikely event I managed to empty the five-shot before someone in the theater located the source of the reports and returned fire. I didn't expect to leave that box alive.

Shooting men isn't like shooting birds. With birds, you start with the one farthest away and work your way to the nearest, that being the sure target. With men, you pick out the most dangerous first, because you might not get another chance. Standing partially behind one of the side curtains, I lined up the Deane-Adams' sights on the third button of Frank Hennessey's shirt, drew back the hammer on the count of nineteen, and squeezed the trigger.

I didn't wait to see if I'd hit him. Trusting to the self-cocker, I swung the muzzle toward Wheelock and fired again. For a ward-heeler, he had fast reflexes; at the sound of the first shot, he'd flung away his stick and hurled himself toward the floor of the stage, and I couldn't tell if he was nicked or if the slug had missed him and gone through the Stars and Bars behind him. It seemed to me the flag snapped as if struck by a gust, but that could have been the wind of the bodies scrambling for cover.

Three shots barked on the other side of the auditorium. I ducked, but none of them came close to my box, and when I heard the wham of a shotgun blast I knew it was Beecher, giving me cover with his Le Mat from a box opposite. I saw the smoke there and knew it was time to leave.

I didn't. I had to know if I'd hit Hennessey.

The stage was a hive, Confederate Sons colliding with one another trying to get to the wings, slipping on blood, which may have been Tom Tulip's. They were bailing out of the seats as well, trampling their fellows and making a mess of their pledge to come to the aid of brothers in need. For Beecher, it was like shooting fish in a bucket.

I searched the stage—and drew a sleeve across my eyes to clear them of smoke. I thought I'd seen Tom Tulip rise from the floor. He was still there afterward, in a cautious crouch. I couldn't fathom that. A head shot at close range leaves no room for uncertainty. Then I saw him sliding backward on his heels, spotted a corduroy sleeve across his chest under his rag-doll arms, and I knew it was Hennessey using Tulip's corpse for cover as he tried for a vantage point. At that instant, smoke puffed over Tulip's right shoulder and a fistful of splinters jumped up from the railing a foot to my right. The guerrilla had spotted me.

I sank down on one knee, steadied my arm in a downward slant across the railing, and fired at Tulip's throat. It offered the least amount of resistance to a bullet intended to pierce his body and hit what was behind it. The Confederate flag jerked. I was hitting high and to the right. I'd messed up the sights when I struck Nero's skull with the barrel instead of the butt. I made the mental adjustment and tried again. Just as I fired, one of the Sons who had drawn a double eagle crossed in front of Hennessey. The Son threw up his hands, ran out from under his body, and fell on his back. I caught a flash of corduroy slipping around the edge of the flag and punched a hole through one of the stars.

Wheelock had spotted me, too. He was standing again, near the front of the stage, shouting something and pointing his stick toward my box. This time I overcompensated, shot low, and shattered a footlight. Fire licked out and found something it liked; a decorative curtain tied back to frame the stage caught. Flames raced up it, across the tassels hanging down in a straight line across the top of the stage, and lapped at the gilded wood of the proscenium. The alderman put the stick to its intended use and hobbled offstage on the double. I tried for him a third time. The hammer snapped on an empty cartridge.

A bullet pierced the side curtain just above my hat and slammed into the plaster near the door of the box. Hennessey, firing from cover, or someone else who had seen Wheelock pointing, had joined the fight. It was time to make my exit.

I leathered the five-shot, scooped up Nero's Peacemaker,

tore open the door, and threw myself across the carpeted passage, flattening my back against the wall on the other side and looking both ways with the Colt raised. I was alone. I ran for the stairs.

Two men in gray were coming up from the ground floor. The one in front had a pistol in his hand. A slug from Nero's .44 struck him like a fist and he fell backward, taking his partner with him. I clattered down, leapt across the tangle they made on the floor at the foot of the stairs, snapped a shot into a crowd of Sons barreling my way toward the exit, and ran out through the foyer. It was filling with smoke. Somewhere on the edge of hearing, a fire bell clanged; that would be Captain Dan's own company, on its way to prevent Barbary from burning down yet again.

"Here's where I make good on that Yankee gold."

That harsh Missouri twang cut through the smoke like water gushing from a hose. The guerrilla's rangy figure stood across the open door to the street with feet spread and his Navy Colt thrust out at shoulder height, the muzzle six feet from my face.

I jerked the Peacemaker's trigger. Both shots roared simultaneously, and I knew we were both dead.

Then the doorway was clear. Frank Hennessey lay on his face on the floor of the Bella Union with a dark stain spreading like crow's wings between his shoulderblades.

Beecher stood on the boardwalk, smoke uncoiling from the Le Mat's top barrel. His left arm hung limp and covered with blood.

"First white man I ever shot," he said. "They'd lynch me for it in Louisiana."

Then he collapsed.

• • •

I knelt over him, found a weak pulse in his neck. The volunteers vaulting down from the firewagon, shining in their oilskin capes and leather helmets, were too busy uncoiling hose and hoisting their axes to help. I shouted to them that there was a man bound and unconscious in one of the boxes upstairs.

"Who the hell done that?" one of them asked. But he was in too much of a hurry to wait for the answer.

Beecher was still conscious. He said he'd shattered his arm when he lost his grip while climbing down the outside of the building and fell ten feet. A shard of polished bone gleamed white where it stuck out of the skin above his elbow. "I think the building hit a downgrade." He grinned weakly.

"Save it for a pretty nurse." I tied my neckerchief around his upper arm and used the barrel of the Colt to twist it tight.

"That ain't proper. Shove over. I seen it done."

Something hard bumped my shoulder. It was an iron ball attached to a chain. Axel Hodge bent over Beecher, undid the tourniquet one-handed, tied a different kind of knot—it looked nautical—and twisted the barrel until the bleeding slowed. Flames were shooting through the Ancient's roof, flickering off his bowler and bearded face.

I said, "He needs a doctor."

"They're all drunks and hoppies hereabouts. He needs the Chinaman."

"What Chinaman?"

"Fat John, who the hell else? Who you think saved me own arm?"

•   •   •

It was my first time in the room behind F'an Chu'an's tearoom in the White Peacock. It contained a cot where I assumed the tong leader slept, some good lamps with glass shades that shed clean light from oil not obtainable from the local pushcart peddlers, a Persian rug ancient by standards unknown in California, and polished teakwood shelves lined with bottles and jars labeled in Chinese characters. It smelled like an apothecary shop. Shau Wing and Shau Chan, the knickknack cousins, helped us lay Beecher on the cot and fetched items from the shelves. F'an Chu'an snapped orders at them in Chinese. He cut off Beecher's sleeve with steel scissors, removed shreds of cloth from the wound with forceps, and poured chloroform into a clean handkerchief, which he spread over his patient's face. When Beecher was breathing evenly, he removed the handkerchief, opened a morocco-leather case, and spread it open on his workbench, revealing a glittering collection of saws, scalpels, and bone chisels. I was feeling faint already, from the fumes and exhaustion, and as the Shaus stepped forward to hold Beecher down by his shoulders in case he woke up in the middle of the operation, I removed myself to the tearoom. That was when I realized Axel Hodge had left. I would not see him again for a very long time.

At the end of an hour, the leader of the Suey Sing Tong joined me. He had removed his apron and put on his green robe. His face was drawn. He was too tired to reach up and pinch his lip when he spoke, and I had to ask him to repeat himself in order to understand what he was telling me. He'd had to remove the arm. Beecher was sleeping, but he'd lost a lot of blood and his recovery was in the hands of the gods. I offered to pay him, as his earlier debt had been discharged. He declined, explaining that there were others to whom he was still obliged. That meant nothing, but then I might not have heard him right. That cleft lip was one more barrier between us.

The night was overcast, but Barbary's jagged edges stood out starkly against the glow of the Bella Union in flames. Fire bells clanged, residents in varying stages of undress bustled about hauling baskets and wheelbarrows piled with clocks, clothing, and other personal possessions, in case the flames spread to their homes the way they had so many times before. I was too tired to care if the place burned down around me. I wobbled back to the Slop Chest and threw myself into my berth. I didn't bother to take off even my boots, but I'd reloaded the Deane-Adams and I lay with it on my chest and my hand on top of it, ready for any of Wheelock's Hoodlums and Confeder- ates who came looking for me. I'd left Nero's Peacemaker in Chinatown.

I awoke well after sunup and went into the saloon without stopping to change clothes or splash water on my face. I was anxious to learn if Beecher had survived the night, but I needed a drink more than news.

The room was deserted except for Pinholster, who was busy playing a game of two-handed Patience against himself. He appeared to be winning. I plunked myself down across from him.

"You look as if you just crawled out from under a charred beam." He laid a six of hearts on a seven of clubs.

"I did. Where is everyone?"

"Billy's helping put out the fire. I'll wager you were unaware he's a volunteer with Wheelock's brigade. The town is filled with such ironies. I haven't seen Hodge since yesterday."

"I saw him last night. Any news about Wheelock?"

"He seems to have vanished. It's unlike him not to make a show of himself on these occasions, directing the pumping crews and working the winch; man of the people, so long as he doesn't expose himself to actual danger. Unlike him, I say, but not surprising. One hears rumors."

That was an opening, and a pretty obvious one for as good a gambler as he was, but I didn't walk through it. "Fire under control?"

"They contained it to the Ancient. I understand it's a dead loss. They'll rebuild it, of course. I heard they pulled a body out."

"Wheelock's bodyguard?"

"No, a stranger. They say he was shot. Another local mystery, like Sid the Spunk's disappearance." He looked up from the card he'd just laid down.

"You forgot that one's solved. So the number of mysteries stays the same."

"I think there are some more. However, it's not up to me to investigate any of them. I'm to Chicago on the noon train. They can spread my ashes on Lake Michigan."

"I thought you intended to stay through tonight."

"There is no tonight. Tonight is canceled. You didn't hear?"

I was tired of hearing him ask questions he knew the answers to. I was just plain tired, but this morning I was more tired of Pinholster than anyone, even Daniel Webster Wheelock. He was too quit of life to make good company.

He went through his deck, looking for the black deuce he needed to win the game. "This morning's edition of the *Call* will be late, I'm afraid. They had to remake the front page twice: first to report the fire, then to carry the tragic news of Owen Goodhue's death."

I felt the same prickling I'd felt when Tom Tulip stepped forward to sing his own dirge.

"Nan Feeny went out first thing this morning," Pinholster said. "One more in a string of broken precedents. It was too early for the cable car, so she must have walked all the way to Mission Street. Mrs. Goodhue, who didn't know her, but who was accustomed to women of her type coming to the reverend gentleman for absolution, let her in.

"There are several versions of what happened next. The least dramatic, and therefore the most believable, is Nan emptied that pepperbox of hers into Goodhue's back while he was kneeling in his cabinet, praying for his crusade's success. She was still there when the widow showed in the police. They have her up at the jail. Ah! There it is."

He turned up the deuce of spades and played it. "Not the ace, but life isn't poetry."

32

The Barbary Coast is no more. The 1906 earthquake managed to do what a half-century of good intentions and sporadic fires could not. A determined rebuilding campaign, followed by journalistic pressure of the Fremont Older type, repressive ordinances, and a beefed-up police presence erected a new city directly on top of the old; one in which there was no place for opium dens, bordellos, and gambling hells in number. It took an act of God to turn the serpents out of Eden once and for all.

I wasn't there to see it. When Edward Anderson Beecher was well enough to travel, I shook his remaining hand at the San Francisco depot, slipped an envelope into his coat pocket containing the money Judge Blackthorne had wired to cover his wages, mileage, and a bonus in partial compensation for the loss of his arm in the service of the United States, and handed him his ticket to Spokane. I was taking a different train to Helena, scheduled to pull out fifteen minutes behind his.

"I reckon I'll have to stay put now," he said. "Can't lug around no steamer trunks with one wing."

"Ask a blacksmith if he can fit you with a ball and chain."

He understood this for the apology it was. "I slipped, boss. You didn't push me."

"It didn't stop you from saving my skin for the second time."

He smiled that thin lost smile. What it lacked in candle-power compared to his full grin, it made up for in sincerity.

"Well, it's pale, but it seemed worth saving both times."

I never heard from him after that. Neither of us had promised to write. We'd been through too much to lie at the end. I like to think that he found his wife and that they took up where they left off; but I'm a sentimental old man who always wants what's best for his friends, having outlived most of them and not having had too many to begin with.

Judge Blackthorne wasn't sentimental. He'd read the report I'd sent, and had only one question for me when I delivered the rest in Helena:

"Are you satisfied with your performance in this affair?"

"I performed it."

He didn't remind me that my orders were to widen the rift between the violent and nonviolent wings of the Sons of the Confederacy so that U.S. authorities could nullify their power in criminal and civil court, and that I'd disobeyed them by taking on Wheelock's killers directly. To do so would have been an embarrassment, because when deputy federal marshals boarded

Captain Dan's train just below the Canadian border and placed him under arrest on more than thirty counts of conspiracy, the entire organization fell apart; Sons from all over the Western states and territories came forward to turn United States' evidence against the killers and those who had directed them. I don't flatter myself that in forcing Wheelock to abandon the security of his position in San Francisco I averted a second Civil War. I just prevented a few more murders and put a dangerous lunatic behind bars.

Not actual bars. Wheelock had still drawn enough water with his former associates to raise ten percent of his million-dollar bail and shot himself in his hotel room in Sacramento the day after he was arraigned. He left a note saying he'd planned to elect himself president in 1884 with the Southern vote. Eight senators and fifteen congressmen from the states that had formerly belonged to the Confederacy issued statements to the press that day, insisting that they'd sooner have backed a Republican.

Nan Feeny stood trial for the murder of Owen Goodhue, was found guilty, and sentenced to hang. Throughout the appeals process and several stays, I pictured her pacing her cell, touching often the ribbon she wore at her throat to remind her how close she'd come to hanging the last time she'd shot and killed a square citizen. (Perhaps not; I picture her as easily untying and discarding it during the long walk from the Slop Chest to Mission Street with the pepperbox pistol growing heavy in her reticule.) Judge Blackthorne wrote a letter to Sacramento at my urging, asking for a commutation to life. Whether it was because of this, or in response to a march on the state capitol building by a ragged band of peg-legged harlots, three-fingered pickpockets, and sundry other shades from Barbary—broken up by some head-smashing on the part of city police, reported in the local papers and carried by wire across the continent—the governor of California granted the request. Nan served ten years in a women's workhouse, then after her release for model behavior opened a restaurant in San Francisco, representing investors who knew how to profit by her notoriety, if not the quality of the bill of fare. The restaurant was the only building on its block not demolished by the big shake; she converted it into a hospital and nursed dozens of the maimed and homeless. When she died in 1916, the supervisors of San Francisco County voted to place a plaque in her honor on the wall of the bank that was built on the site of the restaurant after it was torn down. I'm told it's still there, but I haven't been back to see it.

After San Francisco, I asked Judge Blackthorne for a month's holiday. He let me have three days, at the end of which I was expected to board a train for Oregon; but that's a story for another volume of these memoirs I won't live to finish.

I don't get out much these days. Gout, ancient injuries, and the effects of an intemperate life have banded together to keep me in this furnished bungalow in a dust trap called Culver City, where Famous Players-Lasky pays my rent. In return, I'm supposed to provide expert advice on scenarios for photoplays intended to dramatize life on the old frontier. The producers hardly ever send me anything, however, and I suspect they're trading charity for the privilege of drawing on whatever faded luster my name retains by including it on the title cards. They're fools for their own advertising and think just having it there makes the stories authentic. They're not, the ones I've seen, anyway; not by a rifle shot, but the truth won't play and I'm an old hypocrite, correcting dates and place names and telling myself I'm earning my billet.

A few months ago, someone knocked on my door. I was expecting a courier with a new scenario and stayed put in my chair, calling out that the door was unlocked.

"An old U.S. cove like yourself ought to know better than that," said my visitor. "There's jigger-dubbers all about this padding ken."

The sun was behind him. I couldn't see his face, but he had on a long coat like you seldom see in Southern California, with one sleeve hanging empty. It happened I'd been thinking about Barbary just that morning, and I thought at first it was Beecher, come at last to pay a call on an old comrade. Then I saw the stunted legs sticking out the bottom of the coat and knew him for an old enemy.

"You'd think after forty years you'd learned English," I said.

Axel Hodge wobbled in and closed the door behind him. He was hatless and bald, and his beard had turned white as ash, but his grin hadn't changed. He'd be on his third or fourth set of porcelains by now.

"I was just tipping you the office," he said. "I ain't spoke but a piece of the lingo for years. It never did signify outside Frisco, and now not even there. I meant what I said about locking that door. This town's boiling with border trash."

I slid the Deane-Adams out from under the copy of the *Los Angeles Times* I had spread open on my lap and laid it on the lamp table.

He grunted. "That old barker still bite?"

"Only people get old. What happened to the ball and chain?"

"It got too heavy to pack around. I don't miss it. I was running out of things to bash. Old Nan sure served me hell every time I smacked that bar of hers." He stopped grinning. "You heard she died."

"Years ago. News travels a lot faster now."

"I know. Prohibition agents got radio-telephones." He drew a tall bottle out of his coat pocket and set it on the floor. "A little present from Glasgow, by way of Tijuana. I own the distributorship from here to San Diego."

I said, "I thought you'd be living off your inheritance."

He spread his coattails, tugged at the knees of his trousers, and sat on the foot of my unmade bed. His ankles were no bigger around than striplings. He'd been stumping about on those shriveled sticks for close to sixty years.

"The Hodges never did have two coppers to rub together. I told you my granddad was a convict."

"Your granddad was the father of a soap manufacturer, who named you in his will. You don't have to lie to me, Seymour. Sid the Stump isn't wanted anywhere now."

He showed his teeth. "Too bad it weren't that way when I could collect. Seymour couldn't put in a claim without digging up Sid, and Sid couldn't be dug up without stagging the tappers. When'd you smoke me out?"

"That last night, when you helped me with Beecher. You said Fat John saved your arm. You forgot you'd told me you lost your hand aboard a ship from Australia. I had my suspicions before that; you talked too much about Brisbane. It was as if you were trying to convince yourself you weren't Seymour Cruddup from Exeter. You're the one who overheard Pinholster asking me about Sid and told F'an Chu'an. And you knew that last night you'd made a slip. That's why you left town."

"I felt bad about that. I never told Nan good-bye."

The conversation threatened to become maudlin. I asked him if he knew who killed the old forty-niner in the White Peacock.

"Flinders? I always thought he was Wheelock's."

"Captain Dan wouldn't be caught dead in an opium den, or doing his own killing. I figure it was Tom Tulip. He did it on his own, to please Wheelock. He wasn't pleased. It brought in Goodhue, and in order to hold him off, the Sons of the Confederacy had to alter their plans to include Goodhue's list of scapegoats. That's why Tulip was the first to go."

"Poor ponce."

"Why'd you do it?" I asked.

He wrinkled his bald head. "You just said it was Tom."

"I don't mean that. Why'd you help Beecher? Before that you tried to talk Nan into letting you kill us both."

He nodded.

"I thought about that. Still do, time to time. I figure I owed God an arm."

"What's that mean?"

"There was a fire, and a man with his arm gone and him set to follow. Fat John didn't have to help me in that same spot. I didn't have to help the colored bloke. But he done, and I done. Fat John'd find a better way to say it, wherever he wound up. Under

six tons of Chink's Alley would be my guess." He scratched his
stump. "You ever hear from him?"

"F'an Chu'an?"

"Beecher."

"Not a word."

"Maybe he struck it rich up North and won't truck with our
like."

"You're a sentimental old man."

"Well, stow that under your shaper. I got to keep up me own
south of the border."

We talked a bit more about Barbary and then he left. We
didn't have anything in common beyond that. He didn't ask
why I hadn't told Pinholster that Sid the Spunk was alive; I
wouldn't have had an answer that would satisfy him any
more than his had satisfied me. It might have been enough
for Sid, who had offered his arson skills to F'an Chu'an free
of charge for the memory of a mother forced into the streets
of Brooklyn. I wasn't sure it would be enough for Axel Hodge
the bootlegger.

A week or two later I read a small piece in the *Times* about a
rumrunner named Hodge, slain by U.S. Prohibition agents during a gun battle on the Mexican border. The agents said they'd
returned fire when Hodge opened up on them with a submachine gun. Submachine guns require two hands to operate.
Some things about crime and politics don't change, earthquake
or no.

I took a drink of his *postizo* Scotch to his memory. For all I
knew, we were the last two people on earth who'd remembered

the Slop Chest, the White Peacock, the Bella Union, and all those who passed through their doors. The rest are as dead as Pinholster, whose lesion must have done for him long ago.

There was no follow-up to the story, and the entire account took up just two inches on an inside page near what we used to call the telegraph column, with its news of Washington, miners' strikes, and beer-hall revolutions in Munich. Another column on the same page announced the monthly meetings of the local chapters of the various fraternal orders. It listed the Sons of the Confederacy along with the Elks, the Freemasons, the Rotary Club, and the Knights of Columbus. The current members are doddering veterans and younger men who wish they'd been born early enough to fight for States' Rights. They've never heard of Daniel Webster Wheelock, and I'm not about to educate them. His bones and Barbary's can rot together.

A GUTTERSNIPE GLOSSARY

During the nineteenth century, the English language developed more rapidly than during the thousand years that preceded it; and most of that development took place in the gutters of London, New York City, Sydney, Australia, and San Francisco's Barbary Coast. The special vocabulary of the career criminal had its origins in the cockney rhyming slang of the East End ("twist and twirl"=girl; "whistle and flute"= suit) and spread throughout the Western Hemisphere when the police cracked down and those who spoke it fled by sail and steam to safer venues, bringing with them the tools of their unlawful trade.

While most dialects evolve by accident, the terms and phrases that baffled Page Murdock and Edward Anderson Beecher upon their arrival in San Francisco were coined deliberately, in order to avoid arrest. Employing this code, a pair of "tobbies" (street toughs) could plan to "stifle a stagger" (murder an informer) within a police officer's hearing without alerting that authority to the fact that a homicide was being discussed; assuming, that is, that the policeman was not a "fly cop" (an officer who knows the score). This subterfuge would be borrowed by killers for hire during our own gangster era, when U.S. racket busters scratched their heads over conversations on wiretap recordings about "putting out a contract for a hit."

Thieves' cant has changed. Much of the terminology common to Spitalfields, Hell's Kitchen, Murder Point, and Sydney Harbor is as incomprehensible to us today as it was intended to be to the swells and squares outside Barbary. But much of it remains, sprinkling spice on the American vernacular, crossing all class barriers, and piercing even the walls of the White House. If the reader has doubts, perhaps he'll reconsider the next time he "fobs off a shady deal on some oaf." It's also more than likely that just moments ago he replied to a question in the affirmative, using the once-trendily misspelled phrase "oll kerrect"; although he probably referred to it by its initials.

For details about the fascinating hell that was shanty San Francisco, as well as his introduction to the idiom, this writer is indebted to Herbert Asbury's *The Barbary Coast* (New York, Alfred A. Knopf, 1933), still the standard work on its subject after seventy years. However, a Rosetta Stone was required to unlock the secret of what in blazes half the characters were talking about, and this was found in two sources: *A Dictionary of the Underworld* (New York, Bonanza Books, 1961), first published by Eric Partridge in 1949 and updated in a new edition twelve years later; and *The Secret Language of Crime: The Rogue's Lexicon* (Springfield, Ill., Templegate Publishers, 1997), compiled in 1859 by George W. Matsell, a former chief of police of New York City. From "Abraham" (to pose or sham) to "Zulu" (a vehicle employed to transport an immigrant's personal effects), these invaluable references provide a history of the evolution of the crooks' code from 1560 through the Great Depression.

Unfortunately, the entries are not cross-referenced, and the process of writing dialogue, normally a breezy affair for this writer, slowed to tortoise pace while he searched for the proper crude term for "throat" and stumbled, at weary length, upon "gutter-lane." Perhaps in later editions the editors will take pity on their readers and bring out the equivalent of an English-to-sewer-rat dictionary.

Although efforts were made to use this special slang in a rhythm and context that would guide understanding (except during the conversation between the two Hoodlums in chapter thirteen, which was presented as nearly impenetrable for demonstration and comic effect), some readers may still be at sea. (This is in no way a condescending remark; it means they are square citizens, who wouldn't be caught dead cracking a ken or munging a duce.) For them, the following terms and definitions may be of use.

> ARTICLES . . . Clothing
> BARKING-IRONS . . . Handguns
> BEAK . . . A judge or magistrate
> BENISON . . . Blessing
> BLACK OINTMENT . . . Raw meat
> BLACK-SPY . . . Satan
> BLOW . . . To inform upon someone

BLUNT . . . Money

BOB MY PAL . . . Ladyfriend (Gal)

BOOLY-DOGS . . . Police officers

BREAK A LEG . . . To bear a child out of wedlock

BUFE . . . A dog

BULLY . . . A lump of lead, handy for bludgeoning

CALFSKIN . . . The Bible. ("Smack the calfskin"—
Kiss the Bible and swear)

CALLAHAN . . . A billyclub

CAP . . . To join in

CHANT . . . One's name

CLY . . . A pocket; also, to pocket

COLE . . . Money

CONIAKERS . . . Counterfeiters

CONK . . . One's nose

COVE . . . A man

CRABS . . . Feet

CRANKY . . . Insane

CRIMP . . . A recruiter for a sailors' boardinghouse

CRUSHER . . . A policeman

CUES . . . Points in a game of chance

CULL . . . A man

CUT ONE'S EYES . . . Become suspicious

DADDLES . . . Hands

DANCE AT MY DEATH . . . May I hang

DARBIES . . . Manacles

DAWB . . . A bribe; also, to bribe

DEAD GAME . . . Certain

DONEGAN . . . A privy; also, it can't be helped

DOSS . . . A bed

DUFFER . . . A man posing as a sailor

DUSTY . . . Dangerous

EARTH-BATH . . . Burial

EASE . . . To rob or kill

EMPEROR . . . A drunk

ETERNITY-BOX . . . A coffin

FACER . . . A glass filled so full that one must bring one's face to the glass instead of the other way around

FAMS . . . Hands

FINIFF . . . Five dollars

FISH . . . A sailor

FLAPPERS . . . Hands

FLASH . . . Knowing; to speak knowingly ("Patter the flash")

FLIMP . . . To wrestle

FLUSH . . . Rich

FLY . . . Wise

FRIDAY FACE . . . A glum visage, Friday being the traditional day of hanging

FUNK . . . To frighten

GABS . . . Talk

GAGE . . . Money; a pot

GRIM . . . Death

HANDLE . . . One's nose

HEDGE . . . To bet on both sides; to side with God and Satan at once

HICKSAM . . . A fool

HOIST A HUFF . . . To rob violently

JACK . . . A small coin

JACK COVE . . . A worthless, miserable fellow

JACK SPRAT . . . A small man

JADE . . . Hard time in prison

JOLLY . . . One's head; also, a sham

JOSKIN . . . A country bumpkin

KICK . . . A pocket

KNOCK-ME-DOWN . . . Strong drink

KNOLLY . . . One's head ("Knowledge-box")

LAMPS . . . Eyes

LAY . . . One's particular scheme; M.O.

LOPE . . . Run away

LURCH . . . Get rid of

MADAM RHAN . . . A faithless or immoral woman

MAWLEYS . . . Hands

MOLLISHER . . . A woman, usually a harlot ("Molly"; "Moll")

MONAGER . . . One's name or alias

MUMMER . . . One's mouth

NEB . . . One's face

NIP . . . To rob

NODDLE . . . A fool

NUB . . . One's neck

NUG . . . Dear one

OAK . . . Strong; dependable

OFFICE . . . A signal ("Tip the office")

OLD SHOE . . . Good luck

ON THE SHARP . . . Smart and not easily cheated

PACKET . . . A lie

PADDING KEN . . . A rooming house

PAD THE HOOF . . . Walk or run away

PANNAM . . . Bread

PANTER . . . One's heart

PEACH . . . To inform

PECK . . . Food

PEERY . . . Suspicious

PEGO . . . A sailor

PERSUADER . . . A weapon; a spur

PHARSE . . . The eighth part

PLUMMY (or PLUMBY) . . . All right

POLISH IRON . . . Go to prison ("Polish iron bars with one's eyebrows")

PONCE . . . A kept man

PONY . . . Money; to post one's money

PRAD . . . A horse

PRIM . . . A handsome woman

PUPPY . . . Blind

PUT . . . A clownish fool

PUT UP TO ONE'S ARMPITS . . . Cheat one of his possessions

QUEEN DICK . . . Never ("The reign of Queen Dick"; a nonperson)

QUEER . . . Counterfeit money

RABBIT . . . A rough, rowdy fellow

RAMMER . . . One's arm

RED RAG . . . One's tongue

RHINO FAT . . . Rich as Midas

RUB . . . Run

RUSTY . . . Bad-tempered

SCOLD'S-CURE . . . Death

SCRAG . . . Hang

SCRUB . . . A cruel man

SEA-CRAB . . . A sailor

SCOT . . . A young bull

SCOUR . . . Run away

SCREAVES . . . Bank notes

SERVE OUT . . . To thrash someone

SHAPER . . . A hat

SHINERAGS . . . Nothing

SHOP . . . Prison

SINK . . . To cheat

SKEP . . . A money cache

SKIPPER . . . A barn

SKYCER . . . A worthless parasite

SLAG . . . A chain (also, "Slang")

SLANG . . . To chain something (also, a chain)

SLINGTAIL . . . A chicken

SLUICE ONE'S GOB . . . To drink ("Wet your whistle")

SMICKET . . . A woman's skirt

SMOKY . . . Suspicious

SNAGGLE . . . To wring the neck of a chicken or other fowl

SPEEL . . . Run away

SPLIT OUT . . . To end one's association

SPOONEY . . . Gullible

SPUD . . . Worthless coin

SQUAIL . . . A drink

STAG . . . To inform upon

STIFF . . . A letter

STRETCH . . . One year

STOW ONE'S WID . . . Be silent

STUBBLE . . . Hold ("Stubble your red rag"="Hold your tongue")

STUN ONE OUT OF HIS REGULARS . . . To cheat one of his rights

SWABLER . . . A filthy fellow

SWIG . . . A drink

TAPPER . . . A police officer

THIMBLE . . . A watch

TICKRUM . . . A license

TOBBING . . . Waylaying by striking one on the head

TOMMY . . . Bread

TOP . . . To cheat

TOP-CHEAT . . . A hat

TOPPER . . . A blow on the head

TOP-ROPES . . . High living

TRINKETS . . . Burglar tools; weapons

U.S. COVE . . . A man in the employ of the United States

VAMPERS . . . Stockings

WARE HAWK . . . Beware

WHIFFLE . . . To cry out in pain

WHISKER . . . An elaborate lie

YACK . . . A watch

The following is a rough translation of the conversation Page Murdock overheard between two Hoodlums in Daniel Webster Wheelock's reception room (pages 113–114):

"I'll be hanged if it isn't old Pox. I heard you were in prison."

"No, Freddie, that was a lie. Some sharpers impersonating police officers tried to cheat me out of my goods, but I saw it was a swindle and ran home."

"You always were a smart fellow."

"Well, I'm not blind. How's your girl?"

"I haven't seen her in a year. We broke up."

"The devil you say. I thought you were all right."

"As did I. She informed on me to the police. Cheated me out of my rights, she did, and I gave her a good thrashing."

"I'd have bet my shirt she was honest."

"You'd be a fool if you did. I tell you, she's as bad as they come."

"You must have felt yourself a clown."

"Shut your mouth, Pox. You wouldn't know a no-good woman if she picked your pocket right under your nose."

"Don't take offense, you young bull. If she betrayed you, why aren't you in prison?"

"I had good luck. I was facing a long sentence sure as death, but Captain Dan bribed the judge and arranged for a not-guilty verdict."

"Do you swear to that?"

"Look at my hands. Am I in manacles?"

"What does Captain Dan have in mind?"

"That's why I'm here. If he wants me to hit people on the head and rob them, I'm his man."

"He can get anyone for that. He'll want more for his money."

"The old fox keeps his plans to himself, that's for sure."

"I agree with you there, Freddie, my friend. Throw me over for five dollars if I don't."

The first novel in an exciting new mystery series

FRAMES

Loren D. Estleman

Valentino is a film archivist at UCLA whose discovery
of a long-lost film reel leads him into a world of lies,
corruption, and the faded glamour of classic Hollywood.

**"Estleman marvelously mixes movies and mayhem
in a way sure to please film buffs and mystery fans
alike. *Frames* is another winner from a master."**

—John Jakes, *New York Times* #1 bestselling author

A May 2008 hardcover

978-0-7653-1575-5 • 0-7653-1575-0

www.tor-forge.com

Meet your favorite authors at the

WESTERN WRITERS OF AMERICA CONVENTION

JUNE 10–14, 2008
CHAPARRAL SUITES HOTEL
SCOTTSDALE, ARIZONA

Founded in 1953, the Western Writers of America promotes literature, both fiction and non-fiction, pertaining to the American West.

Some bestselling authors who have attended the convention are:

C. J. Box ★ Don Coldsmith ★ Loren D. Estleman
W. Michael Gear and Kathleen O'Neal Gear
Tony Hillerman ★ Elmer Kelton ★ Larry McMurtry

And many, many more!

EVERYONE IS WELCOME!

For more information please visit www.westernwriters.org
and click on "Convention."